Meet Me in the Middle

Meet Me in the Middle

Ravinder Singh Presents

Vaṇi Mahesh

HarperCollins *Publishers* India

First published in India in 2021 by
HarperCollins *Publishers* India and Black Ink
A-75, Sector 57, Noida, Uttar Pradesh 201301, India
www.harpercollins.co.in

2 4 6 8 10 9 7 5 3 1

P-ISBN: 978-93-5422-350-1
E-ISBN: 978-93-5422-358-7

This is a work of fiction and all characters and incidents described in this book are the product of the author's imagination. Any resemblance to actual persons, living or dead, is entirely coincidental.

Vani Mahesh asserts the moral right
to be identified as the author of this work.

Typeset in 11.5/15 Minion Pro at
Manipal Technologies Limited, Manipal

Printed and bound at
Thomson Press (India) Ltd

MIX
Paper
FSC® C010615

This book is produced from independently certified FSC® paper
to ensure responsible forest management.

To Neethi and Akshara

1

Anu was thirty years old. She had been married for six years and was the mother of a four-year-old. She quite enjoyed being married to her childhood friend Sanju and being a mother to Vicky. She equally loved the breaks she got from being a wife and mother, thanks to Sanju's travel and her parents' free babysitting services. Anu was a kindergarten teacher in the same school that her son went to. She loved her job too. The principal, who was her mother's childhood friend, compensated for Anu's underpay with less work.

Anu was born, brought up, and married into an old, predominantly Kannada suburb of Bangalore, called Vijaynagar. She could have lived in New York, London, Sydney, or even some remote African country because suitable grooms from Vijaynagar were all over the globe. But she loved living in Vijaynagar. Its middle-class living and easy-thinking mode suited her fine. Too much of anything—wealth, intelligence or success—made Anu uncomfortable. Those who possessed too much of these things failed to understand someone like her whose twin missions in life were to stay happy and not work too hard.

That morning, Anu had an issue that had put a bit of a dampener on her spirits. To discuss that matter, she had taken a day-off from school to eat breakfast with her best friend, Shwetha.

'Sanju was acting totally weird yesterday.' Anu took a sip of her coffee. Sanju, a techie like everyone else in Bangalore, was currently in California on a short-term assignment.

'How so?' frowned Shwetha, with her glasses all steamed up from coffee.

'For starters, he hadn't shaved in two days.' Anu dipped a crisply fried Vada into a bowl of hot Sambar, pushing the plate of Idlis towards Shwetha.

'Oh, that is very worrisome.' Shwetha nodded, pushing the Idlis out of the way. 'Why steam the batter into an Idli, when you can fry it into a Vada?'

'Because Idli takes the guilt out of eating Vada. Now stay with me. See, we had a video call last night and Sanju said the house was filthy. He also said I eat too much junk food.' Anu shoved more Vada into her mouth.

Shwetha pursed her lips. 'Though it is true, I can't imagine Sanju saying something like that to you. That is very shocking.'

'Hey, my house is untidy, not filthy. If you see pee-stains on the bed, it is filthy. If you see underwear on the bed, it is just untidy.' Anu shrugged. 'Coming back to Sanju, something is wrong if he said such ruthless words. Is he having an affair?' She asked Shwetha the question that had gnawed at her all night.

Shwetha disagreed immediately. 'Sanju thinks you are way above his league. Misconception, but that is what he thinks. So, he won't cheat on you.' She added as an afterthought. 'Also, if a man is having an affair, he is nicer to the wife.'

Anu nodded. 'True. And, he would shave too. Sanju is not the cheating type. Is he dying of some disease, then?' Worry had now crept into Anu's voice.

'Hmm. Hypothetically, what do you prefer? Him cheating on you or dying of a disease?' Shwetha asked curiously.

'Dying.' Anu was confident of her answer. Well, only momentarily. 'No … I don't want him dead. If he is cheating on me, I can always make him grovel for my mercy.'

'Which is worse than death for him. Now, how was he with Vicky? Also, why didn't you ask him?' Shwetha got into an investigative mode.

'Vicky was asleep when he called. And of course, I asked him. You know Sanju. Mr Opaque. He said it was just work.' Anu beckoned to the waiter for the bill.

'That is a lie. Sanju belongs to a creed that gets energized by work.' Shwetha dismissed it immediately.

'I know, right? Good that you agree with me. I will have to nag an answer out of him.' Anu drained the last sip of her coffee, paid the bill, and got up to leave. 'I have to go now. First to the library, then to pick up Vicky from school.'

'I got to run too. Keep me posted. But don't get your knickers in a bunch. Worry doesn't suit you.'

Anu and Shwetha went back a decade. In a multi-national bank where Anu worked briefly as a receptionist, Shwetha was a junior officer. She was fresh off her MCom with a gold medal, and Anu her BA in first class. At first, Shwetha had ignored Anu steadfastly. But Anu hadn't given up. She had brought her coffee, shared her lunch, extended tickets to movies. Finally what worked was Anu having helped Shwetha pick an outfit for a flashy wedding she had to attend. Why had Anu jumped through hoops to become Shwetha's friend? Anu honestly didn't know the right answer. Maybe she found Shwetha's Sameer kind of no-nonsense attitude very appealing, or because she felt Shwetha could use a friend with a sense of fashion. Besides, apart from Anu, Shwetha was the only one at the bank who read. When Anu saw a reader, she always got a bit overexcited.

Shwetha, as she had admitted later, had thought Anu was an attention-seeking pretty face and she stayed away from those kinds on principle. But soon, again according to Shwetha, their mutual distaste for the office coffee and the boss had made her bond with Anu.

Anu felt better having spoken to Shwetha. She was not the type to bottle things up. Hurrying up the familiar steps to the library with the musky smell of old books, Anu took a deep breath and waved to the librarian. She had been going to that library for at least fifteen years now. The library had witnessed her transition from reading Enid Blyton to Harry Potter to John Grisham.

That was where she and Sanju had their first real conversation—where she had mumbled and he had stuttered. Smiling quickly at a few known faces, Anu got busy rummaging through the shelves. She had to find the twentieth book in the Stephanie Plum series. She had been able to find all parts up to the nineteenth and beyond the twenty-first, but not the twentieth. As her search intensified, so did the beeps and dings of a video game. A kid with a mobile! If she could suffer through the boredom of entertaining her son with toys, so should other mothers.

Anu tapped on the shoulder of the woman next to the child. 'Can you put your son's mobile on silent?'

The woman, with her face buried into a book, replied, 'I would if he were mine.'

Tendering an apology, feeling sheepish, Anu went back to her search. Two minutes later, the kid hugged the same woman. 'Mumma, the phone is not working.'

What an ingenious liar! While Anu gawked, the woman smirked, fixed the phone, and moved to a different aisle.

Anu went up to the librarian and whispered. 'Can you throw that lying woman out?'

The librarian shook his head. 'No, ma'am. But you can take this.' He pushed a brand new Leanne Moriarty towards her, with a conspiratorial smile. 'This had been reserved for her.'

Anu was happy with that sweet revenge. Billing her books, she started to the door. The kid had had now moved on to emanating thuds and crash sounds from the phone. Anu stopped. She had to save the world from that auditory assault. Walking up to the kid, Anu took his phone, turned it off, and left it on a top-shelf. Before he could recover and scream, or smack her cold, Anu handed him a miniature dinosaur she had bought for Vicky. 'Here, play with this.'

Anu felt delighted when she looked at the time. She still had good two hours before she needed to pick Vicky. She could spend this time on her bed with the book—could life get any better than that? Well, it could—if you throw in a bag of potato chips to the mix. The Hot Chips shops in every nook and cranny of Bangalore might be a weight watcher's nightmare, but they were Anu's delight.

Walking towards the car, Vicky told her how he had made a clay robot that his friend said looked like a cockroach, but how it really didn't. Just as Anu began unlocking the car, Vicky spotted McDonald's, 'Mumma, I am hungry.'

But Anu had a perfect afternoon meal planned for the two of them. Vicky was going to be served the chapati and curry the cook had made the previous night. He was a growing boy who needed his nutrition. Meanwhile, she was going to set herself up with a honey cake and aalu bun she had planned to pick up from the bakery on the way home.

But Vicky went on a repeat mode. 'I want burrr-ger. I want burrr-ger.'

Anu relented. She could have the burger now and the cake later.

'Mumma, look, Padma aunty!' Vicky's delighted squeal made Anu freeze. That was Sanju's aunt, who made no attempts to conceal her dislike for Anu. It seemed that Anu's perfect day had come to a halt.

'Vicky!' Padma aunty planted a slobbery kiss on Vicky's cheek, which he duly wiped away. 'Where are you going?'

Oh, no! Anu groaned inwardly. She was not ready for Padma aunty's lecture on how evil fast food was. So Anu quickly intercepted Vicky's truth with her instant lie. 'To buy some fruits, aunty.' Waving her hands in a random direction, Anu added. 'From that organic store. You know how bad fertilizers are.'

'But that is not an organic store. That is a fertilizer store.' Padma aunty raised the glasses on her hawk-like nose. Anu was tempted to shove her to the side and run.

'No … Mumma. No fruits. We will eat burgers.' *Vicky! Stop!*

Padma aunty's eyes narrowed, and nostrils flared. 'Anu, you must know better than to feed Vicky such harmful foods. You can make tasty and healthy burgers from millets at home.'

Argh! Millet burgers! Even the thought made Anu's stomach churn. But she nodded in agreement to get out of there as fast as she could. 'Yes, yes, aunty. I will take the recipe from you.' Anu had to find a way to get rid of Padma aunty. Luckily, the woman removed herself from the scene, citing bank work. Phew, between McD and Padma aunty—the winner was, for a change, McD!

After having the 'burr-ger', Vicky fell asleep in the old Santro stuck in the narrow streets of Mudalpalya. It was one of the clogged arterial roads that connected Vijaynagar to the rest of Bangalore. But you would know that only if you, like Anu, lived in Vijaynagar.

When she neared the Iyengar Bakery, a place that smelled of bread, butter, and belly fat, there was no parking anywhere within a hundred yards. But in Bangalore food was sacred; to buy it, it was okay to stop the vehicle anywhere, even right on someone's toes. Bearing with the horns blaring at her, Anu double-parked her car and honked. The owner, who looked like an oversized version of the buns he sold, was Anu's classmate before he failed the seventh standard. Catching her eye, he waved at her with delight and sent his boy to take the order.

Soon equipped with two honey cakes and two aalu buns, Anu felt pleased. Her heart thudded in excitement thinking of the sweet combination of her bed, the cake, and the book. But Anu's joy turned out to be very short-lived. Just as she got inside her car, there was a rap on the window. When Anu rolled down the window, staring right down at her was a traffic policeman.

'What, madam? You look educated, and you obstruct traffic like this? Give me your license and registration.'

Anu prayed to every god she knew for the documents to be in the glove compartment; she had no idea what the car registration even looked like. Anu harboured an aversion to papers of any kind. Managing to find a folder, Anu handed it to the man who had decided to zero-in on her, ignoring a thousand other more worthy traffic offenders.

'Are you joking, madam? These are receipts from hotels.' The policeman growled but went through the papers intently. 'You must be very rich.'

Oh, shoot. Sanju must have been saving them for reimbursement. Now this man was going to ask her for a hefty bribe. Usually, the traffic police looked at her battered Santro and let her go with only a fifty or hundred rupees. Anu now pretended to look for the documents in her handbag, though it never contained anything other than money and chapstick. Then a voice alerted her.

'She is my niece, and she is a good driver. I say you let her off with a warning.' Anu pinched herself. Padma aunty! Was the woman stalking her? More shockingly, was she defending Anu's honour? While Anu struggled to recover from those multiple shocks, she heard Padma aunty continue sternly. 'Look at the child in the backseat. You must have compassion.'

The policeman, who was twice the size of that frail woman, looked bewildered. Barely finding his voice, he managed to mumble. 'I am letting her go for you, Ajji. Tell her—'

Padma aunty cut him off. 'I am not your grandmother for you to call me Ajji. Now, go. Catch real thieves.' It didn't matter to her that traffic police didn't catch thieves.

'Anu, you just had burgers, and now you are buying the bakery stuff?' Anu looked at Padma aunty dumbfounded. Was unhealthy eating a bigger crime than not having official papers? Sometimes all a girl needs is a tub of ice cream and a packet of chips to perk her up.

'Sorry, aunty. I will give this away to the maid.' Anu offered quickly, though she fully intended to consume it entirely by herself.

'Hand it to me. I will give it to our maid.' Padma aunty fixed a scary stare on Anu. Before she knew it, Anu's bag of joy was whisked away by a bony hand. Those were the times she called that woman Padzilla in her head. Luckily, Padma aunty was leaving on a trip to Europe soon. Such peace!

Even if her afternoon was a lost cause, her night was not. She was going to her mother's house for an overnighter and have a beer with Sameer.

2

Tring, triiing.

'Oh no ... Oh, no ...' Anu muttered to herself, scrambling for the phone to see the time. Why didn't she wear a watch for heaven's sake! It was ten minutes past five! She was late for her yoga class. It had to be Radha, her cook-cum-nanny, at the door. Why hadn't she set an alarm before napping?

Extricating herself from Vicky's tiny arms curled around her, Anu tumbled out of bed. The doorbell had now stopped ringing, which made her sprint to the door. She couldn't miss Radha! When she opened the door, Radha was standing right there waiting. God bless her!

'I was afraid you left, Radha,' Anu panted tying her hair up in a knot. There was not a minute to even wear her new pants—which was a bummer because she had bought two pairs of them recently paying full price. If she now bolted like Usain Bolt, she had a chance to make it to the class. She could not miss the class after all the burgers and finger chips she had scarfed down in the afternoon. For that matter, Anu never missed the class, though even after a year, she was just average at even the basic poses. Some in the class could bend

11

as if they had no bones, but Anu had no qualms sitting in Sukhasana and simply watching them. She was not great at it but she loved it, and she loved her teacher.

Anu's tryst with Yoga had started quite accidentally. Two years after Vicky was born, when her Lee Cooper jeans still rode up only to her knees, Anu, like any smart phone user worth her salt, had started researching on YouTube—for ways to lose ten kilograms in one day. Well, she was may be just five kilograms overweight, but didn't hurt to lose more, did it?

Sweaty and vigorous workouts like jogging or gymming were not to Anu's liking. She was not big into dieting either. What was life without eating what you liked? Then YouTube had thrown the word Keto diet at her repeatedly and it sounded good. All you can eat is fat! But unfortunately, that didn't work for her either. All that butter, cheese and paneer had got her South Indian gut into a tizzy.

On one lazy YouTube-browsing day, Anu misspelt 'Keto' as 'Keno' and stumbled upon a waif-like woman bending her body aesthetically while explaining the poses in a beautiful accent. Video after video of the Keno woman, along with hundred other perfectly toned Yoginis (including Shilpa Shetty with a wide grin) propounding Yoga had left Anu mesmerized. And she had begun right away, pulling up Keno on the Smart TV screen. After a week of practising with Keno on YouTube, Anu asked Shwetha to video her poses. To Anu's horror, she was like an antonym to Keno. Keno's Triangle pose was Anu's Slouched duck. Keno's Lotus bend was Anu's topple-to-the-ground pose. Shwetha's uncontrolled laughter had not help the matter. Shwetha still had the video just as a way to blackmail Anu someday.

Giving up on YouTube tutoring, Anu joined a class. A guru was what she needed. Someone who gently corrected her and made her body supple and toned, like Keno's. But, the forty-something lithe instructor turned out to be a monster in a white kurta. He shamed people in the most ingenious ways if their bodies did not bend to his will. A few examples of his insults being: 'You can audition for the role a hunchback'; or, 'Your arms are so jiggly, they can double as wings.' His favourite for Anu was, 'I said touch your toes, not look at them.' Anu still shuddered at the thought of him. She had stuck on for three months. But after yet again being reprimanded for not holding the toes with her teeth and rubbing the face on the ground, or some such impossible thing, she had quit. He was ruining her zen instead of adding to it.

But Anu hadn't given up her hunt for a gently-correcting-guru. She tried another place, but here the instructor made them meditate more and bend less. Anu ended up dozing off through the entire class. After that, there were a few more disappointments. One, where the entire class was a thousand Surya Namaskaras, another, mostly talks on Patanjali's Yoga Sutras.

Then, at last, her prayers were answered! A year ago, this extremely gentle woman, Supriyaji, had moved into their apartment complex and sent out an email about starting classes. Anu was the first one to visit her. And, it was love at first sight. Supriyaji was oh-so-perfect. Anu's dream gently-correcting-guru. Anu felt like Buddha inside and Keno outside after the class.

Rushing out the door, Anu remembered to instruct Radha. 'Vicky hasn't eaten anything. Please give him something healthy when he wakes up. I will see you at six-thirty.'

Anu almost ran the small distance from her building to the next where the class was held. She was in her homewear, with the hair in a bun. She probably still had drool stains from the nap. And she felt disoriented without coffee. *If only I had woken up half-an-hour early.* Reprimanding herself, Anu hurried into Supriyaji's house. Why was time so elusive? What some called time-management, Anu called punishment.

She entered that tranquil room as quietly as she could. Though the prayer had started, Supriyaji gave Anu a warm smile and beckoned her to a spot in the front. Anu reached the spot, hopping over some, stamping on someone's hair, and stepping on someone's toes. Only then it occurred to her that she had forgotten to bring her yoga mat. She had bought a top-of-the-line one as a first anniversary gift for herself. Now she had to borrow from the stash kept for slackers. Since the mats were at the back of the class, Anu again started the exercise of hopping, stamping, and stepping over people.

Deciding to stay at the back of the room, Anu spread the mat. Yuck! What was that large stain in the middle? She flipped the mat over where there was no stain but enough dust to instantly send Yashoda aunty next to her into a sneeze-fest. Sending a look of sincere apology, Anu settled down. The good thing was, neither Supriyaji nor Yashoda aunty threw any dirty glances at her. Rather, both of them smiled at her. Thank god for these godly women. That was how their apartment complex was. Mostly people from her parents' generation who loved Anu and Vicky. They would have loved Sanju too, but he spent most of his time at work.

Anu decided to skip the chanting. It was already so off-key, one less person joining did not matter. Now that she was sitting without doing anything, her mind started going back to Sanju. She could not relax and unwind in that fabulous room like she always did.

Anu believed she had highly precise instincts and now they were on high alert, warning her that the situation with Sanju was not ordinary. Anu had mind-blowing epiphanies in two situations, one – when she had had a drink, and second – when she lied down in Shavasana in the Yoga class. She felt like a Yogin with great wisdom in both the situations. Recently, after a beer or two, she was struck by the thought of watching movie adaptations of all the books she had read. What a fabulous week that was! The time before that, when she had lied down in Shavasana, it had come to her in a flash where her next long vacation was going to be. The Himalayas! That was another fabulous week when she had put in a thousand-hours watching YouTubers trek the Leh, Ladakh and whatnot. Since she had terrible mountain sickness, watching the videos had taken care of her Himalayan cravings. But today, she was sensing something not so pleasant and there were no YouTube videos to solve her problem.

Anu tried to calm her nerves by taking a deep breath and looking around the room. Supriyaji had the same house as hers but it looked a billion times more beautiful. Maybe, she could do the same. How hard can doing up the interiors be? She must start by buying some brassware. And the colourful cushion covers, and then, of course, that deep rosewood table to host a brass lamp. That would show Sanju how great she was at interior decorating. With that determination, Anu began to feel calmer. Her next YouTube binge was in place.

Anu could hardly focus on the asanas. In her absent-mindedness, she tried the head-stand, toppled, and made three more ahead of her fall like dominoes.

Apologising to the people she had knocked off, Anu tried to relax. Why had she tied herself up in knots? Maybe Sanju was just overworked as he said.

When the class got over, Anu rolled her mat and stepped out. 'Anu, that is not your mat.' Yashoda aunty's words sent a sliver of shame run down Anu's spine. How crazy that she was about to take home the mat that was not hers!

But Yashoda aunty was the least judgemental person Anu had ever met. 'Aunty, I have become so absent-minded!' Anu said, embarrassed.

Yashoda aunty smiled kindly. 'You are very busy, Anu. That is why small things skip your mind.'

Me? Busy? Is Yashoda aunty joking? Anu looked at Yashoda aunty quizzically.

'You work, you take care of Vicky, you take care of the household. That is a lot.'

Thus far, nobody had pegged her job or her mothering as stressful. In fact, in Bangalore, if you were not a techie, or at least worked in a Tech company in the HR, PR or some such department, you were as good as jobless.

Anu smiled. 'Do you want anything from the supermarket, aunty? I can drop them off before going to Vijaynagar.' Yashoda aunty was a widow who lived alone, with both her kids settled in the US.

'See, you are so kind, Anu. You help me despite being busy.' Yashoda aunty's praises that day were a tad too much. Probably, she was trying to make Anu feel better.

'You send me the list. I will buy them for you.' Anu offered. She had taught Yashoda aunty to take a photo of her grocery list and WhatsApp it to her.

Now Yashoda aunty got a bit emotional. 'Anu, I thought I could never use a smartphone, but you helped me with it. Now I can even make video calls to my son!' It was a different matter altogether that Yashoda aunty had now started making video calls to everyone. Most often she called when Anu had henna on the hair or a charcoal mask on the face.

'You should learn how to order groceries online, aunty. I will teach you sometime.' Anu smiled. 'Did you try booking a cab?' Anu had taught her to do so recently.

'Not yet. I have not been going anywhere. But ordering groceries online will be such a great help, Anu. Let me know when you can teach. I will make your favourite poori and chhole. Now, enough about me. Tell me how is Sanjay?'

Anu hesitated and was almost tempted to pour out her woes to the kind elderly woman. That was how she was—when something bothered her, she had to tell everyone, get their advice, and finally end up with a severely messed up brain. This time around, Anu had decided to confine her confessions to Shwetha and Sameer.

'He is fine, aunty. He will be back soon.' Anu smiled a smile she did not feel.

'You go with him next time, Anu. Not wise to leave men alone for long!' Yashoda aunty gave a slightly naughty smile, which sunk Anu's heart further. *Oh boy, oh boy, that was the end of me. Yashoda aunty suspects foul play too? What would I do now?*

Anu walked into the house that looked as messy as ever. Radha confessed sheepishly. 'I could not tidy the house, akka. But I have fed Vicky chapatis, and I have made a mixed veg curry.' With that, Radha handed Anu a hot cup of coffee. She had settled Vicky in front of the TV to watch Popeye.

'I should have married you instead of my husband,' said Anu sipping coffee and Radha laughed loudly. Well, another reason to marry her—Radha laughed at all of Anu's jokes.

'Are you okay, akka? You look a little dull.' Radha asked with concern. Another reason to marry her. Anu again had an urge to pour her heart out to Radha but restrained herself.

'Just a headache. Tomorrow you come at four-thirty sharp. I won't be asleep.'

Radha hesitated. 'Akka, I am not coming for a week from tomorrow. I had told you last month.'

'Oh, right. You go and have a good time. The maid is not coming either for a week,' said Anu wearily looking at the dirty dishes.

'Akka, I would have washed these if you had told me about the maid. Now I have to run. My bus is in an hour,' Radha sounded genuinely sorry.

'It is okay. I will manage.' Even as Anu said the words, she kicked herself mentally. Why couldn't she be more organized? All she had to do was tell Radha to help with the dishes.

Then she decided that from then on, her life was going to be different. She would lead it with the precision of a military man. She would make a to-do list and remember everything. How nice it would be to get ready ten minutes early! Anu dreamed—she could drink coffee, wear fancy footwear, keep a water bottle, play catch with Vicky because they were ready too early.

Deciding to execute the plan of not being late or rushed, Anu resisted picking up the book she had just started. That would melt away hours like ice-cream. Instead, she went into the bedroom to pack an overnight bag to stay at her mother's house. While she packed, trying to be mindful as Supriyaji always insisted, Vicky walked in looking dazed and plopped right on the clothes she had just folded.

'Popeye the sailaaa man …' he hummed sleepily. Well, kids his age watched Doraemon and Shinchan, but Vicky liked the old-world ones like Popeye and Tom & Jerry, thanks to his father. When Anu looked at him, he was trying to do the Popeye wink. He was so adorable—Anu kissed him and picked him up. Then her heart sank a bit—watching cartoons with Vicky was Sanju's thing. If he was having an affair, what would happen to his equation with Vicky?

Anu shrugged off the thoughts and walked to the kitchen, with Vicky trying to sleep on her shoulder. She had told her mother that she would be there by seven. Since it was already six-thirty, it was humanly impossible to keep that time; punctuality had to be postponed. But she was going to be efficient nonetheless. She took a small notebook and wrote.

1. Wash the dishes – 30 minutes
2. Get Vicky ready – 30 minutes to 300 minutes
3. Get ready – 30 minutes

'Vicky, here. Chocolate Horlicks and Nutella toast. Eat and drink fast, okay?' Anu made an offer to Vicky he could not refuse. Chocolate on chocolate was his thing. But not that day. Not on a day when she had made a firm resolution to be on time.

'I want strawberry milk and cheese toast.'

'You have this now. I will make what you want later.' Later his eating would be her mother's headache.

'No … I don't want this.' Vicky crinkled his nose. For a moment Anu contemplated guzzling down the fare herself. She was no less a chocoholic than her son. But she was not in the mood to squander her calories burnt during yoga on Nutella. She had to save those for the dinner with Sameer.

Anu spent another ten minutes to serve her little kingpin what he wanted. Next, she had to tackle dressing him.

'Vicky, you need to change. What do you want to wear?' It was best to give him the choice.

'I don't want to change.' He began to get more and more comfortable playing with his trucks. Though he looked adorable in his monster-truck nightshirt and jungle-print underwear, her mother severely disproved of such cuteness. She would say, 'Not enough if you dress up, Anu. You must make Vicky ready too. If you don't teach him now, he will turn into one of those boys with spiky hair and torn pants.'

The negotiation went on for five minutes before Vicky agreed to wear a Superman T-shirt with red shorts. Luckily, with the underwear inside. Then Anu got dressed and decided to leave the dishes as they were. *What could happen in a day?*

Finally on the road, Anu turned on the radio. 'Mumma, no your songs. Play rhymes.'

Anu sighed turning on yet another rendition of wheels-of-the-bus. Lately, her bathroom singing started with Bits-of-Paper and ended with Twinkle-Twinkle. She spent most of her time with Vicky at home and twenty more Vickys at school.

Parking the car, Anu pushed the door open to her parents' house. Seven-thirty, not bad at all. Anu felt very pleased with herself. Her parents never bolted the front door because they had a steady stream of visitors. Even if a thief walked in, her mom would automatically serve him coffee and snacks.

'Did you park the car properly? Our street is a mess— every household has three cars and zero parking space. The corporation does nothing about this menace.' Anu's father greeted her from behind the newspaper.

'Papa! Can't you first say hello like all normal people? Then vent about parking and current politics?' Anu went into the kitchen.

Her father had a spot bang in the middle of the living room—an oversized sofa chair right in front of the TV. All the other furniture stood awkwardly around the chair.

'Veekuu! Come here to Tata!' His tone changed to a silly singsong when he saw Vicky. The boy went running to his grandfather. Anu wondered what was wrong with Vicky! How can someone find her father entertaining enough to rush to?

'Anu! My beautiful girl!' Ah, that Anu liked. It was her maternal grandmother who lived with Anu's parents. She had lost her husband ten years ago and had moved into that house soon after. Anu's father was not too thrilled to have his mother-in-law live with them, but the good thing was that he too busy to remember that she existed.

'Ajji! You find me beautiful in these track pants?' Though Anu tried sounding nonchalant about the remark, she was pleased. They were no ordinary tracks, they were black Benetton ones, and they hugged her bottom better than any pair of jeans. And, she had worn her best-fitting Lee Cooper T-shirt too because she was planning to meet Sameer for a nightcap. He was just a friend, and she didn't have to dress up for him, but Sameer was someone who noticed the finer things in life. Moreover, he styled himself like a movie star.

Not in a gaudy, Ranvir Singh-way but in a very subtle and classy way. So, she had to dress up.

'You look pretty in anything you wear.' Her grandmother was generous with compliments. That made up for the lousy gifts she gave on all her birthdays. 'You look eighteen. Who can say you are married with a child. Most girls become so fat after a child.' Her grandma shuddered. She did not worry about body-shaming.

'Stop praising her, Amma. She already spends enough time preening herself.' That was Anu's mother. She was lousy with compliments but highly generous with money. Anu was okay with that too.

'I am going out with Divya after dinner. At eight. Feed me soon.' Anu had to lie about meeting Sameer. Her mother did not endorse friendships with old admirers.

'You never spend more than ten minutes with us, Anu. Why didn't you come at seven, as you had said?' Her mother's unhappiness was nothing Anu hadn't expected.

'I had my yoga class.' Anu bit into a *Kobbari Mithai* her grandmother handed her fresh from the stove. Happy with that thousand-calorie-a-piece sugar and coconut mixture, Anu plonked herself on the gleaming part of the counter. That was always her place when her mother or grandmother was in the kitchen. That was where all the food tasting happened.

'Then, why did you say you were coming at seven?' Her mother remarked, mildly angry.

'Because I didn't want you telling me to skip the class.'

Her mother went silent. That was how she hid her irritation.

Then Anu's phone pinged. 'Will pick you up at eight-thirty.' That was Sameer.

'Street corner. Not from home.' Anu typed back, feeling light and happy even before a drink. After Vicky was born, going out at night was a luxury. For the time being, she forgot to even worry about the Sanju situation, imaginary or otherwise. Staying at her parents' house and meeting Sameer for a drink was her ideal night. Shwetha called it unambitious, Sameer called her easily pleased.

Anu's friendship with Sameer was as old as her. They were neighbours who went to the same KLE school. Sameer being a year older than her had worked out quite well for Anu. True that she had followed him around and hero-worshipping him the first few years of her life, but that was a worthy investment. Sameer, when she was seven or eight, had not only noticed her but assigned himself as her guardian. He made her life easy in more ways than one—from making sure she got the window seat in the bus to nobody making fun of her when she had braces and bushy eyebrows.

By the time he was in tenth, being the bike-riding, long-haired, long-limbed, football captain, Sameer enjoyed a superstar-like popularity at school. And Anu made sure she hogged some of that limelight.

'Sameer, ice cream today evening?' She would purposely ask loudly and nonchalantly to flaunt her camaraderie with the school hero. For the record, he never missed his evening football practice to have ice cream with Anu but he humoured her nonetheless. 'Yeah … be ready at six sharp. My bike.' He would wave back. So the kids at school were extra nice to Anu because she knew Sameer. She got plum roles in plays even though she was as emotive as a piece of wood, and got selected into the throwball team even though the balls she threw never crossed the net. Everyone thought she was going to marry Sameer. Then why did she choose Sanju is a story for another time.

3

Like always, Sameer's car smelled good and felt cool. His perfume, bodyspray and the dozens of things he used had come together charmingly well.

'Your car is quite a babe magnet.' Anu took a deep breath.

'I thought I was the babe magnet.' Sameer objected.

'You are thirty-one. You can now attract only the babes' mothers.' Anu giggled.

'You are jealous that I am still hot and available and you are a married aunty.'

'Speaking of which, did you chat with Sanju recently?' Anu was not the type to wait.

'Chatted with him last night.' Sameer cranked up the radio for Atif Aslam's crooning.

Well, the topic of Sanju had to wait since Anu loved Atif Aslam. She listened quietly while Sameer managed his large car on the narrow Vijaynagar suburban streets without swearing at anyone. He knew better than to talk when Anu was mouthing to Atif. When several songs of Atif Aslam followed one after another, Anu realized Sameer was playing from a USB.

'You made an Atif Aslam playlist for me!' Anu touched her heart. 'Touched, my friend.'

'Don't flatter yourself, I am a fan of Aslam too.'

'Right. But I introduced you to him.'

'You are my entertainment guru, Anuji. Now tell me what do I watch on Netflix? Done with *Breaking Bad*, loved it, so the drinks are on me.'

'Glad you accept my superiority. And the drinks should forever be on you for the amount of gyaan I give you. Watch *Better Call Saul*, then watch *Lethal Weapon* on Prime. Both are your type.'

'What is your type lately? Into sad romances because Sanju is not in town?'

'When Sanju is not in town, I am into naughty, Mister Old-Fashioned.' Anu smacked Sameer's hand on the gear. 'Why do you think I have to mope and cry when my husband is enjoying his married bachelor days?'

'Fair enough. But your naughty is movies rated 18+. They don't qualify as naughty.' Sameer squeezed his large car into an impossibly narrow space, which only he could do. As they climbed the steps to Drink and Dine, Anu felt a rush of familiarity wash over her. Anu and Sameer's evenings out were always the same—the same restaurant, the same table, and the same sips (Smirnoff with Fanta for her, Old Monk with soda for him) and dines (Peanut Masala and Egg Pakoda). They used to do the same routine along with some weird club dancing with a gang of friends on Brigade Road a decade ago, but now there was no charm left in either the drive or the dance.

'Hey, Sanju sounded very down and out when I spoke to him. Wonder why,' said Anu as casually as she could. She did not want Sameer to pick up that she was worried. He would either tease her for years to come or get over-protective.

'Because he has to come back home. Give up his married bachelorhood.' Sameer remarked wickedly. 'Why would he be happy?'

'That would be you if you ever get married. Sanju is into home and hearth.' Anu retorted before asking the next question. 'But why do you think he is upset?'

'Maybe he misses Kshama,' Sameer said seriously making Anu almost jump.

'Where is she now? In the US? He never told me!' Anu almost sprung out of the chair. Kshama was Sanju's old flame. Well, he had chosen Anu over her but who knew about them being together in New York!

Sameer began to laugh. 'Got you, babe. Kshama is right here and almost about to pop a baby. I was only messing with you.'

Anu bent forward and hit him on the head with her empty glass. 'That was a crass joke. I will get even, buster.'

Sameer stared at her intensely. 'You already did—six years ago.'

Awe ... Anu's stomach gave a small lurch. He was referring to her marriage with Sanju. Sameer never was averse to voicing how he felt. Why did she pass him up for Sanju again? For a thousand reasons and the main one being that Sameer was a footloose and fancy-free Casanova, and Sanju, Mr Reliable. Sameer adored the entire clan of women while Sanju only her. Then she felt panicky. Did he still adore only her?

'Do you think Sanju is having an affair?' Anu asked hesitantly.

'Sanju is Sri Rama, a sworn one-Anu-man. Why are you suddenly overthinking things? That is not you, babe.'

'This is a question of my marriage. *Tu kya jaane ek chutki sindhoor ki keemat.*' Anu quoted that famous Deepika Padukone dialogue.

Sameer laughed. 'Your Hindi is hilariously wrong. It sounds like Kannada!'

Anu rolled her eyes. 'If you insult my Hindi, you are insulting the holy land of Bollywood.' She waved spoon at Sameer sternly. 'Remember that every bit of my Hindi has come from the stars crooning about ishq and pyaar.'

'Well, Sanju may be depressed about a lot of things but trust me, he is not capable of cheating. Too straightforward a guy.'

Sameer's reassurance and the Vodka working its magic, Anu's happy hormones began to rise. Biting into a crisp egg pakoda, Anu thought of her mom. She would throw a giant-sized fit if she knew that Anu was drinking, eating eggs, and all that with a man who was not her husband.

'How is it going with Snigdha?' Anu asked. 'Shagged? Proposed?'

'Broke up,' Sameer shrugged, taking a large swig of his extra large whiskey. 'She was not my type.'

'Nobody is anybody's type. Go with the flow.' Anu smiled. The vodka was relaxing her muscle by muscle. Sanju insisted that the deep relaxation she felt with one small peg of alcohol was only her imagination. But she knew differently.

'I will go with someone Mummy chooses. Someone who stays at home and does my bidding.' Sameer smiled crookedly and beckoned the waiter for his next drink.

'Very forward-thinking. I will marry that person too. Someone who does my bidding.'

'We will make a fantastic threesome.' Sameer winked, and Anu rolled her eyes.

Sameer patted her hand. 'Look, I wouldn't worry about Sanju. When we chatted yesterday, he was his normal boring self. Not suicidal.' Sameer finished his drink. 'But I don't understand why you hide from Sanju that we meet. I knew you before he did.'

'Because he gets upset even at the mention of your name! Why invite trouble?' Anu smiled. 'I prefer a non-belligerent living.'

Sanju liked Sameer, but he did not like Anu having anything to do with Sameer. Complex equations. But Anu met Sameer whenever she stayed at her parents, which was once a week. Sameer was a part of her DNA. She had to tell him everything that made her happy, sad or worried.

Sipping and dining in silence for some time, Anu watched the giant TV playing Big Boss while Sameer answered messages on Whatsapp. They were like family. They could just comfortably eat and watch TV if they didn't have anything to say.

The next morning, as Anu got dressed leisurely, life seemed pleasantly unhurried; as it used to be before motherhood. Vicky was getting pampered by his grandparents and Anu had only to take care of herself. Usually, the mornings at home were always a blur. Wake Vicky up, get Vicky ready, feed Vicky, hurry Vicky in the toilet. After that Anu had to get dressed in the one-and-a-half minutes left. So today felt like an ultimate luxury. Brushing her hair till it shined, Anu admired herself, and then considered staying back at her parents for a few days. There were only two more days of school and then it was the Dasara/ Dussehra holidays for ten days. Sanju was coming back only by the end of the holidays.

Anu thought of her life back home. Except for the rushed morning, the rest of the day was nice and easy. If she had to be out in the evenings, Radha babysat but only till eight. Radha cooked too, but she was as bad as Anu.

If she stayed here, her life would be one jolly good ride but she would have to report to her mother on a half-hourly basis if she went out after seven. She would get fantastic food but she would also put on at least two kgs. More than anything, Vicky would be taken care of round the clock and that was nowhere but here. Until you become a mother, you don't realise the value of freedom; especially the freedom to do forbidden things like watch trashy movies and talk on the phone non-stop.

Anu weighed the two options and the staying back won hands-down. The major motivator being both Radha and the maid being absent.

Anu shouted from the room, 'Amma, I will stay here for a week. I will stop at home and pick up a few things.'

Her mom shouted back, 'Good you came to your senses. Come eat breakfast.' The joy behind her mother's semi-rude words was unmistakable. Her parents acted as though Anu was doing them a favour when she hoisted Vicky on them!

Anu's mother decided that Vicky was skipping school that day to accompany her to some social event she was attending. Anu's parents had a function to attend to almost every day—wedding, death ceremony, naming ceremony. If, God forbid there was nothing scheduled, they would host a lunch with Satyanarayan Pooja themselves. Attending religious events was their main profession lately. Her father was a well-known chartered accountant who was as enthusiastic about social gatherings as he was about taxes.

Vicky was now clearly torn between school and the function. He loved going to school, which was more like a play zone than a school, but he also loved the attention he got at these gatherings. He finally decided that going out in Ajji's Innova was a better deal for the day. Anu had no problem with Vicky's decision to skip school that day. She was not one of those who believed that kindergarten was a stepping stone to IIT. But Sanju did think so. He thoroughly disapproved of how Anu let Vicky sleep in a few mornings and skip school. In her defence, some days Vicky looked too cosy under the quilt to be woken up.

Anu turned on the TV holding a plate of hot *Uppittu* and chutney. Her mother took food very seriously and couldn't till date understand why Anu hadn't inherited her love for cooking. Anu had inherited her mother's love for food but not for cooking.

Anu reached the school ten minutes early. EARLY! That was what she needed. Small goals that were met. Feeling a tad too happy, Anu parked her Santro on the street and waved at the security guard, handing him a fifty. 'Wipe the windshield, Dasappa.' That was not in Dasappa's job description, but all the teachers got their vehicles cleaned from him. Anu had started the trend and the principal had turned a blind eye to it. That was how friendly her school was. Anu loved working there.

'Hey Anu, looking like a movie-star, ya!' That was her colleague Smitha. 'Your hair looks fab!' Anu had great colleagues who weren't petty at all. According to Shwetha, none of them made any real money so there was no scope for fights or for being petty.

Anu beamed. All that effort she had put into dressing up that morning was already paying off. She had to meet somebody or go somewhere that evening. When you are having a good-face day, you have to flaunt it. A dozen names came to her head, but she picked Shwetha.

When she was about to enter her class, a helper asked her to meet the principal after the class. Anu wondered what it could be. She anyway met her at the end of the day every day. She was not just her principal but she was Sumitra aunty. Someone she had known all her life.

When Anu entered the principal's chamber, Sumitra aunty looked a little hassled, which was very unlike her.

'Anu, sit down. I have asked a few other teachers to join in.' Sumitra aunty rubbed her temples.

'What is wrong, aunty?' Anu felt alarmed. Something was not right.

Four other teachers walked in before the principal answered.

'A few parents are objecting that we aren't affiliated with any board.' Sumitra aunty spoke wearily. 'They are demanding a meeting after the holidays.'

Anu did not understand the fuss. Most kids were only four or five in their school. Why bother with big things like the boards with little kids?

'Some of the kids are entering fourth grade this year. I had never promised the parents that I am going to align with any standard board. But they insist that I had. I might have said that it was a consideration.'

How could anyone blame Sumitra aunty of foul play? Anu had an urge to shake sense into the parents.

'If they don't want the open school system, then they can change schools,' Anu declared.

'Not so easy, Anu. If there are protests or if someone goes to court on some frivolous account, I don't have the strength to fight it out. We have to resolve it peacefully.'

'We will be with you, ma'am,' Anu said and immediately all the teachers joined in. 'We will make sure you don't fight this alone.'

'Thank you. Tomorrow morning bring in your thoughts on why our system works. We will go over it once before talking to the parents.' Sumitra aunty looked slightly relieved seeing their show of support.

4

Dasara holidays. Now in the social media age, everyone spelt it Dussehra but Anu still liked to call it Dasara, like she had done all her life. She loved the holidays. Not that her job was stressful or anything, she mostly played with three-year-olds and taught them rhymes but still, holidays meant lounging, eating, and being sloppy. Sameer claimed that she worked as a teacher just so that she could get holidays.

Out of the ten days, four days had passed like quicksand. Anu's stay at her parents' house was as though her childhood was back. She could sleep however long she wanted and could step out anytime for shopping, coffee or dinner. Dinner! The most coveted event when you are the mom of a young child.

That was the fifth day of holidays and Anu woke up with a start, suddenly remembering her house and its chaotic state. It was on her to-do list and she did stare at it for a couple of days initially but had forgotten all about it eventually. Making a to-do list is fun. But the fun quickly turns to angst when all the incomplete tasks start to glare at you angrily. Sanju was coming back in three days. She had to clean it.

Anu rushed back home, leaving Vicky behind with her mother. Now, standing in the middle of the living room, Anu looked around in despair. The house looked like a pig-sty, a chicken coop, or whatever metaphor one could use for a place that had things strewn around and had a mysterious odour emanating from some corner.

Her books and newspapers covered most of the sofa and all of the centre table and the dining table. Vicky's toys took care of the floor. Anu walked to the bedroom with a foreboding that it was not going to be much better than the living room. She was not wrong—the bedroom had at least ten pieces of her unfolded clothes lying around, plus the new arrivals from her recent online shopping spree. There were more piles of Vicky's clothes, some washed and some not that she could no longer tell apart without smelling.

Anu took a deep breath and wandered to the kitchen. As if her clutter wasn't enough, some old brass vessels stared at Anu from a corner. In passing, Anu had mentioned to her mother that she wanted to buy some brassware to make her house look like Supriyaji's. Her mother had acted on that immediately. 'Anu, I have sent some brass things I had in the attic to your apartment. Shivanna has dropped them off.' Anu now vaguely recollected her mother's words. Her mother had palmed off the old things she had inherited from her mother-in-law. Now those dim, old, squarish vessels sat in a corner looking gloomier than Anu felt. *What would Shivanna, her father's lifelong office assistant who always wore ironed pearly-white shirts, have thought of this house?* Anu wanted to crawl into a hole.

Anu sat on the sofa and thought. The only way to finish work is to start right away. She looked around to see where to begin newspapers—that was easy. The thing was, Anu loved newspapers, not so much for the main news but for the supplements that carried interesting stories of celebrities. She picked up an armful of papers and walked to the utility area where they stored them. Once she was at the spot, Anu knew why she hadn't been putting the papers away. That area was already overflowing with papers. The glossy magazines had made a large chunk of papers slide off the pile. Anu sighed and marched back to the living room with the pile.

Dumping the papers on an already crowded table, she looked around again. Plates and cups. A dozen of them. Picking up the caked plates and cups, Anu walked to the kitchen sink. Why didn't she put them away as soon as she ate? Well, because she watched TV while eating and how could she take a break in the middle of a show? Usually, the maid collected them from around the house and washed them. Once Anu reached the kitchen, she remembered there was a reason why she was leaving her plates about. With the case of the absent maid, the sink had more than its share of the burden.

Dumping the plates on the countertop, Anu bit her nails. It was a holiday and Vicky was with her parents, so she had the day to herself. Should she waste that time cleaning the house? Sanju was coming back in three days and that was more than enough time to clean her tiny apartment. Now, shouldn't she enjoy the day eating, sleeping and being sloppy?

The hot October sun was blaring down. Even that small effort to clean up the house had made sweat trickle down Anu's back. A cold beer with Shwetha would clear up the head. Though Anu came across as an extrovert, she only had two good friends. Sameer and Shwetha. Somehow they were not fond of each other at all.

'SOS' Anu messaged Shwetha. That was their code for a quick drink.

'2 O'clock, Jake's Club.' Shwetha pinged back after an hour. With Sameer, Anu's go-to place was Drink and Dine, and with Shwetha it was Jake's club. Shwetha was now a fund manager, but she still managed to meet Anu the way they did a decade back.

Shwetha lived alone but had a fiancé tucked away in London. *Your engagement is longer than Pam and Roy's in The Office*—Anu often teased Shwetha. Not many would get that reference, but Shwetha did. She watched everything Anu suggested and complained that Anu never returned the gesture. But Shwetha suggested financial thrillers which put Anu to sleep just like her math classes from high school.

When Anu contemplated what to do for the next couple of hours before lunch, her phone rang. Yashoda aunty. Maybe she was calling for a tutorial on online grocery shopping. Anu picked up the phone only to hear a panic-stricken voice.

'Anu, can you come to the gate?' Anu could hear Yashoda aunty gasping. 'I tried to book a cab and—' The phone got cut off. Anu rushed, locking the door behind her. What could possibly go wrong while booking a cab?

When she neared the gate, Anu saw a haggard-looking Yashoda aunty with a mobile in hand and two cabs and an auto in front of her.

'Anu, see, I booked a cab but they have sent three of these!'

'What! Let me see.' Anu's suspicion was right. Aunty had booked three vehicles. Two of the drivers glared at them angrily, while the third started his cab. 'These old people just ruin our rides.' He muttered.

'Hey! She is learning to book, okay? Be patient.' Anu glared harder at the insolent driver.

'Where are you going, aunty? You have booked one cab to Mahalakshmi Layout, the second one to Lakshmi temple, and the third to some place named Lakshmi's Villa. These places are in three different corners of Bangalore!'

The drivers began to laugh and luckily Yashoda aunty had a sense of humour. She joined in the laughter and mumbled that she was going to her sister Lakshmi's house.

Anu cancelled all the three rides and requested the auto driver to drop Yashoda aunty to her destination. Yashoda squeezed Anu's hand. 'Thanks, Anu. You help me like a daughter.'

Anu smiled back. 'Make sure to include me in the will, aunty. Now get going!'

'You are a princess. What can a pauper like me give you?' Yashoda aunty was a retired English teacher, so she quoted from the classics. And, she loved it that Anu got her.

Smiling, Anu headed back to her flat, stopping at the children's play area. Vicky loved playing there even though it was such a basic one. Two yellow ducks, a swing and a slide. But all in working condition. Not just the playground, but their apartment complex was a basic one—elevators with manual doors, corridors without CCTV and a security guard who sat on a plastic stool and snoozed. No tennis court, swimming pool or gym. It even had a very basic name; not lake-view, valley-view, air-view, or any such. It was called the Ramesh Apartments, named after the owner who had razed a coconut grove to build it.

But it had residents who were exceptionally nice and friendly. Since her paternal grandparents had lived there for close to a decade, Anu knew almost every resident of the fifty houses. After his parents had passed away, Anu's father had rented out the place for a few years and then he had gifted it to Anu. So no EMI or rent, which was a sweet deal!

'Hi, Anu! Same pinch, ya. We are wearing the same kurta today!' That was Kavitha who was a huge admirer of Anu since high school. Yeah, they too went to the same KLE school. Though twice Anu's weight and half her height, Kavitha had been mimicking Anu's wardrobe since forever.

'You look nice.' Anu waved a hurried goodbye. If Kavitha got talking, Anu would not only miss her lunch but also dinner.

'Anu, wait. Where did you buy the white shirt you were wearing yesterday? I looked at both Amazon and Myntra but couldn't find!'

'Kavi, stop buying the clothes that I buy. I will help you choose a wardrobe for you, okay?' Anu meant what she said. Not that she was a supermodel or anything, but Kavitha had a body type that was well, not Anu's.

'No, ya. I like what you wear. Tell me where you got it.'

Luckily for Kavitha, Anu was too cheap to be a designer babe. 'Jayanagar. The store next to Motilal.' Anu sighed and gave away the source. This time a tad reluctantly. That shop was her find.

'What shade of lipstick are you wearing?' Kavitha came to a kissing distance.

'I will WhatsApp you the shade.' Anu hurried before she could get scrutinized for her innerwear.

'Anu, but we can go shopping. When? Tomorrow?' Kavitha's eyes lit up in eagerness.

Anu didn't have the heart to dim that child-like light in Kavitha, though going shopping with her was a painful act. Every single thing Anu picked up, Kavitha would order and pay for two of those—one in medium and one in XXXL. One may think to get so many gifts was fun but Anu was like the Lannisters in Game of Thrones—she always paid her debts. Which meant, each time Kavitha paid, Anu had to match.

But Kavitha was like a child, she wouldn't leave Anu alone until her wish of going to shopping was fulfilled. Anu gave in. 'Tomorrow it is. Meet you here at 11. Bye.'

Kavitha's obsession with Anu went back to when they were fifteen. The usually lethargic residents of Ramesh Apartments came alive during their resident's day, which they took very seriously. Taking part in any of the activities was considered to be prestigious. There were dance performances but mostly the middle-aged women who were once-upon-a-time dancers dominated the scene. There were dramas but older men and women who nursed theatrical ambitions when young would be all over it, singing was the

domain of the music teachers in the apartment and their
students. In Bangalore music is big—every street has at least
two Carnatic music teachers with at least twenty students
each. So one can imagine an apartment complex with a
hundred houses.

One event that was left for kids was a beauty pageant
of ethic wear. Every year it was same deal – contestants
strutting awkwardly in strangely draped sarees. Tamilians
and Coorgis sashayed confidently because their mothers
knew how to work the pallus. Then some proclaimed their
drapes were Gujarati or Rajasthani which nobody contested.
It was before the internet era so nobody knew the difference
between Gujarati, Rajasthani or Marathi. Kannada kids had
it hard. Their style was too everyday but their mothers didn't
know any better.

Only girls fifteen years of age and above could audition
and finally, Anu had qualified that year; but so had Kavitha.
The audition was held in the car parking lot and the aspirants
had to walk the slopy ramp. The selectors were older girls
who were also the self-nominated fashionistas. Boys,
uninvited of course, gathered all around passing comments.

Anu's grandmother had draped her in a Kanjeevaram
saree. Kannada style. Anu wasn't happy about the non-exotic
nature of it, but that was the only way her grandmother
knew. Anu, determined to make it to the event, had watched
enough Femina Miss India shows on TV all year long. When
the time came, she made herself proud by walking down the
steep ramp with a hand on the hip and head-tilted upwards.
She had secretly practised not to tumble at the end of the

ramp. Whoa! She even got a big round of applause when she finished.

Walking after her was Kavitha, also draped in a Kanjeevaram saree, Kannada style. Only one girl was selected for a particular style and Anu, though not proud of her thoughts, was happy that her competitor was Kavitha.

But nothing had prepared Anu for what befell the poor girl. When Kavitha waddled down the ramp, the selectors showed no interest in her while the boys were savage. 'Try the elephant costume!' 'Don't walk. Roll down the ramp, fatty!'

Kavitha was in tears and Anu was enraged. She began to think of many different ways to get back at the boys but before she could come up with a plan, the selectors read out the list of the chosen ones. Anu was in but she felt miserable looking at the tears rolling down Kavitha's eyes messing up her make up.

Forgetting for a moment how much she wanted to be in the show, Anu had held up her saree and walked up the ramp. 'I will not participate. Instead, I want Kavitha to do the walk.' Even as she uttered the words, her heart sank to the pit of her stomach. All her effort was a waste. Did Kavitha have to be in the same costume as hers? But when she had looked at Kavitha's stunned but delighted face, Anu had sighed and tried to be happy.

But the catcalls and booing against Kavitha had made Anu, what Sameer termed, pull-an-Anu on the boys. The usually non-belligerent Anu went livid. 'What is your problem?' she had shouted at the boys. 'Do you think you are perfect?'

Her little speech was as ineffective as the dainty little hankerchief she was using to wipe the sweat pouring from her face. Boys were now even more encouraged to catcall and boo both Anu and Kavitha. But luckily, Kavitha's grandfather who had come in to check on them became their knight-in-shining-Rayon pants. When he stood next to Anu and stared, the boys had quietened down instantly. The fashionistas agreed to include Kavitha in the pageant along with Anu, on the grandfather's insistence.

But that particular incident had also resulted in two disasters. The overzealous grandfather had next insisted that Anu and Kavitha walk the car ramp again, but this time together. Individually both the girls had manoeuvred the slope but now, together, with Kavitha holding on to Anu's hand in glee, they both had toppled and rolled.

The second disaster was Kavitha's newfound love for Anu. After that, she wore what Anu wore, went to the same college that Anu went to, and lived in the same apartment complex that Anu did. The only time Kavitha failed to mimic Anu was in her pregnancy. She had her son Adi two years earlier than Anu had Vicky. But to make up for that, Adi too was now in Dew Drops.

Anu sighed. Though she felt stalked by Kavitha, it was not all that bad having her in life. She found Anu household help, hunted for yoga classes when it became Anu's obsession, and she willingly sipped Fanta when Anu had a drink and drove her back. Everyone needs someone who makes them feel special.

Anu hurried home. She needed to get dressed before heading to Jake's.

4

Jake of Jake's Club was in fact Jagannatha. If you watch a lot of English shows and expect Jake, aka, Jagannatha to be a friendly, suave, six-pack toting, bartending owner, you are in for a surprise. Jake here is a sixty-something short and burly man, with a ring on each finger. He walks around in a white-suit without making eye contact with any of the patrons. He does not believe in being a friendly owner who chats up the guests. He is the King of his club and the customers are his subjects. Anu has been going to the club for almost a decade and all she gets from him is an occasional small nod.

When Anu reached the club, Jake was pacing, and Shwetha was already seated and typing furiously on her mobile. She was crunching some numbers for her multinational investment bank employer for sure. Anu waited for Shwetha to finish her work.

A tiny puppy came bounding towards Anu. Before she had a chance to even look at the pup, an equally tiny boy came bounding after to take the puppy away. It was obvious he did not fancy his new dog liking a stranger.

'What is your puppy's name?' Anu asked to break the ice with the boy.

'I won't tell you. Don't be his friend.' The boy, probably four like Vicky, snapped at Anu.

'He won't become my friend. He is only your friend.' Anu tried to put the boy at ease but he ran without casting a second glance at Anu.

Shwetha looked up from her phone and smiled. 'Don't worry. I will be your friend.'

'Fine. You are not half as cute as the pup, but you will do for now.' Anu beckoned the waiter.

'You look nice, Anu. New online haul?' Shwetha put away her phone. 'How much money do you spend on clothes?'

'I spend as much as I can. I can't have online businesses go bankrupt.' Anu grinned at her friend. They were a fun company.

'Regular stuff, madam?' The waiter who came to their table asked with a wide smile. Unlike the owner, the staff was friendly at the club.

'Yes, Anand. Budweiser, peanut masala, and Veg Pakoda.' Anu knew most waiters by name because Jake employed a small staff. 'How is your new baby?'

The man grinned widely, yanked out his phone, and began to show Anu photos of his baby with large black dots smeared on its forehead and the left cheek. Those black dots were to protect the baby from people's evil eyes, a tradition Anu had flouted with Vicky.

When the waiter showed no signs of finishing with the pictures, Anu felt Shwetha's heeled foot kick hers. Note to self: Never ask a new parent for baby pictures; they won't stop until you have seen all ten-thousand of them. 'Anand, leave the phone here and get us beer. I will see the photos slowly,' Anu volunteered.

'That is all, madam. I will get you your beer.' The man ran towards the kitchen stoving the phone into his pocket.

'His gallery probably has more porn than baby pictures! Why would he leave the phone with you!' Shwetha began to laugh.

'I stopped the slide show, didn't I? He could have just said his baby is doing well. Everyone has too many photos to share lately.' Anu shuddered.

'By the way, how come you are drinking today? Breaking your once a week rule?' Shwetha asked when the beer was served. Anu drank two larges of something once a week and no more. Not for any health reasons but because she didn't fancy sporting a large gut and perennial undereye bags.

'Desperate times call for desperate drinks. The house has gone from bad to ugly. I got to clean it now.'

Shwetha nodded understandingly. 'See, cleaning is easy. Dump everything into Vicky's playroom. He anyway plays in the kitchen.'

Anu nodded. 'Gosh, you are so smart! I can clean up in five minutes this way! What do I do with the dirty dishes?'

'Until Sanju is back, eat outside or stay with your parents!'

'Very smart. Let us drink to that.'

One mug led to two. The starters got repeated. Office gossips were shared. So much happened over a drink.

'Don't you need to go back to work?' Anu asked Shwetha who was all too comfortable sitting cross-legged removing her heels. Usually, she ran after one beer.

'Have taken the afternoon off. Let us order more beer.' Shwetha beckoned the waiter. 'What are your plans for the afternoon?'

'*Gilmore Girls* on Netflix,' Anu grinned. 'You know, when Supriyaji asks us to thank the universe, I say a special thank you to Netflix and Prime. What would I do without their no-brainer funnies?'

Shwetha raised a toast. 'To Netflix.'

'What do we eat for the main course?' Anu eyed the menu. 'Paneer this and that. Biryani this and that. Naan, roti, this and that.'

'Indian lunch menu is the one thing that doesn't change worldwide. Order Maggi, Anu. And add Maggi at Jake's to your thanksgiving list.'

The puppy yet again came back to Anu and so did its possessive owner. Anu tried smiling at the boy, who only frowned. 'How come that boy isn't charmed by me?' Anu asked puzzled. Usually, people warmed up to her when she smiled.

'Wait till he hits puberty.'

'I will be too old by then.' Anu giggled. This was phase two of drinking where they both started talking nonsense and giggled over nothing.

'How is Sanju?' Shwetha asked taking a long swig.

'However he is. I will assess when he is back,' replied Anu. Somehow, Sameer assuring her that nothing was wrong with Sanju had put her at ease.

'I think we should stop drinking,' said Shwetha tentatively.

The problem with buy-one-get-one deals was one always over drank. So did the girls. 'Got to hit the loo,' Anu got up.

She felt her stress from having to clean the house melt away. She could now go home to *Gilmore Girls*. Cleaning could wait till tomorrow. A perfect day so far—Anu smiled contentedly.

As she moved by the poolside to get to the restroom, she saw the puppy follow her wriggling its nonexistent tail. Anu couldn't resist anymore. She bent down to pet it but the springy creature in its excitement started to climb all over her, finally succeeding to grasp her feet firmly with its paws. Anu shook her leg trying to pry her foot free and the weightless little thing landed straight inside the pool!

Anu gasped—had she killed a little dog? When her breath returned, she squealed for help looking at the puppy struggling to stay afloat when a nearby swimmer set him on the ground. Sighing in relief, Anu tried drying the little moaning bundle. The next thing she knew, someone thudded into her and a moment later she was the one sinking to the bottom of the pool. Anu wiggled and tried crying but the words wouldn't come out. What had just happened? Was her death going to be in this manner? Vicky! Was she never going to hold her little Vicky again?

Then someone yanked her to her feet. 'Madam, it is three feet here. Just stand.'

Anu looked at the amused faces gathered around the pool and then at Shwetha who was about to burst out laughing. Anu looked at herself. Her pink bra showing through her white shirt. What was she thinking when she wore it? Her jeans, now soaking up all the water, weighed a ton. *How did these things happen only to me? As Sameer often said, I am a disaster magnet!* Shwetha gave her a hand to get out of the pool. As Anu stood dripping water around her, a hand that carried a robe came towards her. Jake, aka, Jagannatha! 'Return it tomorrow.' The man handed the robe and walked away.

'How did I land in the pool?' Anu asked with her head now light inside and heavy outside.

'You pushed the poodle into the water so its owner,' Shwetha subtly pointed at the boy, 'returned you the favour. Anu, it is like straight out of a comedy movie, man!'

Anu wrapped the robe around herself, disappointing a few lunchers who were enjoying her wet t-shirt show.

'Say sorry to aunty,' the boy's mother pushed him gently towards Anu.

Anu bent down to face the reticent little boy and smiled, 'I had a good swim. So don't bother saying sorry.'

Now the boy looked up at her, still without a smile. He spoke after a pause. 'You can touch Spot. Only once.' He held his dog towards her.

Anu shook her head. 'No. Spot won't like it if I touch him.' Anu said solemnly. 'He likes only you.'

The boy brightened. 'You get your own dog. He will like you.'

The mother now looked at Anu and apologized sheepishly. 'Thank you for being so nice. I am really sorry. My son is very possessive about his dog.'

'Don't worry. I live closeby. I can be home in ten minutes to change.' Anu waved the haggard mother goodbye.

'Come, I will drive you home.' Shwetha dished out the keys from Anu's handbag. 'And, I will help you clean the house. I have taken the afternoon off.'

'How do I sit in the car? I am going to wet the robe in no time.' Anu steadied herself. Thank god she was a tad drunk. How could she have managed to walk around in a robe in public otherwise?

'Spread a newspaper. Your upholstery isn't some high-quality leather that gets ruined.'

When they began to walk out, Anu's phone rang. Sanju! Anu picked up the call automatically and realized it was a video call only when Sanju's face loomed large on the screen.

'Hey, what time is it? Why are you up till this late?'

'It is 5.30 in New York. Told you I was going to be here for three days before flying to Bangalore.' Sanju's voice held a minor edge. 'Where are you?'

'Jake's.' Anu briefly explained what had happened, fully expecting Sanju to smile and shrug in mock desperation as he always did. But he snapped. 'Why do you keep going to Jake's? Can't you find a better place? How could some boy push you into the water?'

'Sanju! You like Jake's and so does your father. What is this sudden loathing for the place? Also, why are you snapping at me?' In her anger, Anu blurted, 'I know your problem. You are you having an affair and you don't want to come back to Bangalore. So you are on a fault-finding mission.'

Sanju's jaw opened wide. 'Anu! What nonsense! I am just snowed under with work, okay?'

Anu went into one of her belligerent investigative modes. 'Show me around the room. Prove to me you don't have some floozy hiding in there.'

Shwetha snatched the phone from Anu. 'Anu, get a grip.'

Anu snatched back the phone only to see Sanju move it all-around an immaculate hotel room. When the phone zoomed in on him, he was laughing. 'Anu, of all the crazy ideas you get, this must be the craziest! Go home and sleep.'

Shwetha sighed. 'Now let us get you home before another disaster strikes!'

'Shwetha, we will go to your place. I don't want you to waste your afternoon cleaning up my house!' Anu insisted. Shwetha was like Sanju. Obsessive about keeping things tidy and if she saw Anu's house now, one of two things would happen—she would faint looking at the mess, or if she managed not to, then she would clean it till eternity.

Once into Shwetha's cosy warm clothes, Anu picked up the large cup of coffee waiting for her. Tucking her legs underneath her, Anu took a contented sip.

'What is happening with you and Dini, Shwetha?' asked Anu.

Shwetha was quiet for a bit and then shrugged. 'He wants to get married soon and wants me to move to the UK.'

Anu's heart skipped a beat. She knew that day would come and she was the happiest for her friend, but losing Shwetha to the UK was somehow an unbearable thought. 'Shwetha, think about it. I feel you are hoping for Dini to change his mind about living in the UK and move back to Bangalore. But he won't.'

Shwetha smiled. 'I am not like you, Anu. You are very sure of what you want but I always oscillate.'

'You will know what to do, Shwetha. Take a day off from work and think.' Anu lifted her coffee cup in a toast. 'Here is to Shwetha and Dini's happy ending.'

Sanju was going to arrive that night and luckily Radha was back that morning. Anu had to bring Vicky back since her parents were going to an out-of-town wedding. If there was a world record for the maximum weddings attended in a lifetime, her parents would win it hands down.

'Just take care of Vicky for now, Radha. No need to cook. I will bring you food. We will clean the house together.'

Yashoda aunty had asked Anu to take her for a quick round of grocery shopping. Now that Radha was around, Anu felt relieved. Just as she was about to leave, the doorbell rang. Anu knitted her brows thinking if she had ordered anything online. Well, she only ordered in the first week of the month; after that, she was usually too broke for shopping. Radha opened the door, and Anu gaped at the figure that stood before her.

5

'Sanju! You are early!'

'No, I am not! You thought I was coming at 2 in the night, didn't you?' Sanju shook his head in desperation. 'Get the dates and time right, Anu!'

'Where do I even sit here? It looks like a haunted house.' Sanju's voice held despair as he glanced around.

Radha quickly removed the newspapers from the sofa, and Anu shoved the plates and cups underneath it. Then she smiled brightly. 'Here! Sit now.'

To her relief, a smile played on Sanju's lips. 'Very clean now. Where are you going all dressed up?' He asked, stretching on the sofa. 'Where is Vivikth?'

'Daddy! Find me … find me!' The joy in Vicky's voice from behind the door was unmistakable.

Sanju picked him up. 'Hey Champ, what are you doing?'

Vicky wiggled out of Sanju's arms, 'Daddy, play hide and seek with me.'

Anu intervened. 'Vicky! Daddy has just come. He will play with you later. Now go play with Radha aunty.'

Radha handed them both a cup of tea and took Vicky out. Remembering that she had to cancel with Yashoda aunty, Anu picked up her phone.

'I have just come, and you are all ready to head out.' Sanju flashed a look of disapproval.

'Nope. I am cancelling my date with Yashoda aunty.' Anu snuggled next to Sanju.

'So you thought I can still get a girl for an affair? I am quite flattered.' Sanju put an arm around Anu pulling her closer.

'Well, you are a sugar daddy now. You have your appeal with the young.' Anu smiled. 'Sanju, if I die, will you remarry?'

'Hmm … if I am still young and dashing like now, I will. If I am old and gnarly, I won't. You?'

'Just the opposite. If I am still young and dashing, I won't settle into a marriage. If I am old and gnarly, I will.'

Sanju began to laugh. 'I won't die ever then!'

Anu felt good. It was nice to have Sanju back. In a way, she even liked the discipline he forced into her life. But though he was laughing and having a good time, his moodiness in the last few days bothered her. She was tempted to shoot her volley of questions at him right away, but decided to wait. Why spoil a good moment?

But Sanju's good mood was short-lived. He was back to being sulky and snappy within no time. The bedroom was a mess, she had left the laptop plugged in, the bathroom had too many of her clothes—he was testing Anu's patience. Sanju had borderline obsessive compulsive disorder but he never got this irritated with things around him.

Anu decided to let him sleep on it. When she couldn't fall asleep up until midnight, she texted Shwetha. 'Call Sanju's phone in the morning. If he doesn't answer it, I might have murdered him.'

'Done. Hide the evidence.' Replied Shwetha.

But Sanju hadn't cheered up even by next morning. As Sameer had pointed out, Sanju was not one of those chirpy kind of men but even by his standards, he was too mopey. By afternoon, when he was walking around, moodily picking things up and tidying the edges of the sofa covers, Anu decided enough was enough.

'Sanju, why are you looking like death? What's wrong?'

'I am not heading a happiness project like you, Anu. Allow me to be how I am.'

'Well, your ways affect the progress of my happiness project.' Anu flashed him a murderous look. 'So, spill it, Sanju. Did you lose your job? Do you have VD? Do you—'

'Stop, Anu!' Sanju shrugged in despair. 'There is nothing wrong per se. Just that I don't want to live like this.' He pointed around him.

Anu was taken aback. The messy house is causing this distress? He wasn't even around for three months to see the mess!

'Hey, we can clean it up. No big deal.' Anu tried not to sound offended, though she amply was.

'No, Anu. Not the mess.' Sanju added quickly, 'Not just the mess, at least. I want a better lifestyle. Like what my boss has in the US. His suburban house was straight out of a magazine. He dines in style, drives in style, lives in style. Period.' Sanju always acquired an accent and Americanisms like *Period* when he returned from the US.

Anu furrowed her brows in disbelief. 'You want to move to the US?'

Sanju shook his head. 'No. Don't panic. Even if we move there, it will take a decade before we can afford that life. And, with the policies of Trump, moving to the US is not even a possibility. I want to live that life here. It is possible, you know.'

Anu remained silent waiting for Sanju to finish. She could not gauge what his angle was.

'See, we could have lived in the US but you never wanted to move. So I gave that up. Look at the roads here, the traffic, the footpath, the noise—I want to live in a place that at least shields us from all this.'

'Where is such a place, Sanju?' Anu felt an irrational anger rise within her. When anyone criticized Bangalore, her antennas went up. She loved her city with all its trappings.

'Let us move to a nice house in a classy neighbourhood. A villa in North Bangalore, like in Hennur or Hebbal. Like the one Dave rents when he is in India.'

Anu almost jumped back in horror. Her mouth went dry, and her heartbeat became erratic. What is he saying? He knew she did not have the stomach for such drastic changes in life! He knew that for more than a decade. 'Hennur! That is not even Bangalore! Hope you will get over this thought once you are not jetlagged.'

Sanju sighed. 'Anu, I am serious. At least let us look at some houses, okay?'

Anu kept shaking her head. 'I could have married anyone in the US if I wanted to move! I chose you because you wanted to stay around here as much as I did.'

'You do firmly believe that marrying me was an act of kindness, don't you?' Sanju smiled amusedly and ruffled Anu's hair.

'Not just marrying you but making a nice life for us. See, you don't do a thing around the house, except smoothen the edges of the sofa covers. Neither do I. That is because I have carefully collected people who ease our lives. Now you want to throw this all away for some absurd dream?'

'Why are my dreams all absurd? Come on, Anu.'

Plonking on the sofa and stretching her legs on to the magazine table, Anu turned on the TV. She could not continue with the discussion anymore. She could not imagine uprooting her life from Vijaynagar.

'How can I abandon my friends, family, Jake's, Yashoda aunty, Supriyaji, my school?' Anu waved her hands dramatically. 'And, Kavitha!'

Claiming the seat next to her, Sanju muted the television. 'Kavitha will follow you anyway. And the others are not going away anywhere. They will all be here and you can add more people to your collection in a new place. You will think about it, right?'

Anu nodded wearily. Sanju was nice, kind, and adjusting, but was also like a broken record when he wanted something.

He wore Anu down. 'Sanju, is it just the house and the car that bother you or us too?'

Sanju stretched next to Anu and pulled her to him. 'You are perfect. I don't want you to change at all.'

Feeling all warm-fuzzy with the rare compliment, Anu declared. 'Vicky is perfect too.'

'He is. Though you could cut his nails and clean his nose more often.'

'Done. Now can we watch TV? Before your snotty little boy comes in like a hurricane?' Anu smiled. Sanju never prolonged any fight. They hadn't stopped talking to each other even for a day in the past ten years. Well, except for six months once. A story for another time.

'Think about what I said.' Sanju was going to be relentless unless she gave in. She knew it already.

Anu threw the head back, sighed, and nodded. 'Okay, milord.'

When the school reopened after two days, Anu felt quite delighted. Holidays had meaning only when there was work. And, she couldn't wait to showcase her revamped wardrobe after the Amazon Great Indian sale. Luckily, Sanju was so busy at work, he hadn't pestered her with the think-about-it phrase. So she was secretly hoping that he would forget all about it soon.

Dropping Vicky to his class room, Anu walked into her class. 'Anu ma'am, my birthday today.'

'Anu ma'am, I went to the beach.'

'Anu ma'am, I saw a pallot, tigel and fox.'

The shrill excited voices surrounded Anu. It was a herculean task to quieten them down so Anu decided to close the classroom door and let them squeal.

At lunch break, the principal summoned the teachers to let them know that the meeting with the parents was going to be in two days. She looked so worried, Anu had an unreasonable urge to make all the trouble magically go away for her dear Sumitra aunty.

When Anu came home with Vicky, Sanju was already seated on the sofa surrounded by colourful brochures. He looked up and smiled brightly at Anu. 'Look, all I had to do was ask a developer who visited our campus about the houses in the Hennur area. He sent in these many options.' He pointed at the glitzy papers on the table.

'Daddy, make an aeroplane!' Vicky's highly excited voice brought Anu back to reality. Sanju hadn't forgotten about the move as she had hoped. Darn!

'No, Vicky. We will make aeroplanes with the newspaper. Go get some. These are daddy's work papers.' Sanju grabbed the glossies before Vicky did.

'Newspaper not good, daddy.' Vicky pouted.

Anu picked up Vicky and said weakly. 'He is hungry, Sanju. Let me give him something to eat.'

She was tempted to pick up all those brochures and blow them out of the window. They were her worst nightmares in technicolour.

'Come soon, Anu. We will make a map of the places to visit.' Anu did not have the heart to burst Sanju's enthusiasm. But she had her routine in place. After feeding herself and Vicky, she was going to take a nap. Then she had her yoga class. After that, she was going to take Vicky to the playground and chat with Yashoda aunty or Kavitha or someone. Anu sighed. This was the beginning of the end.

Half-an-hour later, Anu put Vicky down for a nap and sat beside Sanju with a heavy heart. He began by holding up four glossies as if they were winning poker hands. Anu picked up the one that looked all white and serene. 'Riviera?' She laughed. 'Seriously, Sanju? Have they created a coast in Bangalore?'

Sanju smiled. 'Don't pick on the names. Look at the credentials. See this.' He showed her a brochure named Helios. 'This is in Hebbal. Built by—'

Anu cut him off. 'Oh, wait! You said Hennur and now you are showing me Hebbal? That is another ten kilometres from here!'

Sanju slightly knitted his brows. 'Why are you measuring the distance from Vijaynagar? We should think about my commute to work.'

As if only his work mattered. Anu felt offended. 'I still have to work here and visit my parents.'

Sanju shook his head vehemently. 'No, Anu. You will work there, not here! Also, I have been commuting twenty kilometres to work all these years! So you can travel twenty once a week to visit your parents.'

Anu looked at him disbelievingly. 'You sleep in your office cab both ways. How does the distance matter to you? I meet my parents five times a week, not once a week!'

When Sanju grew quiet and gathered the brochures, Anu knew she had pushed him too far. 'Hey, sorry. Sit down.' She patted on the sofa next to her. 'We will look through them.'

Finally, that weekend they were going to visit two places in Hennur and two in Hebbal. All of them looked so posh, Anu made a mental note to check if any movie star had a weekend home there. A selfie with Upendra or Yash would look good on the DP.

Anu picked up her coffee from the self-service counter and looked for a table to sit. The meeting with the school parents was in another half hour. Her colleague Disha was going to join her for the coffee. As there were no empty tables, Anu sat on one that was occupied by two women.

One of the women seemed to look distinctly uncomfortable with Anu sharing the table. Anu smiled at her. 'You are not from here, are you? It is common to table share here.'

But the woman instead of smiling and saying it was okay, looked a bit irritated. 'Then thank god I am not from here.'

That was rude! Anu looked at the other woman who looked familiar and mildly embarrassed. Before Anu said anything, her phone rang. Shwetha. Anu forgot all about the women and perked up. Disha too joined her with her coffee.

'Hey Shwetha,' Anu began enthusiastically when Shwetha asked where she was. 'I had told you, no? Meeting with the parents today? Silly that they are worried about the education of their toddlers.'

Anu felt Disha's foot on hers and withdrew hers. Then continued. 'Some parents are demanding that the school affiliates with a central board. Overenthusiastic folks, man. They can't let their children enjoy childhood.'

Disha's foot kicked hard at her shin. Anu moved her chair a little and bid goodbye to Shwetha. Now, the rude woman caught Anu's eye and asked. 'Couldn't help overhearing you. Are you a teacher?'

Anu perked up and enthused. 'I am. Today we have a meeting where we have to convince the parents that our school is good.' Anu rolled her eyes. 'We have the best system. Kids are not stressed with exams or homework.'

Disha whispered, 'Anu, listen—'

But the rude woman cut in. 'So, you don't think the kids need to develop a competitive spirit through exams? Don't we need to teach children to work hard?'

'That will happen with time. Also, children have to work hard if they want to. Not because of parental pressure.' Anu was now feeling uncomfortable with the belligerence the woman was showing.

Disha stood up and walked out and Anu followed her murmuring a bye to the woman. As soon as they were out of the hotel, Disha blurted. 'Anu! One of them is a parent at the school. You went on saying so much!'

Anu blushed in anxiety. What had she done? How damaging were her statements? Disha assured her that nothing was too bad and Anu decided to go with it.

Vicky was playing with the other teachers' kids in the play area, with an Ayah watching over them. Anu peeked in to make sure he was doing all right. He was rolling in the sandpit like a cute puppy. The thing with Vicky was, he was an influencer. Even as Anu watched, two other kids joined him in the roll-in-the-mud game. Anu shrugged and moved towards the meeting room.

'Anu,' she heard Kavitha's voice call her name. The principal had insisted on sending out an email to all the parents to join in. Luckily, there were only about twenty of them.

'Hey Kavitha, why are you here?' Anu waved and stopped.

'Just came. We can go back together, no? We can have a Masala Dosa and coffee on the way home?' Kavitha was like the boyfriend one never had. She was so eager to be with Anu at any given opportunity!

'Okay! See you at the meeting.' Anu agreed. Who can say no to Dose and coffee?

By the time she entered, the parents were seated and the teachers had gathered on the podium next to the principal.

'Why are there only four teachers?' Anu asked the principal in a low voice all the while scanning for the parent she was supposed to have met. They weren't there!

'After school hours. They all must have gone home.' The principal answered a bit dejectedly. Anu couldn't believe the teachers. This was a time to show their support and they went home?

Anu excused herself to go into the school office. Luckily, four staffers were still at work and Anu dragged them to the meeting room, instructing them to simply stand confidently and nod in vehement agreement at everything the principal said.

Sumitra aunty's eyes lit up when Anu came back with the office staff but Anu's heart sank. The two women from the coffee shop were seated right in the front.

The meeting began with the principal welcoming everyone. Then she opened up the floor for questions.

'What is the future of our kids if we continue here?' The questions started hard and rude.

'The same as any child studying in any school! Here children are learning to gain knowledge, not to ace exams.' Anu admired Sumitra aunty's soft yet confident voice.

'But you promised that you will align with CBSE when we started here,' said another not-so-gentle mother.

'I had said I might consider,' said the principal firmly. 'But now we like the outcome of our system. Children are competent and stressfree.'

'But kids do not develop a competitive spirit without exams.' That was the rude one from the coffee-shop. 'One of your teachers I met earlier said she doesn't even believe in kids working hard.'

Anu was flabbergasted. How could her words be twisted like this? 'I never said kids shouldn't—'

Anu was cut off before she even completed by the same woman. 'Quoting this teacher, she says we parents are silly to be even bothered about this. "Silly" was her word.'

Anu's face burned; in anger or distress, she could not tell. 'I did not say that to you. You overheard me over the phone.' Great Anu, now you have stepped right into a trap.

'But you said it!'

'No, I did not mean—' Anu was cut off again.

'If this is how teachers feel about parents, then I don't know what to say.' The woman was now looking triumphantly at everyone setting off a murmur.

'Madam, wait.' That was Kavitha who had stood up shaking a finger at Madam Rude. 'You are not even giving Ms Anu a chance to talk. I am also a parent and I think we should not attack the teachers. Ms Anu, you continue.' Nobody dared defy Kavitha who looked murderous enough to throw punches.

Anu smiled nervously and looked at Sumitra aunty, who subtly nodded at her to continue. 'Kids here are studying at their own pace, they are capable of answering questions based on that learning, and they complete projects that are again based on what is taught to them.' Anu glanced around and everyone looked interested in her little speech. Warming up to her speech now, Anu smiled like an enlightened Guru at the audience.

But historically, Anu never stopped while ahead. 'In fact, my own son studies here and so do most of the teachers' kids. We as parents need not worry about the exam-preparedness of our young ones.'

Anu knew that she need not have added that bit about Vicky but words tumbled out when she spotted the kids lined up outside at the door. She beckoned to Vicky who came bounding to her. She picked him up and well, hoped that he would hug her and maybe kiss her lovingly. He did no such thing. He was in fact in such an urgency to run, he plucked a fistful of Anu's hair out of the clasp and kicked her in the shin while sliding down her arms. It was all unintentional from his part, but Anu wished it had been a tad soberer.

'He looks very well-adjusted.' Madam Rude cocked a brow. 'How old is your son?'

Anu was now growing rather uncomfortable. Why was she the target? Did she have a bull's eye painted on her face?

'Four,' Anu answered briefly. She had to get out of the spotlight.

'At that age, even we didn't worry. Now my child is in fourth grade. I have to think about his education and his future.' Another parent chimed in.

Seriously? Eight-year-olds need to get serious about their futures? But Anu with great difficulty waited for someone else to field the question.

Sumitra aunty did. 'You need not worry is what I am saying. We are teaching them what they need to learn for their grade.'

But Madam Rude would not let it go. 'How many teachers here have children studying in the third or fourth?'

'How is it relevant?' Sumitra aunty asked politely.

'Ms Anu here claimed that most teachers have their kids studying here. If a restauranteur eats at his restaurant, then the patrons feel better about the quality. So I want to know how many of their kids are in higher classes.'

Was that woman a lawyer? Did she think this was some kind of family court? But the truth was, most of the teachers' kids were kindergarteners. Then Anu's eyes fell on Adi snuggling next to Kavitha.

'I have an older son.' Anu declared and signalled to Kavitha to send Adi over. She did not dare look at Sumitra aunty.

'See, Adi is in fourth grade. But I am not worried.'

But Adi was not very cooperative. He stood next to Anu digging his nose for a moment and then asked loudly, 'Anu aunty, can I go? I want to go to Mummy.'

The crowd burst into laughter before Kavitha stood up holding Adi's hand up like a soldier holding a gun. 'He is like a son to Anu Ma'am. We are neighbours and friends for decades.' She said with a flourish. 'We always say we have two sons.'

'Thank God not two husbands!' was Madam Rude's crude reply. But the crowd did not burst into laughter. So the joke was on her.

Later, Anu walked into the principal's chamber sheepishly. 'Aunty, sorry. Didn't mean to stir up so much controversy and bury your words.'

Sumitra aunty laughed. 'Anu, you meant well and that was evident. But recognize when someone is attacking you personally. You don't have to waste energy on them.'

When Anu bit into that Masale Dose later with Kavitha, sipping a hot cup of coffee, Kavitha spoke wistfully. 'Anu, you called Adi your son, ya. I am so touched.'

Anu smiled. 'You saved me from my lie! But he is like a son to me.'

'And I am like a sister, no?' Kavitha asked eagerly.

'Of course.' Anu patted Kavitha's hand and surprisingly, she meant it. Anu began to feel better. She had made a fool out of herself but she hadn't caused any damage.

Then there was a call from Sanju, sinking her mood like the Titanic. 'Anu, we can go see some houses tomorrow. I am working from home.'

'I can't teach from home, can I?' Anu snapped.

'Okay, okay. We will go after you come back from school.' Sanju backtracked quickly. If he fought, she could say no to him more easily. But Sanju was so gentle, Anu most often just gave in.

Anu looked longingly at everything in Jake's club. The pool, the tennis court, the lawn, the rabbits that scurried around the lawn. She knew that place, she knew people who worked there. She knew exactly what to order there. She had come to meet Shwetha to tell her about Sanju's fanciful idea.

'Now, why are you so upset, Anu? You want to die in the greater Vijaynagar area?' asked Shwetha working on the onion pakodas.

Anu took a swig of her beer. 'Shewtha! I can't move! My life is here. I married Sanju because he never had any ambition to move out of the greater Vijaynagar area.'

'You are too low on ambition, Anu.' Shwetha continued to eat, and Anu continued to drink.

'Hey, that is called contentment. I am happy, Shwetha. I am happy with the way I look, the way I live, the people in my life. Everyone I know is unhappy about something or the other. Now, why does Sanju want to rob me of my happiness?' Anu wailed more.

'When you get married, it is the collective happiness that you sign up for. But Sanju is proposing an upgrade to your life. Give it a try. Go see some houses as a start.'

'We see some houses and then we will settle for one. That is the end of me! I curated my life here. It didn't just happen, okay? Left to my parents, I would be an engineer in a faraway country. Left to you, we would never be friends. Left to Sameer, I would just be some girl and not his best friend. Left to Sanju, I would be toiling living with Padzilla.'

Shwetha laughed. 'I agree, Babe. You will do the same things all over again. Don't act as if this is the end of the world. You will still be in Bangalore.'

'You and I can't just meet at the drop of a hat anymore.'

'Yes. But we can still meet. If it makes you feel better, I will wear a hat and drop it for you.'

Anu laughed at that absurd thought but fell silent soon. She liked being close to her parents' house. And her in-laws. Unlike many others, she did not hate them. They were nice people who hosted them every Sunday for lunch. Then they kept Vicky so that Anu and Sanju could catch a movie. Her parents, her grandmother … Anu held herself back from getting carried away. She was acting as though she was dying of some illness! She would only be moving a few kilometres away. Then the thought began to panic her again.

'Shwetha, I love working at the school. What will I do if I move?' When Anu wanted to go back to work once Vicky turned two, her mother's close friend Sumitra aunty had offered her a job at her school. Six months later, Anu had put Vicky to pre-school right there. He loved it, she loved it, and Sanju so far didn't dislike it.

'You can teach at a pre-school in Hennur too.'

'Why are you pushing me to do this? You are my friend. You should support my loathing.'

'I will hate it if you hate living there. Right now your loathing is only in your imagination.' Shwetha finished her drink and patted Anu's hand. 'You are only thirty, Anu. Live a little.'

Sameer was the exact opposite of Shwetha when Anu met him. 'Sanju has gone mad. Don't encourage him.' Anu wanted to hug Sameer.

'He has gone mad. How can we replicate the US suburban life here? All he talks about is his boss and his splendid living. The scotch he drinks every night, the barbeque parties he throws, the Porsche convertible he drives.'

'What barbeque party does your pure-veg husband want to throw? He drinks a pint of beer once a week and curses everyone like crazy driving his XUV. So the Scotch and the Porsche don't matter! Anu, don't get me wrong. But Sanju is someone who can never be completely happy. Even if you move to a mansion and change your lifestyles, he will find some other reason to gripe about.'

Anu sighed. Suddenly, she did not like Sameer's tirade against Sanju and decided to call it a night. 'Hey, don't badmouth Sanju. Let us see how it goes.'

'Don't be upset with me, Anu. I am a friend to both you and Sanju. Here, at least you are happy. If you move, I am afraid both of you won't be.'

6

That Saturday was their first visit to Hennur. Anu hadn't dared tell her parents. Surprisingly, Sanju had asked her not to tell his parents either. Surprising because Sanju told them everything. They were a very matter-of-fact type of family as opposed to Anu's, where the emotions were hyperbolic!

Sanju had short-listed four houses to see and Anu had just found a nice place to have lunch. She had to make good of the situation somehow. If you are to tackle a dreaded task, there better be a good reward at the end of it.

'Do we drop Vicky at your parents' or mine?' Sanju had asked the previous night.

'Yours.' Anu's mom would dig dirt on where they were going, why, what time they were returning—so Sanju's parents were a good choice.

Anu cranked up the music and lip-synced. It was only eight in the morning and Bangalore hadn't yet gone into the Saturday tizzy. People woke up late on weekends so if you had beat the traffic, you had to beat people's wake up time. They arrived at a gated villa in less than an hour.

But the problem was, their real estate agent was probably still sleeping too. Each time Sanju called him, he said he was ten minutes away. The hour-long wait in front of the gate started to get so irritating, Anu was sure she was soon going to pick a fight with Sanju. Because of the man who was ten minutes away for the tenth time, Sanju hadn't let her go have a coffee either. Luckily, before she burst open like a floodgate, a pudgy man in his late thirties or fifties (was hard to tell from untidy beard and bloodshot eyes,) in night shorts showed up on his bike. Swinging the keys like it was Vishnu Chakra, the man gave them both a curt nod and walked to the guard at the gate talking on the phone. 'That is only ten lakhs. I want at least double that, Macha.'

Big shot without a clean shirt, Anu gave a mental eye-roll. The word 'Macha', which was used like 'dude' by all the guys in Bangalore lately, totally got to her too. If this guy talking in lakhs used the word 'Macha', then he was only showing off.

When they entered inside the gate, Anu's mood began to lift. Green lawns on the side, paved roads, kids on cycles—it was like from an old English town. The houses were two-storied, white, and with winding drive-ways and colourful bougainvillaeas spilling over the compound walls. If she could get some ideas for interiors from the houses they were seeing and redo their apartment, Sanju may not even want to move!

But the man did not stop at any of those pretty houses. He kept walking until they reached a stretch with a lone house in the distance. The manicured lawns and curbstones were now replaced by discarded bricks, mounds of mud, and a strong stench. The man kept waddling ahead with his phone, absolutely ignoring Anu and Sanju.

'Where is he going? Is he selling us for organs?' Anu whispered to Sanju. She was a bit scared.

'Shh ... don't be silly. This lane is yet to be built that's all.' Sanju seemed to be convincing himself rather than her. 'The house may be nice. All the houses thus far are.'

The agent stopped in front of that lone house which stopped Anu in the tracks. She could not imagine how someone had managed to turn such a good-looking house into a dump—dried up bushes in the garden, large black garbage bags filled with stuff strewn on the unwashed driveway, worn-out paint, mud-caked front porch.

'Don't you have any other house to show us? This looks like an abandoned godown.' Anu expressed her sentiments to the agent without looking at Sanju.

The agent turned to her, still on the phone. 'You can make it look like a house. The tenents still live here. So expect people inside.'

Anu felt incredulous. Who shows a house which is still inhabited? A lanky teenager answered the door and shouted. 'Someone to see the house.'

A woman, who looked sort of old and haggard in a nightie, turned up carrying a toddler. Anu's heart went out for her. So unfair that lately many working couples dumped their children on grandparents.

The woman looked too tired to even stop the child who was banging two plates together. Anu, to ease the situation, asked her with a bright smile. 'What is your grandkid's name? He is cute.'

The woman knitted her brows at Anu and snapped. 'She is my daughter.'

Ooops. That did not go too well. The agent flashing a look of disgust at Anu beckoned them to see the house. The woman led the way.

'We are moving to Mumbai next week. So in a hurry to find a tenant,' said the woman as she walked up the stairs. Anu noticed that not an inch of the wall was left free of Crayon marks. Ha! The joke was on Sanju. He wanted a nicer house than theirs and look what he found! A hellhole!

The woman pushed open the door to a room where a man was snoring. Anu's bedroom looked like Marie Condo's compared to that! As they moved to the room next to it, Sanju hopped back in horror and screamed, 'Poop on the floor! Anu, watch out!'

Anu had to stifle a giggle that bubbled up. Sanju was not in the mood to see the rest of the house. So walking out, Anu waylaid the agent who was still on the phone. 'Are you showing us more houses?'

The man muffled the phone and looked at Anu like she was a flee. 'What is wrong with this one?'

'Nothing. It was extraordinary!' Anu couldn't help her sarcasm. 'Just want to some ordinary ones.'

Sanju was trying desperately to bring in some peace but Anu ignored him and stared at the agent, challenging an answer. The man finally signed off of his phone. 'The other houses are at fifty-thousand rent. But this one is at forty only because the house needs some repair. If you don't want to take it, no problem.'

Anu, tired of the man's insolence, turned to Sanju and said in a low voice, 'I don't want to see more houses with this guy. Let us go home, Sanju.'

The agent walked off in a huff blurting into the phone. 'Time waste, Macha. They want a palace for cheap.'

Sanju grew silent as they walked to the car. When he headed home, Anu was surprised. 'Aren't we going to see the other houses?'

'Anu,' Sanju looked pained. 'Unless you decide to move, you will not give this a fair try. Let us not waste our time.'

Anu couldn't believe her ears. Wasn't that an awful house and wasn't that man a terrible agent? Why was Sanju blaming it on her? 'You are being unfair, Sanju. That man was so uninterested in showing us any house.'

When Sanju continued to drive silently, Anu began to feel irritated. 'Sanju, you come back from the US after four months and decide that the life we built over decades is not good enough anymore. The people, the locality, the house—everything that is ours is not to your liking anymore. Then you expect me to embrace that idea and come on board immediately!' Much to her chagrin, she began to grow emotional. 'Give me time to digest the thought. Convince me why we need to move. And, get me some coffee for heaven's sake.'

Sanju sobered and stopped the car before an eatery. 'This move is only because it is my wish. You think, mull, digest, and if you are convinced, we will look at the houses.'

Anu hated it when Sanju was reasonable because it made harder for her to be unreasonable. Sanju had hardly demanded anything out of her in the six years of marriage or for that matter, even while they dated. Maybe she should cut him some slack. 'I will try.' She smiled weakly sipping coffee and eating a Vada absentmindedly. 'I wish someone rewired my brain to love this idea!'

'Hi Ajji, why this early?' Anu yawned into the phone when her grandmother called at six in the morning.

'Otherwise you will get busy to go to work.' She continued. 'Can we go to the Lakshmi temple today evening? You wear a saree.'

Anu had been the designated companion for her grandmother's temple visits forever. And, she quite enjoyed it. 'Will there be dinner?' Her grandmother was an A-lister at temples and got invited to mouth-watering festive dinners.

'There will be! Gowri's family is hosting it at their house. Come in the pink saree. Gowri thinks her granddaughter is beautiful. I have to show you off.'

In the modern-day lingo, Anu's grandmom and Gowri were frenemies for five decades. Anu never let her grandmom down when Gowri was involved. 'I will come dressed like Aishwarya Rai. You dress in a pink saree too. We will go to twinning.'

After the call, Anu pondered whether to go back to bed or drink coffee and chose the latter. As she sipped her coffee in the tiny balcony, it suddenly hit her. She will no longer be a call away to take her grandmother to temples anymore. She shrugged off the thought before gloom started to spread through her.

Sanju soon joined her in the balcony. 'Hi, Aishwarya Rai.'

Sanju was looking nice and relaxed. That was how he started the day and his job coupled with the Bangalore traffic sucked the life out of him by the end of the day. 'Dad called. He is bringing jackfruit in the evening. What time are you leaving?'

Anu's parents-in-law bought jackfruits and watermelons that could serve an army. Watermelon was for Sanju's benefit and the jackfruit for Anu. Her father-in-law brought it cut and packed three times a week. 'I will call him to come by before five,' Anu said contemplating a second cup of coffee.

'Sanju, if we move, your father cannot drop by like this anymore. That is sad.' Anu meant it. Not just her father-in-law, her father, mother, mother-in-law, at times even Padma aunty, just dropped by their house to have a chat over coffee. Suddenly, Anu found Padma aunty's visits endearing too.

Sanju grew serious. 'I said take your time to decide on the move.' Well, he didn't say it like he meant it.

7

That weekend Anu came to stay with her parents since Sanju was busy working on some deadline. And over a hot Uppittu breakfast, Anu ended up blurting about the move to her mother and grandmother.

Her mother went silent for a good three minutes, which was very uncharacteristic of her. Then she declared disdainfully. 'That North Bangalore is not even Bangalore. Aren't there luxury places here?'

Anu's grandmother shook her head vigorously to get the water out of her hair. 'There is a Durga Parameshwari temple somewhere there.'

'Ajji!' Anu screamed in despair. 'Do you think we are moving so that we can live close to the temple?'

Anu's father walked in and he was briefed as well. 'The only real luxury in Bangalore is owning a house.' He said before picking up the newspaper. He was a man of very few words. He practised economy in everything.

'You people don't give any concrete suggestions.' Anu snickered. 'Tell me what to do. Sanju is very serious.'

'He is only proposing to rent a house, not to buy one. You can try.' With that, her father was gone.

'Tell Sanju you can't move. You father once wanted to move to Singapore but I refused.' Her mother said with finality.

'That was a great opportunity that I missed.' Her father yelled from somewhere.

Anu's grandmother, now drying her hair vigorously with a towel, chimed in. 'Tell Sanju that I might die any time and so you can't move.'

'You said the same thirty years ago to foil our Singapore plans.' Only Anu heard her father mutter as he passed by.

Anu suddenly felt very dejected and her eyes began to well up. 'None of you are taking me seriously. I am the only one who is fighting to stay back.'

Anu's mother handed her a cup of coffee. 'Men always make these outrageous plans. It won't happen, Anu.'

Her grandmother squeezed her hand. 'I will pretend to get admitted to a hospital. My friend Rathnamma's daughter owns one. Then how can he ask you to move?'

Anu sighed. Her father was too practical, grandmother too impractical, and mother in complete denial. It was her battle now. She considered talking to Sanju's parents but dismissed the thought. They preferred to simply go along with whatever their beloved son proposed. Only Padma aunty could put some sense into Sanju, although she might also convince him to marry someone else. Some battles have to be fought alone because the outcome of it affects only you.

Anu walked on aimlessly through the Vijaynagar main road that evening. She ate Masalpuri at her usual corner (the cook knew she liked it mildly spiced without sweet chutney,) drank Mosambi juice from her regular joint (the shop-keeper knew how she liked it—only fruit, no water, no ice and one spoon of sugar), bought a kurti from a street vendor—well, Anu didn't know him but he still sort of favoured her over a hoard of other customers.

While heading back home, Anu stopped before an ice cream shop feeling all nostalgic. That was where Sanju had proposed to her. From then to now, the shop had severely shrunk. Once big and airy, it was now reduced to a nook with two chairs. The bigger area had been rented out to a mobile outlet. But the owner was the same.

Anu smiled at him. 'Hi.'

He looked at her intently. 'You are Balakrishna sir's daughter. How are you?'

Everyone in that area either knew her or her family. Anu called Sameer. 'At the ice cream shop. Will you come?'

Squeezing inside the nook, Sameer frowned at Anu. 'Ice cream? We are not in high school anymore, Dorothy.'

Anu laughed. 'The only literary reference you can make!'

With her favourite Butterscotch ice cream melting in the mouth, Anu began to feel like a kid again. 'Sameer, I went all around Vijaynagar and now nostalgia is oozing through me!'

'Drama Queen!' Sameer worked on his Pista ice cream. 'You know that all three of them are the same Vanilla with three different colours, right?' He pointed at the colourful tubs of green, yellow, and pink.

'Mixed with hazardous food essence.' Anu pursed her lips. 'But who is complaining? I love it.'

'Why did you want me here so urgently?'

'Not urgently. But for old-times sake. Now hear me out.' Sameer took a deep breath. 'I knew there was a catch.'

'I have to do the pros and cons. Pros of moving? Makes Sanju happy. Cons? Makes me unhappy.' Anu looked up pleadingly. 'I need a sign from God to tell me whether I should choose myself or Sanju.'

Sameer laughed. 'You are going to get the sign while devouring your ice cream?'

Anu screwed up her face. 'God has nothing against ice cream.' Then she added absentmindedly. 'Sanju has never really said no to anything I have wanted. Why is it so hard for me to say yes to the one thing he wants?'

'Because this is a big ask. You never asked him for anything that was against his will.' Sameer pointed out.

Anu laughed. 'You must be amnesiac! I made him move out of his parents' house!'

'Right. But that was before you married him.'

A conspiratorial smile played on Sameer's lips. 'Anu, there is a sign coming your way as we speak.' He was sitting facing the street.

Anu turned back to see what he was referring to. Padma aunty was walking into the shop with a friend. What a hypocrite! Did she think the ice Cream was made up of millets?

'Hello, Sameer.' She greeted him warmly while she nodded coldly at Anu.

'I am leaving on my trip to the US and Europe tomorrow.' She beamed visibly.

'Shall I drop you to the airport, aunty?' No wonder everyone adored Sameer.

'No no, Sameer. I am going with friends. Thank you for the offer.' She cast a you-never-offered glance at Anu. That was not fair! Anu had done the woollens and jackets shopping with her!

When she began to leave, Anu asked. 'Aren't you eating here?'

Padma aunty snickered. 'No. Absolutely not. I saw Sameer so came inside.'

With that, Padma aunty joined her friend who was walking out with two cones of ice cream.

When she left, Anu pursed her lips. 'I wanted to tell Padma aunty about her nephew's grand idea but I don't want to bother her before the trip. Sameer, please give me a suggestion I can't refuse.'

'Let us have a beer.'

That indeed was a suggestion she couldn't refuse. But that evening, not even beer and the grub succeeded in calming her down. When she watched around Drink and Dine, instead of the usual joy, she felt melancholic. She knew she was grieving a little too much but she was never good with changes.

'Anu, it may not be so bad. A better house, posh neighbourhood.' Sameer tried consoling her.

'A change is exciting only when you are craving one. To me, this feels like an unwanted wedding to a millionaire.'

Anu rolled her eyes. 'People move for a new job, a new house, or new life when what they have isn't good enough. But what I have is fantastic.'

'That is because you are fantastic. Come on, Anu. Moping isn't you. Fight, baby, fight.'

As they sipped in silence, Anu gasped. The large-screen TV started blaring about how North Bangalore was a posh and upcoming neighbourhood. What were the odds of that! Anu watched the massive villas and flats on the screen in dismay. 'Sameer, look! The TV here always shows Cricket even if it is a match from hundred years ago. Maybe God is talking to me through the TV. He wants me to see those houses.'

Then the TV screens changed to show the news. 'I don't believe this!' uttered Sameer.

'Kavitha! That is Kavi on TV!' Anu almost screamed. Kavitha was on some sort of highway amidst a berserk crowd and was being pushed back by a female constable.

The news reporter began to talk, 'Actor Sudeep is shooting on the outer ring road near the Hebbal flyover and the fans are going crazy to catch a glimpse of their favourite star …'

Anu sighed. God was talking to her through the TV! Though Kavitha's obsession with Sudeep was nothing new, what were the chances that she was on the Hebbal flyover at almost ten in the night!

Then it struck her. How would Kavitha get back home? Yanking the phone out, Anu called and Kavitha answered the fourth call.

'Anu! Can you believe? I got Sudeep's autograph!' Kavitha was screaming in euphoria.

'That is great, Kavi. Who are you with? How are you coming back home?' Anu started to feel concerned. Kavitha was, well, not someone who planned things.

'I came here at five o'clock. I took an auto then. I will get an auto now. Don't worry.' Kavitha screamed again.

'Fine. Call me if you don't find anything in fifteen minutes.' Anu hung up the phone.

'What do you plan to do if she calls for help?' Sameer cocked a brow at Anu. His dislike for Kavitha was nothing new. For a while, she nursed a massive crush on Sameer and he wasn't happy being followed around by a grinning Kavitha wherever he went. Anu had then manufactured a story to bail Sameer out. That he was engaged at birth to marry his father's childhood friend's daughter. That hadn't gone too well when Kavitha spread that story to everyone in Sameer's college, but it was still okay since it got Kavitha off his back.

The phone duly rang in fifteen minutes. There was no background noise anymore around Kavitha. 'Anu, no autos, man. Feeling a bit scared. What do I do?'

'Is there a bus-stand around you? Stand there. It is safer than the roadside. I will come to get you.'

Anu looked at Sameer and got up. 'Come, Sammy boy. Let's rescue the maiden in distress.'

Sameer shook his head in disagreement. 'No way! I am not getting caught for drunken driving because of that whacko.'

'Hey! What happened to all the chivalrous men? Come on, Sameer. She can't call her husband because he hates her love for Sudeep. Her father doesn't drive.'

'Ask Sanju to pick her up. He will be sober and he works closer to where she is.'

'He is in the electronic city office! It is insanely far for him. And, he is in the middle of some software crisis. Come on, Sameer.'

Sameer picked up the keys reluctantly. 'Why are you the saviour of the crazy world? Who will mess with her? She is large enough to pick up a man and throw him into the traffic.'

'Hey! No body shaming.' Anu poked Sameer in the arm, fastening the seatbelt.

'She calls me a skinny crow. Isn't that body shaming?'

'That is because you broke her heart.'

What usually is one of the most wretched stretches of Bangalore during the day turned out to be a nice drive at that hour on the outer ring road. Anu could see lit-up huge apartment complexes with large empty spaces on either side of the road. Tiny cars and tinier two-wheelers zipped past majestic BMTC buses and trucks. Sameer was enjoying the drive as much as her. By then, Anu's mother had called a hundred times. Anu deftly dodged that bullet by lying that she had gone home with Sanju.

'Lucky we weren't stopped for alcohol testing.' Sameer sighed in relief. They had come past a couple of checkpoints but the police hadn't suspected them.

After being misdirected by Kavitha a dozen times, they were able to locate her sitting in an empty bus stop.

She got in muttering at Sameer. 'Yo, skinny crow. Can't you locate a place properly?'

'I will throw you out of my car if you insult me, Tata Sumo.' Well, that was a mean nickname but that was how the insults between Sameer and Kavitha went.

'You can't even move my little finger!' Kavitha snickered and turned to Anu. 'Thanks, Anu. What would I do without you?'

Within ten minutes of driving, Kavitha had a desire to drink the roadside tea. Anu didn't mind since she had begun to feel drowsy. Sameer was ever ready for a tea so he turned off the ring road towards a tea-stall. But the moment he got onto the service road, Sameer started cursing when a drunken-driving checkpoint stared at them straight in the face. Soon a traffic policeman approached them with a breathalyzer. Anu peered at it curiously and she grew suspicious.

Sameer got off the car and walked a little distance with the policeman.

'That looks like the breathalyzer I got on Amazon to gift to Shwetha. Do you think these are fake police? Are they stopping us to fleece money out of us?'

Kavitha grew all excited. 'You are never wrong when it comes to products sold on Amazon, Anu. Let us call their bluff.'

The next few minutes went by very quickly—with Kavitha accusing the policeman of being fake, a constable getting into their car and driving them to the police station, and

Sameer repeatedly telling the policeman that the women with him are a bit demented.

When they got off at the police station, Sameer glared at them. 'I want the two of you to shut up. Especially you, Sumo. Can't believe I am stuck with you.'

Anu walked around outside while Sameer pleaded with the policeman. Kavitha said she was too tired to get off the car. Anu smiled at a woman, smartly dressed in jeans and T-shirt, about the same age as her.

'Drunk driving?' Anu asked smilingly. A fellow felon.

The woman shook her head. 'No. I am a journalist. Here to find a story.'

'Wow. That is cool. I have never been in the news.' Anu said wistfully.

'Give me a story. I will put you in the paper.' The woman smiled.

'Tonight I am a joke! You can put me in the comic section.' Anu walked away. What if that woman took a picture of hers and published it in under some heading like, 'Educated woman caught stealing.' Journalists did exaggerate.

Sameer had now gone inside the station and Anu saw a man with a parrot, standing before a horse. He was talking to a policeman animatedly. Anu walked towards the scene fascinated.

'Sir, I don't know who gave alcohol to the horse. I don't drink, sir.' The man slurred even as he spoke.

'You are drunk and you were riding a drunk horse. I will put you in the jail for one year.' The policeman was not exactly polite with the threat.

Anu was flummoxed with the conversation. The police station at night was quite exciting. No wonder that journalist woman was hovering around.

'Sir, what if the horse was drunk but not the man? Will you arrest the horse?' She asked out of curiosity but the policeman thought she was joking.

'Madam, you may find this funny but for us, you are all a big headache.' He muttered something and walked inside instructing the parrot-cum-horse-man to stay put.

When the policeman had left the scene, Anu asked pointing at the parrot and the horse, 'Are they both yours?'

'I am a parrot astrologer, madam. Someone gifted me this horse because my predictions are so good. My ancestors were astrologers at the court of the Mysore Maharaja.' That was another thing in the Bangalore-Mysore area. Everyone cited some or the other connection with the Mysore Maharajas. Some were his poets, some taught him or his queens something, some tended to his stable or garden.

'Can you predict my future?' Anu extended her palm.

'I am a parrot astrologer, madam. Not a palmist.' The man gave Anu a look of disdain. 'Wait. I will tell you.'

He sat down on the steps and asked Anu to do the same. The horse was now tied and doing some crazy eye movements.

The astrologer spread some cards facedown, muttered things, and let the parrot out of the cage. It daintily walked towards the deck and picked up three cards. Handing the last card to its boss, it pirouetted and then walked back to the cage. Anu found that little green bird so cute, she picked it up. When the astrologer screamed at her and the parrot pecked at her, Anu, all panicky, let the bird fly. At that very moment, a camera flashed. That was the journalist.

'Come on, madam. Stand in front of the horse and unleash it.' The journalist called excitedly.

Anu followed the journalist promptly and untethered the horse with aplomb, though she had no clue why she was doing what she was doing. The beer had that effect on her. The animal now stood on two hind legs and neighed. That was the next photo the journalist shot.

'Your name, madam?'

'Anu … Anupama Rao.'

'Anu darling, you will be a star tomorrow. Read Times Today.' The journalist zoomed off on her moped.

Now the horse was still neighing standing in place. The silly thing hadn't realized that it was free to run. The astrologer was running behind the parrot that was now walking instead of flying. Kavitha was furiously taking pictures of the astrologers' cards. 'I will interpret these cards, Anu. I can do it. I just need these pictures.'

'Put my cards down. You … you … I will curse you.' The astrologer still ran in circles but was screaming at Kavitha. The parrot now perched on the horse, making it run.

A policeman who walked outside with Sameer threw up his hands in exasperation. 'Sir, please get someone to drive you and take your crazy women home.'

To cut a long story short, Sameer paid five-thousand rupees to one of the men in Khakhi to avoid getting booked and Sanju came forty kilometres to pick them up. The next

morning the *Times Today* magazine had published two
rather flattering photos of Anu—one releasing a parrot
and another looking in bewilderment at the horse on hind
legs. The journalist had written about how Anupama Rao,
an animal activist from Hebbal had got wind of animals in
captivity and had come rushing in the middle of the night
to release them. Anu was quite thrilled with her photos in
the paper and duly bought ten copies of the same. Then she
bought five more for good measure. She had to give them
to a lot of people.

Even after this crisis was over, when Sanju did not utter
a single word of anger or disgust about that dramatic night,
Anu felt guilt flow through her veins. When she was guilty,
Anu's brain turned into mush. So she not only agreed to
see the houses in Hebbal but also promised Sanju that she
was going to move. Why do women get on the guilt-trip so
quickly? The destination of that trip is only disasterville.

The coming weekends were plain dreadful for Anu when
they had to drive a good twenty kilometres to look at the
houses. Even after a month, they hadn't found anything that
appealed to both her and Sanju, some were too big for her
and some not posh enough for Sanju.

As they inched through the Yashwanthpur traffic yet
again that Saturday afternoon, Anu kept quiet. Now that
the guilt had faded, she had turned a little cold and sinister
towards Sanju to express her displeasure at the house-
hunting trips. In a bid to humour her, Sanju was trying his

hands at small talk. Mind you, he loathed talking while driving. But Anu had gone all monosyllable in her responses to him. He asked her if they could have dinner after seeing the houses which she immediately turned down.

After a few more minutes of silence, Anu glanced at Sanju, who was braving that horrendous traffic without a complaint. Again, very unusual of him. Although he didn't fancy talking while at the wheels, he did curse the fellow drivers eloquently. Anu felt a twinge of guilt. Why was she making him so miserable and out of character? What is he proposing that was so evil after all?

Anu touched his hand gently. 'Hey, Sanju. Today we will finalize a place, okay? If it means so much to you, let us do it.'

8

'Sir, ma'am, a house won't get better than this.' The smooth-talking thirty-something real estate agent referred by Dave cooed dramatically, pointing at a Villa.

'This house costs five crores to buy and two lakhs to rent.'

Anu almost tripped and fell. 'Oh, that is a bit too low for us,' she whispered to Sanju eliciting a silencing glare from him.

'But, sir, ma'am,' the man was now purring. 'You are so in luck. I can't tell you how lucky you are.'

You can stop repeating yourself. Anu felt her irritation raise. *If not two lakhs, what is it? One lakh eighty thousand? Now that will be very affordable for us.*

'Let us look at the place, sir, ma'am.' The man bowed dramatically like a butler in an old English household.

Anu butted in. 'Can you tell us how lucky we are before we see the place?'

The man gave the fakest laughter she had heard in recent times. 'No, ma'am, no! I want you to fall in love with the place first.'

As they stepped in, Anu gasped. They stood in a living room as big as their current house. It had a wall-to-wall glass window that overlooked a lush lawn. The rest of the tour seemed surreal to her. It was like the villas the Greek tycoons or the Sheiks owned in romance novels. They strolled upstairs, and Sanju had forgotten to close his mouth. The agent disappeared for a few minutes to take a phone call, leaving them in the massive master bedroom.

While Sanju sauntered to the French window, Anu finally found her voice. Her head spun from the tour. 'Anu,' Sanju's voice had gone all husky. 'This house is straight out of my dreams. I want to live here right this moment.'

'Are you out of your mind? This house is not where people live. This is where celebrities live! I can see myself turning this into a large messy junkyard within a month!' Anu could not believe Sanju wanted to live in an unreal world like that!

'Now, sir, ma'am,' the agent walked in, and his addressing them thus started to grate on Anu's nerves. 'You have seen the house. Shall we see the property now? Verdant Green boasts of five pools, two tennis courts …'

'Multiple clubhouses and at least ten five-star restaurants.' Anu completed the sentence for him, with her best sarcastic smile. 'Can you please tell us the rent?' She could feel Sanju cringe even without looking at him. He was certainly going to tell her later that she was way too crass in the way she spoke. She did not care. She wanted to get out of there before Sanju fell even more deeply in love with the house.

The agent flashed another fake polite smile. 'Yes, ma'am. I was going to get to that. As I was saying, it is a six-crore rupees house and costs two-lakhs in rent. But the owner is relocating to Kuwait, and he is in a hurry to rent it out. So,' he paused dramatically. 'I can't even believe what he is willing to accept.'

Anu got up to leave; she had had enough of the man's theatrics. Sanju could handle the rest of the drama. The agent blurted sensing Anu's determined steps. 'He is willing it to rent it out at one lakh! I can't believe it myself!'

Anu looked at Sanju, who had a silly smile plastered on his face. She genuinely hoped it was the smile of refusal. 'We will take it.'

'Sanju! It is a lakh a month! What do we eat after paying the rent?' Anu didn't care anymore that the agent was around. 'We can't—'

Sanju cut her off quickly. 'Ma'am is nervous for no reason. We will take it. Please draw up the papers, and we are ready to move in by the first.' The first was only ten days away!

'Excellent decision, sir. You are the first one that I have shown the house to.'

'Why did you do that favour, sir? Why did you choose to like us so much?' Anu asked the agent sarcastically. 'Do we have a past life connection with you? For you to bestow this favour on us?'

She knew the agent was doing his job, and she was being a complete bitch, but it was too big a shock to digest. How could Sanju decide on the spot without even talking to her in private?

'Ma'am, I showed you the place because Dave sir referred you to me.' Now the agent sounded pissed. So, was he going to withdraw his grace on them? She sure hoped so!

But there was no such luck. The agent turned to Sanju and started explaining. 'Sir, there is a small maintenance fee of twenty-two thousand a month.'

Oh, that is very small! But Anu said nothing. All she wanted was to get out of there, settle on her cosy sofa in her small apartment and watch *Friends*. Why should everyone dream big? There is nothing wrong with small and easily achievable dreams like buy ice cream and watch TV.

'Anu, I know it is a bit of a stretch for us. But I can manage. It is such a beautiful house. We deserve to live there. We will not be able to save much, but we can live a comfortable life.' Sanju was now almost pleading.

'I am not a finance whiz, Sanju. But something in me says we will be downgrading our lives with this upgrade. We won't be able to afford even a decent dinner or a vacation if we pay so much in rent.' Anu's eyes started welling up. 'Why do you hate our house? Is it because my dad gifted the apartment to me? I can change the ownership. Right away. I will make you the owner. Please let us stay here.'

Sanju looked wounded. 'Hey Anu, is that how much you have understood me? I have no problem that this house is yours. I want to try living differently. We are too young to settle down yet.'

Before she burst into full-blown tears, Anu put on her shoes and stepped out. A good run might fill her with some happy hormones. She had to pour her woes to someone and who better than Kavitha?

Abandoning the run, Anu walked with Kavitha digging into a bag of Potato fritters from their favourite street vendor. Managing not to burst into tears, Anu narrated her tale of two localities, the one she loved and the other she dreaded.

Kavitha took the news much better than Anu had anticipated, at least for the first five minutes. 'Anu,' she spoke swallowing the fritter and taking a sip of Pepsi. 'I will miss you, Anu. You know how much I love you. I love you more than I love myself, much much more than I love my husband. I love you as much as I love my son and my dog.' She stopped for some extra effect. 'But this will be good for you. You are a princess and you deserve to live in a castle.'

Okay, that was the thing about Kavitha. When angsty, she became overly dramatic. 'Go, my love. Go. Rule your kingdom in Hebbal. Leave this place for peasants like us.'

Then she started sobbing. The good thing was, Anu in the process of consoling Kavitha, forgot her woes.

Kavitha recovering after a good ten minutes scrunched up her face. 'I feel queasy, Anu. From almost a week. As terrible as when I was pregnant with Adi.'

Anu gasped. 'Kavitha! Maybe you are pregnant again! Go get yourself checked.'

Kavitha smiled in delight. 'Oh Anu! I never thought of that. You are a genius! If you are right, my treat at Jake's!'

9

Cliché, but the next ten days passed like ten minutes in Anu's life. Even before she could properly lament her fate before Shwetha and Sameer, they were sitting on their old sofa in the new house, with their furniture looking like tiny lilliputs in that large space.

Sameer had come along to help them move. The movers had done all the work. They had packed everything and now Sanju was instructing them where to offload everything. At first, Anu tried not to care what went where but then Sameer nudged her. 'Anu, if you don't tell them where to keep the stuff, you will end up moving the furniture around yourself.'

That had made Anu spring out of the sofa quickly. Sanju was about to move her dressing table and clothes boxes into the master bedroom and Anu made a decision on the spot. 'Move all my stuff into the next room, please.' She always had a room to herself being an only child and she missed that pleasure after marriage.

Sanju looked bewildered as if she was divorcing him. Anu smiled at him reassuringly. 'Why share a room when we can have our own? Look, I am Ms Messy and you Mr Clean. Let us have the liberty to live how we want!'

Sanju nodded but he didn't look too thrilled. 'But Anu, we cannot keep any room unkempt. You have to keep your things tidy.'

'Sanju, relax. If someone wants a tour of the house, we will tell them my room is haunted so we have locked it shut.' She liked the idea of her own room. Maybe she could begin to draw or write. She hadn't done either in her life, but she could start now, right?

Vicky seemed to be the happiest of all, riding his cycle at dangerous speeds all around the house. If Anu didn't stop him, it was only a matter of time before he banged himself against a wall and wailed for an hour.

'Vicky, come I will show you the garden outside. I saw a swing, I think.' She was too tired to engage, but the kid needed to be stopped. When Vicky came bounding, Anu picked him up kissing his sweaty, reddened cheeks. *Maybe it won't be so bad after all …*

Deciding on lunch at the restaurant inside the property, Anu walked silently behind Sanju and Sameer. Her mind was a mess with thoughts. Thoughts she could not even distinguish anymore. Vicky kept going off the path into the lawn eliciting polite reprimands from the gardeners. Sighing, Anu picked him up. It was not easy carrying him but then at least she wouldn't have to worry about him running straight into a giant lawnmower.

By the time they reached the restaurant (a fifteen-minute walk in the sun), Vicky was asleep on Anu's shoulders. Sanju settled him on a couch and the three of them took a quick look at the menu. Anu's heart stopped. It was more expensive than a five-star restaurant! She was not cheap but having to pay five times the regular price for everything seemed highly illogical. She raised a brow at Sanju who was quickly placing an order without meeting her glance. She looked at Sameer who was pretending to be looking all around. He became a different person when Sanju was around, treating her like a stranger.

Anu took in the scene around her. The waiters almost tiptoed and sophisticated-looking patrons talked and laughed in hushed voices. So it did look like a five-star resort. There were hanging pots, standing pots, statues of all kinds of Buddha, a small waterfall of recycled water flowing down like a curtain of white linen. To complete the look, the restaurant overlooked a gleaming blue pool with nobody swimming in it. She looked at the fellow lunchers—with the number of white folks all around, it almost felt like they were in a foreign land. The few Indians sat looking very posh and suave. Anu felt depressed for not dressing up a bit more. Then again, who expected this level of sophistication in a local restaurant!

Anu tried to focus on what Sameer and Sanju were discussing. Something about mutual funds. Sameer was quite an enthusiastic investor and Sanju was still thinking about it. Finding their conversation utterly boring, Anu focussed on her drink. For having paid so much, she might as well enjoy it. The food was good too. She slowly started to forget about the uprooting of her life and began to unwind.

When Sanju excused himself to the restroom, Sameer smiled at her. 'Feeling better?'

Anu nodded. 'For now! Because of alcohol.'

'It won't be too bad, Anu. Once you settle down, you will like the place. It is like living in a resort.'

'I liked my economy hotel of a house,' Anu sighed. 'But I will try not to make Sanju feel bad. He is already punishing himself for having to pay for all the nonsense here!'

'You never make anyone feel bad, kid.' Sameer patted her head from across the table. A few drinks later Sameer became a tad emotional. 'You don't object to things out of ego. Only out of your discomfort. People get that.'

Anu smiled contentedly. 'So you are saying I am egoless but self-centred.'

Sameer raised his mug to hers. 'Something like that.' Anu clinked it.

They walked back towards the house with Vicky still asleep but now on Sanju's shoulders. Sameer had bid them goodbye right after lunch. He had paid for the lunch before they even had a chance to look at the bill. But that was Sameer for you—generous in both kind and cash.

'I can foresee myself getting lost here multiple times,' Anu said looking around. All paths looked the same. All the villas looked the same.

'That is how you figure out a place,' Sanju remarked wryly.

'Sanju, sorry if I am being moody. This is hard for me, you know. I don't cope well with change.' Anu genuinely felt bad that she was unable to enjoy being in the lap of luxury. All because a fear lurked inside her that it was not going to end well.

'You will be fine, Anu. We will be fine. Dave lives round the corner. We will visit him in the evening. My other colleague Smitha also lives here. You can call her if you need anything.'

By the time they reached home, Anu was soaked in sweat. She longed to turn on the AC and take a long nap. But when they were arranging furniture, Sanju had repeatedly remarked how cool the room was. And how they would not need the AC at all there. The future expenses had begun to scare him already! So Anu had refrained from asking why he was sweating buckets if the room was so cool.

The point was, he wouldn't like it if she turned on the AC in their large master bedroom. The thrifty life she had dreaded had begun! Every room was massive in that house. Was there a smaller one that didn't consume as much power to cool down? A servant's room maybe? Finally, Anu decided to sleep in a ground-floor bedroom that was comparatively cooler. She couldn't help notice how their two diwan cots had significantly diminished the beauty of that room.

'Is there anything for Vicky to eat when he wakes up?' Sanju asked putting him down on one of the cots.

'You wake me up. I will make something.' Anu yawned. She longed yet again for her old life that had Radha who would come and cook. She pined for her books that she always kept on the side table. Now except for the one she had in her bag, she had no clue where the rest were. And, she didn't have her library next door anymore. The very thought was depressing.

As the fan started whirring, it also started kicking up a thin layer of dust that had accumulated on the floor. 'The owners got the place cleaned fifteen days back. Now please have it cleaned again before you move in.' The realtor had smoothly palmed off a dusty house to them.

As Anu drifted between sneezes and snoozes, she only had nightmares where she had turned into a full-time housekeeper who wore her hair in a bun and lived in a nightie, all day and all night.

10

Anu woke up to the voices coming from somewhere. At first, she couldn't register where she was; then it hit her. The new house! And the voice was her mother's! She almost ran to the living room. Her mother would make everything all right!

Vicky looked happy eating his favourite Akki Rotti and chatting away with his grandma. Sanju was sipping coffee. Her father was inspecting a pillar that stood in the middle. Her grandmother who was generally pacing around was the first to spot Anu.

'Anu baby! This is such a beautiful house.' That was grandma; one who loved luxury in all forms.

Settling down next to Sanju, Anu sighed. 'Then stay with me, Ajji. I am sure we can fit you in somewhere here!'

Her grandmother laughed. 'I will stay with you, Anu. Soon. I have my kitty parties planned for the whole month.'

Anu's mother handed her a cup of steaming coffee. Her mother loved to take control of things, but not without making Anu feel bad. All through her growing up years, Anu's room was perfectly made and her clothes always washed and ironed. But her mother mentioned every single day how messy the room was before she cleaned it up.

'Anu, your kitchen is not set up at all to even make coffee. I have organized it a little.'

Anu smiled. Nothing had changed between her and her mother. But she was secretly glad that her mother had this obsessive need to take over Anu's life. Who cared about a few harmless reprimands here and there!

'Sanjay, this is a load-bearing wall. Don't drill any nails into this.' Anu's father patted at the column he was inspecting. As if Sanju was ever going to take a drill into hand!

Sanju nodded. 'Sure, uncle. I won't. Thanks for telling me.' Nobody except Anu knew his fake politeness. But that stood Sanju in good stead with her father. He liked people who agreed with him.

Another hour, another round of coffee, and Anu's parents were ready to call it a night. Anu's mother spoke to her privately. 'Anu, the house is too dusty. Get a maid fast. And, get a cook like Radha. Vicky will need his home food.'

Anu's irritation suddenly started mounting. If there is no cook, wouldn't she take care of Vicky's nutrition? Well, okay, a cook would be good. She was not the cook-tasty-and-nutritious-meal type.

'Anu, I have kept dinner for you two and some food for Vicky in the fridge. And …' Her mother added worriedly, '… this house is too big. I don't know how you will manage.'

'I will be all right, Mummy. You go on now. Daddy is waiting.'

Anu suddenly felt too lonely once her parents left. Sanju was trying to get the TV to work and Vicky was busy drawing in the new book with the new set of crayons he had just got from his grandparents. Anu sat next to him on the floor and started colouring the borders.

'Mumma! You are not colouring inside the line. Kavitha ma'am will not be happy with you.' Vicky said all too gravely. That hit Anu—Vicky's school! They had not talked much about it.

'Sanju, we have to send Vicky to school. Have to get his TC and get him admitted some place.'

Sanju nodded. 'Can you ask around tomorrow? I can ask Dave but he has no kids.' Sanju added after a pause. 'Can you also call some Internet provider and get us broadband? And a cable connection for the TV?'

These were precisely the things Anu had dreaded. Sanju would be busy at work and she would have to run around to get things done. She missed her old apartment that had everything they wanted and needed. If your life is mostly good, why change it? It is like throwing out a perfectly good pair of old jeans for a new but ill-fitting one.

Anu, all ready for a jog, looked around the property deciding which path to take. In a bid to belong to that fancy place, she had clothed herself in her best pair of tracks. She had dressed Vicky too in his good track pants and a pullover. Even if she thought so herself, Vicky looked beyond cute. It was eight-thirty in the morning and Sanju had left for work.

Thanks to her mother storing breakfast in the fridge, Anu hadn't gorged on Maggi.

Anu was not really in the mood to even walk, let alone jog but she had to get out of the house. She had things to do and a maid to find.

As if by a miracle when she had just about crossed her street, a woman in her fifties clad in a saree appeared before her. 'Are you the new ones who have moved in?' The woman asked brusquely in Kannada.

Who was she? Anu sized her up quickly. Her saree was quite nice and bright, the blouse was a perfect match, and she dangled a designer handbag. But she was certainly not a resident, Anu knew, but she decided to be careful. What if she was the poor relative of a resident? She smiled. 'We just moved in. How about you? Are you from here?'

'I work here. I thought you may need a maid.'

'Oh, I do!' Anu instantly regretted the over-enthusiasm in her voice. That showed her desperation.

'I have seen your house. I used to work there.' The woman was all business. 'I work with my daughter. We can cook and clean for you.'

Really? Do wishes really come true this way? 'Okay. When can you start?'

'As soon as we settle the salary. The old owner used to give me eighteen thousand. But that was six months ago.'

Anu's head started spinning even before the woman finished talking. She used to get ten thousand to teach! Maybe she should take up cleaning for a job.

The woman noticing Anu's ashen face added. 'See madam, nobody will work for less than that here. If you want to get only the floors cleaned, I will work for ten thousand. If you want cooking too, then eighteen.'

'What about washing dishes and clothes?'

'You have machines for that, no?' the woman asked suspiciously. 'If you pay twenty, I will run the machines for you.'

Now Anu got curious. She had to know how this alien land worked. 'What about folding clothes and ironing them?'

The woman was now losing her patience. Anu was sure she had already labelled her a cheapskate and dismissed her off. 'Here is my phone number.' The woman expertly produced a small chit. 'You call me. My name is Rathnamma. But soon. I have other offers.'

Vicky, bored with that wait, started tugging at her shirt. Anu thought of going back home but the state of it scared her. She made her decision. If they lived in a high-class place, they should be able to afford a high-class maid. 'Rathnamma,' she called after the woman. 'Come back. You can start work now.'

Sanju would have a near heart-attack if she told him about her deal with the maid, but was there a choice?

11

Rathnamma insisted that she go for a walk with Vicky while she worked her magic. Anu agreed gleefully. There was nothing worth stealing in their house. Also, Anu was sure Rathnamma owned a better TV and a laptop than them.

Anu could not believe her eyes after two hours. The house was sparkling. There was not a speck of dust and the woman had made their furniture look decent. Who knew stacking everything up and fluffing the pillows would make such a big difference. 'Madam, my daughter has made Chapathis and Bhindi curry. I will clean your barbeque area and the patio tomorrow.'

Anu nodded, trying not to look too thrilled. Who was she kidding! That was not her—squealing with delight was her. Throwing caution to air, Anu almost hugged Rathnamma. 'Thanks so much. You have made it look so good. It even smells good.'

Rathnamma looked a little bewildered with this display of affection. 'Madam, I brought all the cleaning supplies. You have to give me six-hundred rupees for that.'

Anu felt a little sheepish with her over-enthusiasm. Handing Rathnamma the money, Anu asked, 'Will you help me unbox these? I will pay you extra.'

Rathnamma agreed. 'Five hundred per hour, madam. I charge more but you are still new.' What she actually meant, Anu was sure, was *you are poor.*

'Change this furniture soon, madam. The last owner had some really good stuff.' Said Rathnamma inspecting the house with a slight frown. 'Nobody has this type of stuff in this complex.'

Anu wondered why she was not even offended by that remark. 'No. We can't afford to change anything now. All our money is going towards the rent.' She refrained from adding, '*and your salary.*' She was sure Rathnamma too refrained from adding, '*Then why are you here?*'

Sanju almost squealed in surprise. Very unlike him to display emotions. 'This is neat, Anu! You found someone to clean the house.'

The delight on Sanju's face was worth what Rathnamma was charging. 'Well, the woman charges a bomb but she is good.'

'How much?' Sanju asked with a bit of panic. When Anu explained the various rates, he fell silent. When he spoke, his voice was low, like it was coming from a cave. 'Anu, I will cook in the evening and do the dishes. Hire her only for cleaning the house.'

Anu was dumbstruck. *Was he for real? When had he ever cooked or cleaned?* She almost blurted how she had anticipated this dreadful life even before they moved here.

She wanted to add how she knew Sanju would not be able to bear such fancy bills. But she stopped herself. There was no point arguing. She had to lie to him. (White lie - dictionary meaning - a harmless lie that saves someone from hurt. Real meaning - a harmless lie that quickly comes back to bite you in the ass.)

'Let me negotiate with her. I am sure she was just bandying the numbers and did not really mean it.'

'Not a rupee more than ten thousand, Anu.'

Yes, sir. Thought Anu, all the while quickly calculating how much she had in her account. She had to pay the extra eight thousand herself or she could become the Rathnamma of the house.

All the boxes unboxed and the items put away, Anu felt a weight lifted off her chest. Her wallet felt lighter too after coughing up thousand-five-hundred rupees towards Rathnamma's charges for unboxing. But it was worth the money spent. Now she had the onerous task of finding Vicky a school. The sweet smiling receptionist had handed her a list of four schools, eight tennis coaching centres, two each for archery and shooting arenas. Anu picked a school closest to home. She was visiting them at three that afternoon.

Anu started her Santro after three days. Vicky looked too happy to be going on a car ride finally. It sputtered and coughed a little but then started, as it always did. As she eased it out of the driveway, there were curious glances cast at her.

She was driving a cheap relic. Most houses had their Audis, Benzes, and BMWs parked nonchalantly outside. The car of the least denomination in that community was an Innova. Anu couldn't wait to get out of the complex and get on a public road where a Santro was normal and a Jaguar was not.

The school visit failed spectacularly for both Anu and Vicky. The facilitator, who showed the school around and informally interviewed Vicky, said smoothly at the end. 'He is a bright child but looks like he has been through traditional schooling. Here we emphasize on overall personality development.'

Anu was tempted to ask what aspect of four-year-old Vicky's personality wasn't round enough for her. Instead, she smiled and said, 'That is wonderful. Personality is everything.'

Then the proud-as-a-peacock facilitator handed Anu the fee chart. The first few rows sounded unbelievably unreasonable. Academic fees—60,000, sports—5,000, Computer lab (*Really? For pre-schoolers?*)—5,000.

After a lot of these five to eight thousand rupee rows, the sheet continued onto the next page. Building fees—50,000. Fast-track Kids—1,00,000 (*What was this anyway?*) Scholarship fund—1,00,000.

They were the big ones. As Anu glanced at the total, hidden way at the bottom, the fee per annum came to six lakhs!

'That is too steep for LKG!' Anu's voice sounded a bit too whiney to her own ears. Why couldn't she say the same thing with more verve? Like she did in Vijaynagar? Were these posh-looking coordinators and facilitators making her nervous?

'We don't call it LKG here like in traditional schools. We call it Development Level 2. DL 2.' The woman corrected Anu. 'Also, you can pay it in three instalments!' The woman said brightly. *Oh, that is fantastic but the total still remains the same*—Anu didn't say any of those things. What was the point when she knew she was not going to put Vicky there? The usually bouncy Vicky had sat quietly in a corner. As if the whole scenario had overwhelmed him too.

The woman now turned to Vicky and cooed. 'Vivith, do you like this school?'

'Vivikth,' Vicky corrected her. He had an unusually sharp hearing when it came to mispronunciations of his name. 'I don't like this school. You are not my friend.' He stated matter of factly and lurched at Anu.

Anu controlled her laughter but did not apologize for Vicky. Why demean his firmly stated opinion? Politely murmuring a thank you, she started towards the exit. Then she stopped, remembering something. 'What is Fast-track Kids?' She couldn't leave without knowing what it was!

The woman brightened up again. 'They are our co-curricular partners for maths and science. They even start teaching concepts of Trigonometry by class four!'

That did it. Anu vividly remembered how Trigonometry had tortured her in the tenth standard. That very Trigonometry had made her take Humanities instead of Science. That decision, in turn, had resulted in her mother's deep disappointment for months. Her only daughter was not going to be a software engineer while every other kid in Vijaynagar was.

Vicky found his bounce the minute they left the school building. What next? Anu felt her panic spread all through her body. The other schools on the list would not be any different from this one. Was every little task going to be this hard in her new life?

12

Sanju came home in a good mood. It was Friday after all. Anu, having gotten over the traumatic experience at the school with a good nap, was in a good mood too.

'Hey, Dave asked me if we wanted to go out for dinner with him and a few of his friends. I have already agreed. Get ready, babe.'

'Where are we going?' Anu had to know every detail. 'We, as in a few couples? Children too?'

'I think Mariott.' Sanju beamed. 'Dave's girlfriend is in town. So I am sure it is a couple's thing. But I don't know about taking kids.'

'Can you call and ask if we can take Vicky? If others are bringing their kids, we will too.' Anu started working out the details in her head. Leaving Vicky with her parents would take insanely long. She could ask Rathnamma but she would charge an insane amount of money.

'Ask the maid to stay with Vicky. We will have a nice evening out. See, this is the kind of life I was talking about. Living in a luxury house, going out for classy dinners with friends.' Sanju looked so visibly happy, Anu decided not to point out any negatives to the situation. She could think of many, like for example, the cost of dining at Mariott. But they could afford that. It was just dinner.

Rathnamma's daughter agreed to stay with Vicky for a thousand rupees for three hours. Anu brought it down to seven hundred. But the fact was, she had begun to lose a sense of money after moving here. Seven hundred would seem exorbitant a week ago but now, after dealing with Rathnamma and the school, it sounded reasonable.

The dinner was all good and friendly when it was just Dave and his girlfriend. Soon the other two couples joined them. Since Anu had already had a cocktail, one of the wives looked familiar but she couldn't place her. Anu had a strange sort of memory. She could remember incidents even from her past life but not faces.

The woman now stood squarely before Anu and frowned. 'Oh! You are the teacher from that school in Vijaynagar.'

Anu gasped when she recognized the woman before her. What were the odds! Anu stared blankly and asked, 'How come you are here?'

The woman gave a short laugh. 'I want to ask you the same! I heard you are a new resident at Verdant. I am Meena by the way.'

Now the whole conversation from before unravelled before Anu. There really was a small-time god who was playing pranks with her and having a good chuckle at her expense.

'I heard we are meeting two old residents from Verdant. So, you live here and send your child to Dew Drops?' Now Anu was truly intrigued.

Meena laughed derisively. 'That is my friend's son. My son goes to school here.'

The man who stood next to Meena urged her forward. 'You can chitchat later. Now take a seat.' He seemed to be in a terrible hurry to begin drinking.

With everyone's attention converging on her, Meena bent down and whispered to Anu. 'I have much to ask you! Later, okay?'

The cool breeze, live DJ, perfect lighting, swaying palm trees—all the pretty things Anu was enjoying thus far lost their allure that second. This woman Meena was trouble.

Anu glanced around to see Sanju nurse his first pint of beer and the other men down Vodka in gallons. Soon Meena and her yes-woman started chugging swanky cocktails one after another. Ginny drank in moderation and so did Anu.

Meena asked Anu where they had put Vicky to school. Anu, hoping for a half-decent conversation, made the mistake of being honest.

'Yet to find a school for him. Went to Indigo International today morning. Six lakhs for kindergarten! Can you imagine? We paid sixty thousand in Dew Drops.' Anu rolled her eyes.

'Oh,' the two wives exchanged glances with each other. Meena spoke relaxing her bulk into her chair. 'Don't even compare the two schools. Indigo is high-quality education.'

Anu was baffled. The nerve of this woman to insult Sumitra aunty's school. 'Dew Drops gives a world-class education too. The principal has modelled it after Shantiniketan.'

'Then why did you move here? You said the school was so fantastic that you sent your son there.' Meena the Meanie looked at Anu challengingly. The men were in their own world to be a party to this, Ginny squirmed at this attack, Meena's yes-woman assumed a pose similar to her boss— head tilted, brows raised, lips quirked up.

Anu decided to stay away from that line of conversation. 'I had my reasons to move. Not because I wanted a better school.' With that, she picked up her drink and gulped it down.

That conversation tipped the whole balance. Anu could feel how the two women degraded her even more in their minds. Anu was as good as dead to them. They spoke about a new Pilates-with-props program that had started in the community Yoga Studio and they made sure to ask only Ginny if she wanted to join in. Then they spoke about a spa they were visiting with their other friends on Tuesday and again they craned their necks and invited only Ginny. Anu was never one to take offence easily but these women were good! They made sure Anu was miserable. Soon, Meena changed the seating arrangements so that Anu was now pushed to a corner. This sort of adult bullying was all new to Anu. The only time she was bullied was in the sixth standard. A ringleader had taken a dislike for Anu and had made sure nobody spoke to her the entire year. Except that, nobody had disliked her this strongly and openly.

Instead of focussing on what was stressing her out, Anu decided to read the menu. The food sounded good and she made a mental note of what she wanted to eat. When the time came to order the main course, only she and Sanju turned out to be vegetarians.

'No veg food for us, please!' Meena declared with aplomb and the others laughed in agreement. Since she knew the place like the back of her hand, she offered to order for everyone. Courtesy Meena the Meanie, while the others enjoyed platters and platters of food, Anu and Sanju had to be happy nibbling on a plate of salad and a small pizza. Meena was the ringleader of the group, all right! It was sixth grade all over again. Anu had to suffer debarment having fallen out of the leader's grace.

Anu watched Meena and her friend gorge on fried fare while waxing eloquently about their fitness regime. Well, clearly, food had won over fitness in their lives.

'How much is this Pilates program at the Yoga Studio?' One of the men asked.

'Some 10K per month. Not much.' Meena shrugged. *Ouch*, Anu thought. *Not much at all to do something that old Chinese people do in a park! Okay, fine, that was tai-chi. Thank God I hadn't blurted that and made a fool of myself.*

Anu, the one who was seldom nasty to others, changed by the end of the night. Rather, the large Whiskey on the rocks she chugged down changed her. 'If you eat the "Veg Food" (she made air quotes for emphasis), you won't need to do the expensive "Pilates" (again she made air quotes). Even Kareena Kapoor turned vegetarian to turn size-zero. You should try, Meena.'

Suddenly a complete silence pervaded all around. The men too had stopped talking and gawking at her. Was she too loud or did she choose that precise moment to speak when there was a lull in the other conversations?

Oh please! I am not shaming her. I am only getting back at her. Anu wanted to scream at the men who now looked at her like she was a complete villain.

Meena was not the one to give up easily. 'I would much rather afford a good meal than be thin!' Now everyone laughed good-naturedly, nobody but Anu noticing the insult packed in her statement. She glanced at Sanju and he was sporting his look of disapproval. *What did I do wrong?*

Anu thought the miserable night ended when Dave asked for the bill. But far from it. When the bill arrived, Sanju picked up the fancy leather case where the bill was placed. 'Tonight is on us. To our new beginnings at Verdant Green.'

Dave objected. 'No Sanjay. Let us split the bill. It is too huge for one to bear.'

Sanju did not budge and quickly placed his credit card inside the fancy case. Anu was shell shocked even to say goodbye to Ginny, the only decent person at the table. Meanie and co. strode out without as much as glancing at Anu.

'Sanju! You just spent eighteen thousand on strangers! Are you out of your mind?' Anu was livid when she looked at the bill in the car. 'You object when I turn on the AC in the afternoon for an hour and you splurged so mindlessly?'

'Can you get angry with me after what you did? Just because you are not fat, you can't shame someone.'

Anu did not know whether to laugh or to cry. 'Sanju, have you ever seen me shame anyone? Is that how much you know me?'

'I thought I knew you but tonight you proved me wrong. My mistake to think you would cooperate. You are vengeful because we moved against your will.'

Anu's heart sank at Sanju's accusation. She did not want to cry. She did not even want to explain to him why she did what she did. Ten years of togetherness and he did not even give her the benefit of the doubt.

That night as Anu stayed awake late into the night in the guest bedroom, she felt depressed and lonely like never before. They were not a couple who bickered. They had mild arguments but they had never gone silent on each other. As she tossed and turned, her mind rewound to how they had met, dated and married.

13

Sanju was the new kid on the block while Anu, Sameer and four others were born and raised in adjacent houses and knew each other all their lives. Sanju moved into their neighbourhood when Anu was twelve and in the sixth standard and Sameer in the seventh. Sanju was in the eighth—fair, lanky and bespectacled.

While Sanju was an awkward teen, Sameer was a charmer. Everyone wanted to be his friend. He rode a motorbike at twelve, played football with older boys, and listened to rock bands like Linkin Park and Coldplay. Both girls and boys envied Anu for the special status she enjoyed with Sameer.

Sameer was the first one to invite Sanju into their group. That should have made him get accepted easily, but it did not happen that way. Most of the time Sameer went off to play football and Sanju was stuck with Anu, two other girls and two boys who did not like him at all. He did not know the games they played or their inside jokes but he had tried to fit in. After a week of making efforts, he stopped joining them.

'Anu, why isn't Sanju coming to play with you guys?' Sameer asked her when he remembered Sanju after a month.

'Ask him. You know, he goes to NAFL! May be that is why.' NAFL was a school for the rich kids with high IQ. Everyone else in the neighbourhood went to KLE or Vani Vidyalaya or some such.

Sameer somehow took to Sanju. It was a classic case of opposites attracting each other. He made sure to visit him once a day. 'He is super smart, Anu. He reads books on astronomy in his passtime!' Sameer filled her with details about Sanju. 'He is not coming to play here because he is going for tennis classes in the Vijayanagar club.'

That was how it was between Anu and Sanju for at least three years. They never met, they never talked, but Sameer gave her accounts of Sanju. How he was working hard to get into an IIT, how he assembled a computer with parts bought from SP road, how he was building a website. Was Anu impressed? Of course, she was! That was mostly because if Sameer liked someone or something, he made sure Anu did too.

Then one evening, Sanju and Anu spoke to each other. She still remembered everything from that evening vividly. That was the summer vacation of the ninth standard. Most kids in the neighbourhood, including Sameer had gone on vacations to their grandparents' or cousins' houses. She had discovered Georgette Heyer in the neighbourhood library and was devouring all her books. Of course, Mills & Boons too had just happened but she had to hide those from her mother.

She met Sanju at the library and he smiled making her almost drop her books in shock. She never thought Sanju would be the kind to smile at girls! That evening she only picked Georgette Heyer and no Mills & Boons. Somehow it was important to her that he did not think of her as frivolous. He had waited for her to take her books and they walked back home together. He had taken Isaac Asimov.

'Do you read a lot?' Sanju asked.

'I do but not any great literature. How about you?'

'I read mostly non-fiction or science fiction.' But he stated that as a fact and not in a I-am-superior-to-you way. Anu liked it. She liked him.

After that walk, Anu made sure to join him and Sameer whenever they went out to get ice cream. Then, a year later, Sanju went to IIT Chennai, but met her and Sameer whenever he came home for holidays. In the meanwhile, Sameer was busy being flamboyant and changing girlfriends every six months. He went to St. Joseph's College because they were big on sports. Anu toyed with the idea of changing her college but decided against it and continued her thirteenth year in KLE.

After nearly eight years of knowing each other, one day Sanju asked her out. 'Anu, shall we go out for lunch tomorrow?' He had added hastily. 'Just you and me this time.'

Anu was more shocked than surprised because she had given up on both Sanju and Sameer; they treated her like a backslapping buddy and never a girl. It did annoy her occasionally that Sameer had courted everyone decent in the neighbourhood but had never asked her out. But Sanju was different. He did have a few super brainy girls for friends but as far as she knew, nobody was special.

She agreed to go out with him. There was no reason not to. He looked good (not in a macho way like Sameer but in a decent-guy kind of way), and he went to IIT. IIT held a different type of glamour in Vijaynagar.

That lunch oscillated between awkward and more awkward for the most part. Sameer wasn't there to keep the conversation moving. Then Sanju had asked her abruptly. 'Are you and Sameer together? You know what I mean.'

Anu had laughed nervously. 'We are good friends. But that is all we are.'

'He likes you a lot.' Sanju had added.

'I know.' She had smiled. 'I am his agony aunt every time someone breaks his heart or something goes wrong with his hair or he loses a match.'

'I am sure he is your agony uncle too,' Sameer had tried joking but she could sense anxiety in his voice. He would have loved it if she had denied her fondness for Sameer but how could she! Sameer was a part of her, like an arm or a leg.

'He is more like my saviour when I am in dire straits.'

Then Sanju had asked her suavely. 'If you both are just friends, will you be my special friend?'

Anu had blushed and then gaped at him open-mouthed. Is this really Sanju? The nerd of the century, the boy who loved astronomy, the guy who courted Computer Science?

'This is a surprise!' Then Anu had asked him, 'Why me? I mean, you know—'

Sanju had added after a pause, looking into his water cup. 'You are pretty, kind and uncomplicated.'

Anu still remembered her heart skipping beats and sinking to her stomach. Other boys had confessed their eternal love to her but somehow the way Sanju said it was very endearing. He had called her uncomplicated—that felt nice!

They had become 'special friends' from then on. When he did M.Tech in Chennai, they texted at midnight. They went out in his father's car when he was in town, indulged in minor dalliances but all through their courtship, Sanju was a gentleman who respected her boundaries. She knew he was not happy about her friendship with Sameer but he never objected. For that matter, he never objected to anything she did.

In his own inimitable way, Sameer had refused to acknowledge her relationship with Sanju. They had continued to be friends but Sanju was never discussed between them anymore.

14

At around 1 a.m., Anu gave up on sleeping. She would have a cup of coffee and read something instead of chasing an elusive sleep. Then she remembered pinging a hello to both Sameer and Shwetha a few hours back and she had forgotten to check for their replies. There it was—a reply from Sameer.

'How goes, babe?'

She was so tempted to pick up the phone and call him. There was a high possibility that Sameer would still be awake. Then again, Sanju could be awake too! They already had enough trouble brewing. She pinged back Sameer instead. 'Free for lunch tomorrow, Casanova?'

She got an immediate reply. 'Yes. Also for dinner now.'

She smiled to herself. Her tomorrow had already brightened. 'Me too. But Drink and Dine closes by 11 in the night. So lunch it has to be.'

She gave up on coffee and curled up next to Vicky. She thought about Sanju sleeping alone in that massive master bedroom. A pang of small guilt peeked inside her but she was not in any mood to make up with him yet. Also, she was too sleepy.

When Anu woke up the next morning, for a moment she thought it was still midnight. Her phone showed 5.32 a.m. and she decided to get out of bed. Making her coffee, Anu stepped outside the house into the garden. Her breath caught in her throat. It was such a perfect morning! The sun had just about risen, the wind was cool and the garden looked so pretty. Settling down on the circular stone bench that was built around a tree, Anu sipped her coffee slowly and thought about Sanju.

How excited he was to move into this house and what a dampener she had put on his happiness. She thought of all the times when he had been supportive of her—how he had told her it was not the end of the world when she gave up on her master's degree halfway, convinced her irate father when she did not want a wedding until she was twenty-five, consoled his parents when she wanted to leave Vicky in a daycare and not with them. Most of all how he had agreed to take up a different place and not live with his parents after the wedding. Sanju agreed with her on almost everything.

Just when she was about to get up to go inside the house, Sanju stepped out into the garden. He still looked grim and greeted her with a nod. He paced around but did not sit next to her. So he was in no mood to make up either. How was this impasse going to end?

Anu broke the silence. 'I am going to Vijaynagar to get Vicky's TC.'

He gave a curt nod. *Oh, come on! I am making an effort to be nice here and it would be helpful if you tried too.*

Just as she got up to leave, he asked her, 'Are you coming back here tonight?'

Anu was taken aback. 'Why wouldn't I?'

Sanju shrugged. 'You do vanish when you don't like something.' He was obviously referring to the time when they almost didn't get married.

'Are you spoiling for a fight, Sanju? This is not you.' Anu felt exasperated.

'See you at night, then.' Sanju strode inside the house, leaving her half seething and half dejected. Till then they had never fought a real fight, never played mind-games, and never belittled each other. She hated the cold war that had started between them now.

Vicky got ready in record time when she told him he was going to Dew Drops. 'Mumma, I want to show this butterfly to Chandan!' He dangled the dead and stiff butterfly he had found in the garden.

'You should!' Anu played along. 'You should also show that diamond stone you found.'

When Vicky had gathered all his prized possessions, Anu sat him in the car and fastened the seat-belt. She was as excited as him about the visit. Weering and cutting off through the mad traffic, Anu managed to reach Vijaynagar in an hour and fifteen minutes. Her car was too old to power the AC so by the time she got off, she felt her face was crusted with dust. There was a time when she reached the school in ten minutes looking immaculate. The moment they entered the school, Vicky ran off to meet his friends. Anu didn't mind since she couldn't wait to talk to Sumitra aunty either.

'Anu! Welcome. So good to see you!' Anu enjoyed the welcome, the hug, and the familiar smell of Pond's powder emanating from Sumitra aunty.

'Good to see you too, aunty.' Anu sat down. 'You won't believe who I ran into!' Anu narrated in a single breath the incident with Meena.

Sumitra had a hearty laugh. 'Anu, such impossible things happen only to you! A parent did email me today asking why the teachers are pulling their kids out of the school! Your friend has a quick network.'

'Aunty, I am so so sorry. I will ask her to stop this gossip-mongering.' Anu had an urge to shake sense into Meena's head. What does she know about the efforts and ideals of Sumitra aunty? She had quit the job of a principal in an esteemed school to start Dew Drops. 'What is happening with the parents of the fourth graders?'

Sumitra took off the glasses and rubbed her eyes. 'Not very good news, Anu. Almost half of the parents have given letters to withdraw their kids. The coming academic year, we will have a single section.' Sumitra paused and added hesitantly. 'You know how I bought high-end Montessori materials for that class. Now, half of that is a waste. The seller is refusing to take it back. It is almost five-lakh rupees worth of stuff.'

Anu felt a jolt. This should not happen to someone as good as Sumitra aunty. Anu's head whirled when her mind generated a million thoughts a minute to make it better for Sumitra aunty. She spoke after a pause. 'Aunty, new parents will come to you in due course. But for now, I will help you get the money back. We must create a demand for these products so that the seller comes crawling to you for a buyback.'

'Thank you for caring so much, Anu. Don't take too much trouble over this. Now tell me, how are your new house and new life?'

Anu smiled dryly. 'Aunty, that place is for top Bollywood actors or ultra-rich politicians! We must be the poorest in that neighbourhood. The schools charge six lakhs for LKG! I don't know that to do.' Anu poured her heart out to Sumitra aunty.

'Anu, this is India. There is no place where only the rich can exist. I do know a school in Hebbal, run by a friend. I don't know how far it is from your house.' When Sumitra aunty dawned that I-will-solve-this-for-you face, Anu started to relax.

'Aunty, will you ask if I can also work there? Being at home is snuffing the air out of me.'

'First things first, Anu. Let us now take care of Vicky. You relax in your new place for a while and settle down.'

Anu nodded and looked around longingly sipping the tea that was poured from a flask. Old-world bookshelves filled with books about Tagore, education and Montessori methods. Anu had helped Sumitra aunty set up the library and other rooms when she had started Dew Drops seven years back.

As Sumitra aunty had suggested, she was going to make an effort to relax and enjoy her life in Verdant Green. But there was a premonition that it was going to be a very short-lived life.

Anu left Vicky with her parents-in-law, so she could take as long a lunch break as she could with Sameer. He was going to pick her up from the school.

'Did you make time for me or were you free today?' Anu asked once they settled down with a drink.

'I would have made time for you but I was free today. No shoots.'

'Smooth.' Anu smiled. 'No shoots of both kinds?' Sameer did some part-time modelling and also some professional photography. But his full-time occupation was lazing around.

'So how is it going there? Settling down? Has Sanju started enjoying his luxury living?'

Anu scrunched up her face. 'Let us not talk about it, Sameer. It is not a pretty scene.'

'Done. Let us just drink to Anu's happiness.'

They drank quietly for some time. Anu exceeded her normal two mugs and ordered a third and then a fourth. That was when she started unravelling. She told it all to Sameer. The snooty crowd, her fight with Sanju, and how miserable she was, the trouble Sumitra aunty was in.

Sameer listened quietly. When she finally calmed down, he shook his head. 'Anu, don't act like the martyr you are not! Big deal you got into a catfight. And it is high time you and Sanju fought. For how long can you remain the Romeo and Juliet of the twenty-first century? Now, go back and live. Go out more. Meet more people. You can't brand an entire community snooty because of two immature women.'

'Hey! Don't trivialize my problems.' Anu's head started to spin with the extra beer.

Sameer laughed. 'I am not trivializing them. I am saying they are solvable. Come on, Anu. You are a fighter. Fight to have a good time as you always do.'

Anu began to giggle. 'You sound like a fortune cookie!'

Sameer smiled. 'I am feeling like one too! Do you remember Teju?'

Anu squinted at him suspiciously. 'Of course. The air-hostess who turned you down.'

Sameer smiled. 'Not any more. Now she is all turned on and around. We are seeing each other.'

Anu smiled. 'Sameer, you have to live a little less! Get married, have children. Join the married people's club for all-things-sedate.'

As soon as Sameer dropped her at her parents' house, Anu crashed on the bed. She would pick up Vicky later when she felt sober. Also, her mother-in-law was like a sniffer dog (a gentle one, though) and would smell beer on Anu from a mile. And she was someone who boasted to everyone that her son, though had been to so many countries, never touched alcohol or meat. Well, the meat part was true.

Sleeping on her old bed, Anu thought about what Sumitra aunty had said, that she needed to relax for a while. Then thought about what Sameer had said. That she had to get a life. Determined to do both, she texted Sanju. 'To our new beginnings.' She put the emoji of two mugs clinging.

Sanju immediately sent two smilies in return. Then he wrote more. 'Come to my parent's place. I am here with Vicky.'

Anu felt abnormally happy. She and Sanju were back to being Romeo and Juliet! She only had to hatch a plan to live a little more now. Then it suddenly occurred to her. She could take up tennis! There were two courts in Verdant Green, according to the realtor. She had after all taken tennis coaching (though she missed more than she attended) for a year in high school. She would pick up Sanju's racquet from her in-law's place. That was a lot more Verdant Green-worthy than the one her parents had bought for her.

15

Anu's mother-in-law offered to keep Vicky for a few days so that Anu could focus on getting the house in order. Then, as a return gesture, Anu invited her in-laws over for dinner on Friday night. Her mother-in-law had very exacting standards but Anu had Rathnamma and her daughter who could meet those standards. Her mother-in-law looked pleased with the invite. Unlike Anu's mother, Sanju's mother only very occasionally showed up uninvited.

Anu and Sanju made good use of that alone time that night to watch some non-stop TV till late into the night. With the TV still blaring some episode of *Suits*, they collapsed and slept off on their respective TV-viewing sofas.

The next morning, as soon as Sanju left, Anu sat down to make some calls. She was going to get Sumitra aunty's money back.

She called the first Montessori school on her list of fifty. 'Hi, I am looking to put my son into fourth grade.'

When the receptionist chirped that they would be happy to take her on a tour of the school, Anu asked. 'I was wondering if you have a complete kit for upper elementary classes. Materials that help children move from concrete to abstract thinking? The Dew Drops school has them.'

As Anu had expected, the receptionist asked what exactly Anu was looking for. Feeling pleased with her ingenuity, Anu gave the name of the kit Sumitra aunty had bought and the name of the seller. 'I heard this is the only place where it is sold.'

She made the same call to ten other schools before she got super tired. She could call the others later. For good measure, she also called the seller posing as a school owner and asked for that same kit.

Then she got dressed all determined to start tennis. She had picked up her sports shorts from her parents' house that she had worn just once to run a marathon. That was a few years back before she had Vicky. To cut a long story short, Anu had to abandon the marathon after just a kilometre because she thought she was having a heart attack. Sanju had to stop too and rush her to the hospital where they said she was not having a heart attack but was just not used to running.

When Anu wore those shorts and a matching dry-fit T-shirt that morning, she suddenly felt ultra-sporty. Then she made the mistake of looking at herself in a full-length mirror. The horror of horrors! She looked like that chubby dancer who gyrated far behind Madhuri Dixit in the eighties. Anu knew she wasn't fat (no way!) but probably not yet toned enough to look good in those shorts.

She settled for something a lot less ordinary—track pants and a loose-fitting T-shirt. Picking up Sanju's racquet, she peeked into the mirror again. Now she looked quite nice to herself. She had read somewhere that one had to be a great player or a girl in a ponytail to be accepted into a sports club. She prepped up her high ponytail once more before stepping out.

Rathnamma flashed a dispassionate look at her new avatar but said nothing. Anu missed Radha who would have gushed and said how pretty she looked. That didn't matter. She was going to start a new life. A life full of tennis, swimming, and fancy eating to compensate for the calorie loss. Anu strode confidently towards the tennis court.

She went to the gate that she knew opened into the tennis court. She had done that research the previous evening because she didn't want to look foolish walking all around the property searching for the court. She flashed a bright smile to the Jackie Chan-lookalike guard and walked towards the gate. She had seen people do the same the previous evening.

But Jackie Chan, who never stopped anyone thus far, stopped her! 'Madam, have you signed up for this session?'

Anu was stumped. What was this signing up thing? 'Hmm … no. I can do that now.'

The guard flashed her a wicked smile. 'No, madam. You have to book the court in advance.'

Already people walking inside were casting condescending glances at her. Mostly men with a salt-and-pepper beard and well-preserved women in their late forties or early fifties. To Anu's chagrin, they were all in short skirts looking nice and toned. She was the grandma there in track pants! Then she heard a voice behind her.

'Anu! Surprise! Who are you playing with?' Anu wanted the earth to break open and swallow her. It was Meena.

'Mmm ... not with anyone in particular. Thought I could come here and find a partner.' To Anu's relief, Meena looked quite comical in her skirt.

'Okay. Let her inside. She can play with us today.' Meena ordered the guard pompously. Anu knew the sane option at that point would have been to just run home, but she followed Meena meekly.

After a quick round of hellos and hugs with her friends, Meena turned to Anu. 'You warm up for a bit. By then we will play two games.'

'Sure,' Anu mumbled. Somehow, leave alone warming up even moving herself seemed like a herculean task. She felt unbelievably self-conscious. Taking a chair, Anu glanced around. It was beautiful just like everything else in that place. Three courts next to one another, lined by palm trees and flowerbeds. The people in the other two courts looked very professional. Mostly men but some women battling it out with men. It was almost ten in the morning and that meant the players were mostly retirees or homemakers.

Anu focussed on Meena and her friends. Much to her chagrin, they turned out to be quite good! No Serena Williams but at least her cousins hundred times removed. She still had an opportunity to turn tail and run but Anu decided to stick around. When she played in high school, she was not bad at all. How hard can it be to whack the tiny ball around with a huge racquet?

Meena walked up to Anu and told her to take her place. Anu was sure it was only to assess her skill-level and not out of any benevolence. But that was still all right. She at least got to play. Taking a deep calming breath, Anu walked into the ground on wobbly legs. *Why hadn't she run?*

The woman who was her partner flashed the most unfriendly smile while doing some kind of twisty, jumpy warm up. Then even before Anu had her racquet in place, the woman served. As Anu watched in horror, the ball got returned by the opponent and raced towards her at a thousand kilometres per hour. Nobody hit that hard in high school! At first, Anu tried to duck the ball and then out of sheer self-defence, held her racquet to it. By some miracle, the ball crossed the court and landed in the opponent's court.

Anu, remembering what her coach used to say, did a tiny jump and was all ready to receive the return. Then, the world around her began to dance and she started to see twinkling stars before her. Did someone shoot her point-blank? Nope. The ball was smashed right onto her face. That is all.

When she opened her eyes, a woman in a saree was fanning her with a newspaper. May be an attendant. Meena stood next to her trying to look concerned.

'Anu, I thought you knew how to play! So sorry I got you into trouble.' When she cooed, Anu wished someone had shot her point-blank. Then she wished someone had shot Meena point-blank.

Anu sat up and murmured. 'You go ahead and play. I am all right. I am out of practice, that is all.'

Meena walked away with a friend making sure Anu heard her loud and clear. 'Doesn't look like she was ever *in* practice to be out of it!'

Anu had no more anger or humiliation left in her. Grabbing her racquet, she walked out. That was when she noticed a man walking in step with her.

'Rough morning, ye?' The man said. He was a fifty-something white man.

'Don't rub it in.' Anu, to her surprise, actually laughed. The man had very kind eyes and he was not mocking her. 'Not a rough morning, it is a disastrous morning.'

'Nope. Disastrous would have been if the ball had killed you. 'I am Pete, by the way.'

'Anu Misfit.'

The man laughed heartily. 'Welcome to the club, then.' He raised an imaginary glass in a toast. 'To Anu not dying.'

16

'Do you want to have a cup of coffee? I am headed to the coffee shop.' Pete made an offer Anu couldn't refuse. She could use some company in that strange land that was in Bangalore but not Bangalore.

As they sat down with coffee, Pete asked. 'So what is the story behind the forlorn look you are sporting?'

Anu sighed. 'How much time have you got?'

Pete shrugged. 'How much coffee can you buy?'

'I will make it short then.' Anu twirled her coffee to dissolve the creamy heart they had made. 'I don't want to be in Verdant Green. I want to go home but I can't.'

'Hmm, where is home?'

'You wouldn't know. Vijaynagar. The real Bangalore.'

'Real Bangalore, is it? What is this place then?' Pete sounded amused but he also looked curious.

'This is a pretend western suburb. Where are the cows, the dogs, and the street vendors?' Anu sounded like Arnab Goswami to her own ears. She had to become a little less animated.

'I went to Gandhi Bazar,' Pete spoke. It took Anu a moment to understand Pete's mispronunciation of the place. 'It was so vibrant with flowers and fruits and whatnot. But along the way, there were also piles and piles of garbage and construction debris and horrendous traffic.' Pete was not being snobbish about what he said. He was just sharing his awe mixed with horror.

'I love the city with its chaos, traffic, processions and noise. I don't like to live in this isolated bubble where I have to pay five-hundred rupees for a coffee.' Anu put her cup down. 'Nice meeting you, Pete. And, thanks for the coffee.'

'Wait, Anu. I didn't mean to offend you.'

'None taken. I just want to sleep off the humiliation at the court.'

'I am sure nobody even remembers you by now. So don't feel humiliated.' Pete patted Anu's hand. 'Come back to the court at three. I will play with you.'

Anu's eyes lit up, as they always did when she was excited, giving her away completely. 'Will you?'

'Don't look so hopeful! I coach two kids at three in the afternoon. You can join in.'

'How old are they? Kindergartners?' Anu rolled her eyes but she was going to take up on the offer.

'Close. Fourth graders. They could beat you, though.'

'Very comforting. What do you charge?' Anu looked at him suspiciously. 'An arm? A leg? Liver?'

'Heart,' Pete replied solemnly. 'A heartfelt thank you is all I take.'

'That is what he said.' Anu smiled, quoting Michael Scott.

'Michael Scott fan, ye!' Pete laughed. 'Nice meeting you, Anu.' He quite mispronounced her simple name too.

'Did I tell you the twins I coach are my grandsons?'

Anu laughed. 'I would have remembered if you did. If it is all in the family, can I bring my son too sometime?'

'More the merrier. Bring him along! By the way, a smile suits you better than a frown.'

Anu had the best time that afternoon. 'Thank you, Pete.' Anu smiled all sweaty and pink after hitting a few balls that Pete fed her very very slowly. 'I feel like a champion!'

'You are what you feel! See you tomorrow. Same time, same place.'

Feeling light and fit, Anu walked home through the calm winding paths, flowering trees on either side, kids biking. Somehow everything looked beautiful. So beautiful, it felt surreal. This was a slice out of some European countryside. She had gone on a twenty-one-day package tour to Europe with her parents. Her family was considered affluent in Vijaynagar for doing so. But probably only the maids and gardeners took such package tours here. She thought of Vicky and how excited he would be to play tennis with Pete's grandkids.

Then her eyes fell on a building that stood a little distance. The red-tile-roofed building stood in stark contrast to a sweep of green grass around it. Anu looked at it mesmerized and started walking towards it. As she neared it, she squinted against the evening Sun and read the word 'Karma' etched artistically on a brass signboard. Her reverie began to crumble slowly as she realized it was a yoga and Ayurvedic health centre. She would probably have to sell herself to even set foot in there. As Anu was about to turn back, a tall and very graceful young woman in a saree sashayed towards her.

'Ma'am, Good Evening.'

Anu felt like an ungainly pig facing that woman. She returned the greeting and stopped to hear what news that nymph had for her.

'Are you here for the trial yoga class? The class has just begun. You can join in.' God, even her voice was so melodious.

Anu decided to go along. It was her lucky day, after all! Free tennis classes and now a free yoga class in that gorgeous building. She was curious to see how it looked from inside. Probably had all kinds of vintage stuff with posts to pillars hauled from old houses in Kerala. She loved those.

'Sure. I would love to go in.'

The woman took her tennis racquet and led her inside the beautifully carved door. The moment Anu stepped inside, her smile vanished. It was hot as hell in there! People were sitting cross-legged, with their eyes closed and profusely sweating. Hot Vikram Yoga! Anu started to feel so claustrophobic, she was certain to faint soon. Before she even had a chance to escape from there, the instructor, an older and a lot sterner version of the woman who ushered her in, signalled Anu to take a place bang in the middle of the room. Great! Now there was no escape.

17

Wedged between a slim girl on her left and a large woman on her right, Anu closed her eyes as per the instruction. 'Breathe deeply. Inhale … hold … exhale … hold.'

Well, Anu could do all that easily if only she was not getting roasted to a crisp. Sweat trickled down her back and face. She tried wiping her face with the back of her arm but the next instruction, gentle but stern, stopped her in her tracks. 'Do not move. Hands in Chin Mudra and breathe.'

How long was this breathing thing! Anu suddenly felt nostalgic remembering Supriyaji's classes. It was so nice and airy in her house. And all her routines were just about right.

'Now, take a break and have a sip of water.' The tone made Anu remember the movie Hunger Games, where if you didn't follow the instructions you would have to die. This was no different.

She had no water. It was in her tennis kit. Anu got up to get her water when the instructor raised her dainty brow. Anu signalled with her hand that she was going to get water. With a nod, the instructor asked Anu to sit back down. Handing her a glass of water, the woman moved back to the front of the class. She was the kind that scared Anu. Mid-fifties, slim, pursed-lips, crisp cotton saree, grey hair tied into a bun. The kind that did not look very kind.

Anu could feel the others staring at her. To make matters worse, everyone had wiped their faces with their hand-towels and only Anu poured sweat like a leaky tap. She looked at the woman on her right. Mistake. She looked at Anu not just disapprovingly but with contempt. The way people did when Vicky cried in the movie halls.

Anu looked to her left. An eighteen-or-so girl looked at her and smiled. The girl was quite a plain-looking one. But she was so well turned-out in expensive, bought-from-abroad printed leggings and a T-shirt, she looked smart. Rich never looked plain actually. Even her mat looked the designer kind. Anu realized that she was the only one sitting on the plain mat spread by the Yoga Studio. Everyone else had swanky mats with elegant steel or glass bottles next to them. Anu was secretly glad she hadn't brought her green Tupperware bottle inside. That would look so out of place.

'Now, I want everyone to stretch your legs out and try to hold the toes. Stay in the position until my next instruction. And breathe.' Anu sighed at the words. At least she knew how to do that and she even knew it was Paschima Uttasana. Didn't the woman know the names of the Asanasas or was she deliberately not using them? Anu decided to go with the former. Labelling that pretty woman as ignorant made Anu feel better.

The stretch and hold were fine with Anu. The girl on Anu's left had managed to hold the toes but the woman on

Anu's right was struggling to even reach till her knee, with her ample bosom resting on her thighs. The girl, catching Anu sizing up others, smiled. Anu smiled back feeling smug that the woman next to her was as flexible as a wooden stick.

But soon the stretch turned into a never-ending saga. 'Stay in the position until I instruct.' The woman kept announcing. Anu, soon unable to bear with the screaming back, bent her knee, at first slightly, then generously. The girl on the left did the same and so did the others in the row.

'End the stretch and go to the crossed leg position.' The instructor spoke looking begrudingly at Anu. As if Anu inspired the others to cheat on her. *Nobody can stay stretched forever—even a rubberband would snap!*

The girl handed Anu a tissue paper to wipe off the sweat. Anu mouthed a thank you, eliciting another glare from the instructor. Then the class resumed. Just when Anu had started feeling like a cooked tomato with the skin half peeled, the class ended. The teacher, glancing at Anu frequently, gave a short speech. 'I hope you enjoyed the class. Those of you taking this as a trial today, please do sign up outside for regular classes. See you all on Friday, same time. Hari Om.' Of course, the yoga instructors had to end with a spiritual salutation. But Supriyaji just said bye. Anu liked that because she could also just say bye. She could never say something like *Hari Om* back naturally.

Anu got up along with the girl. When they walked out, the girl asked. 'Are you signing up?'

Anu laughed. 'Are you serious? I will sit in an oven instead!'

The girl burst into peels of laughter. Just the way youngsters do. 'I am not coming back either. My mother has already paid I think but she can think of it as a charity.'

Anu walked with the girl until she got on her cycle. Anu recognized the brand, it was a Tata Stryder 7 Speed. Sameer had bought one last year. When Anu said it was too expensive for a cycle, he hadn't stopped defending it for months. Now it was collecting dust in his driveway just like Anu's ordinary BSA cycle did in hers.

When the girl bid goodbye, Anu thought of asking for her number but didn't. What if the girl thought Anu was a stalker?

The girl peddled away but then stopped and looked back at Anu. 'Aunty, do you play every day?' She pointed at Anu's racquet.

Aunty! Anu had to get used to getting addressed thus by teens. She shook her head. 'Started only today. So I don't know yet how long I will last! Do you?'

The girl now stopped and started pushing the cycle next to Anu. 'I learnt for a couple of years. Then I gave up. It was too competitive, so it was no fun.'

'What do you do?' The girl asked after a pause.

Anu smiled. 'As of now, trying to get used to this place. We just moved here. How about you? I am Anu, by the way.'

The girl shrugged. 'I am Pooja. I finished my twelfth. Waiting for my results. We are quite new here too. Moved in only last month.'

That explained why a teenager was striking up a conversation with Anu! She had no friends yet. 'Enjoy the holidays. Join me for tennis if you want.' But Anu quickly explained to her that it was not a great playing situation.

The girl laughed. 'So I will be playing with fourth-graders? That will help me look hep.'

Anu smiled. 'You will also be playing with a middle-aged woman and an older man. You will be the most sought after girl in your circles once you get spotted with us.'

'I will think about it. I will see you if I see you!' When the girl peddled away, Anu hoped that she would join them. She liked that kid.

18

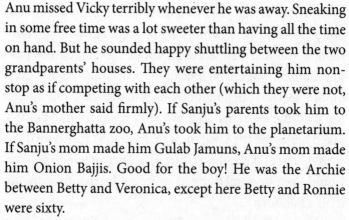

Anu missed Vicky terribly whenever he was away. Sneaking in some free time was a lot sweeter than having all the time on hand. But he sounded happy shuttling between the two grandparents' houses. They were entertaining him non-stop as if competing with each other (which they were not, Anu's mother said firmly). If Sanju's parents took him to the Bannerghatta zoo, Anu's took him to the planetarium. If Sanju's mom made him Gulab Jamuns, Anu's mom made him Onion Bajjis. Good for the boy! He was the Archie between Betty and Veronica, except here Betty and Ronnie were sixty.

The next morning Anu called Sumitra aunty to enquire if anything had happened with the materials. After a bit of hesitation, Sumitra aunty spoke, 'Anu, the seller called a couple of days back and said someone from our school was trying to play games with him. He said the call was coming from "Anu DewDrops".'

'Oh, no. Aunty, I was only trying to create a scarcity for that kit. I forgot that TrueCaller now gives away everyone's identities.' Anu felt and sounded miserable. 'Everything I do seems to backfire.'

Anu tried to forget that incident. She would think of something else to solve the issue later. Now she had to get the school checked out for Vicky. Anu texted Shwetha if she was free to go with her and then for lunch. Shwetha texted back immediately. 'Yes and yes! Have to see your paradise too. See you at ten.'

Shwetha would be impressed with Verdant Green, Anu had no doubt. That girl loved luxury. Well, Anu did too but not at the cost of an empty bank account. Talking about money, she had lied to Sanju about how much she paid Rathnamma. She had to figure out a way to absorb that extra money she was shelling out. She had also lied about what she paid the gardener. The property manager had politely asked her to get the lawn mowed. He hadn't mentioned the consequences if she didn't, but Anu knew it would be dire. Could even be something as grave as Meena announcing it on a bullhorn.

'Oh, my God! Anuuu!! This place is better than most high-end resorts. What were you mopey about, you stupid one!'

Shwetha stood out in her all-red outfit. She had been going to the gym and had developed some really good calf and arm muscles. Many, including Anu, thought she looked like Bipasha Basu but somehow Shwetha didn't like it. *Can I look like someone younger than me? Not a yesteryear star, please*—was her gripe. That made sense.

'Look at you, Shweth! You look fabulous. I want you to punch Meena the Meanie with your newly toned arms.' Over the daily conversations, Shwetha was up-to-date with Anu's woes.

'Let us find her.' Shwetha did some ridiculous looking kicks and punches in her tight dress. Anu smiled. She missed Shwetha and the fact that she could not meet her at an hour's notice anymore.

Anu drove to the school Sumitra had suggested, with Shwetha taking over the navigation. Despite the Google Maps, Anu got lost wherever she went the first time and the second. But by the third time, she always nailed the place. Shwetha had an equally bad sense of direction.

'Head left in twenty metres onto first crossroad.' That was the Google lady.

'Is it this left?' Anu asked panicking. What were twenty metres anyway?

'Maybe not ... oh, wait. That was it. The map has now gone into a tizzy and says it is redirecting us.'

Anu put the car into reverse and started moving back with every vehicle behind her blaring their horns. It was a one-way street. As long as you manoeuvred very slowly, you could move any way in Bangalore.

A police officer knocked on her window just when she turned left and asked her to pull over. 'Sir, please sir. Job interview. Already late, sir.' Anu pleaded very helplessly.

'You girls have no traffic sense. Go. Leaving you only because you said interview.'

Anu grinned at Shwetha. 'He called me a girl.'

Shwetha sighed. 'He has eye-sight issues.'

'Now, Miss Direction. Tell me where to go now.' Anu grinned at Shwetha. 'Accept it. It was a good pun.'

After getting lost another five or six times, they landed before a building that looked like an old house. The address matched but that place looked nothing like a school.

'Are you sure this is not a job interview for a housekeeper?' asked Shwetha.

'We will decide once we see the owner. If it is Brad Pitt, I will do the housekeeping.' Anu walked inside but a guard stopped her and made her sign the guest register.

The house was like a mysterious mansion. They walked into a foyer and an attendant idling on a stool looked at them quizzically. Anu asked to meet the principal, and the attendant directed them to a woman almost the same age as Anu. She walked them to the principal's chamber. So easy! No marketing, no trying to sell the school to her, no smooth-talking associates in matching sarees. Nobody was in a uniform—neither the staff nor the kids. Anu was already falling in love with the place.

Walking on, Anu peeked into the rooms. Children were sprawled on the floor or sitting around large desks working on things. Some were younger but most seemed to be Vicky's age. This is how it was in Sumitra aunty's school. Though Sanju did not believe in that type of free learning, Vicky had fun. He need not learn anything at four, does he? His fulltime job must be to run around and laugh.

'I love it here.' Anu gushed to Shwetha who shushed her.

'Happy hormones cloud your thoughts. Stop feeling good.' Shwetha thought just like Sanju most of the time.

Anu instantly liked Principal Janaki and the assured way in which she spoke. Vicky would love it here! And, the fee was in thousands, not in lakhs.

'But, there is no bus facility. You have to drop and pick your son up.' The principal concluded. 'Sumitra told me you were teaching in her school. Currently, I have no vacancy but I will keep you in mind.'

That was a bit deflating. Coming all the way to only drop Vicky. It was a good seven kilometres in some horrifying traffic. But Anu nodded chirpily and added. 'That is okay. Kids here look happy and Vivikth will be happy here too.'

Janaki smiled. 'We try not to control them too much. I can't say they are happy all the time, but for the most part, we let them be themselves.'

Anu saw Shwetha knit her brows. 'How so? What if a kid is not happy doing maths?'

'Then he can leave the class and do what he likes.' The principal smiled with ease.

Anu wished she was in a school of that sort. No, she wished she was in a life of that sort. 'I am yet to get his TC. I will get him over as soon as we do.' Anu visibly beamed.

On the way out, Anu was on cloud nine and Shwetha was highly unimpressed. 'Anu, what will Vicky learn there? To string beads and pour rice from tumbler to tumbler? I don't think Sanju will approve.'

Anu said with finality. 'I am quite certain of two things. Vicky will love it here and Sanju will hate it. But Vicky, at four, should not be sad. So he is coming here.'

Shwetha quickly clicked a few pictures of the building. 'Show these to Sanju and ask him what he thinks. You should put Vicky in a proper school.'

19

'Sanju, the school that Sumitra aunty suggested is nice. Vicky will like it there,' Anu broached the topic tactfully when they were in the middle of a good pasta dinner. Rathnamma's daughter, Geetha, was Master Chef calibre.

Sanju, obviously pleased with the food, looked at Anu and smiled. 'If Vicky is going to like it, then it cannot be good.'

In a way, Sanju was right. But he and his family were the kinds who expected kids to know tables till ten by the time they turned two. Well, Vicky, on his good days, could count till ten.

'Anu, please put him where all the kids here are going. If it is six lakhs per year, so be it. Education is important.' Sanju said firmly. 'No more mom-and-pop school for Vicky.'

Anu glared at him. 'Don't insult Sumitra aunty's school. Also, I am not a genius in maths, Sanju. But even I can count that it comes to fifty thousand a month. Have we come into some hidden gold suddenly? Till last month, you objected to buying even things like Twinings teabags!' Then she remembered to add. 'There is nothing wrong with

Sumitra aunty's school. I taught there too. Now, don't say case in point.'

'You said it. I didn't! And, Twinings tea tastes like water and is double the price of Tetley!' Sanju put his fork down in irritation. 'Why is everything about money now, Anu? You spend so much on bags and shoes and teas but when it comes to important things, you become stingy.'

Anu was stung. True that she bought an occasional (well, once in three months at best) Hidesign or a Caprese. But was that any comparison to the expenses Sanju was talking here?

After a pause, she nodded her agreement. She didn't want to drag on the fight and make Sanju quit dinner. The credit card bill would do that anyway. 'Fine. I will put him in Indigo International. Let him become an unhappy Einstein!'

Sanju smiled. 'Say Jeff Bezos or Nadella. Einstein is long dead.'

Anu smiled too, as the cloud between them began to lift slowly. 'Sanju, how much is your actual take-home salary? After the taxes, retirement and other hidden expenses?'

Sanju didn't like to reveal the numbers. She never knew how much he made. He got up and ruffled her hair. 'Don't worry. I won't make you spend your inheritance.'

'I will need your debit card to pay the first instalment of fees.'

Worry flashed on Sanju's face momentarily. She was sure he hadn't thought of actually having to pay!

Pooja hadn't shown up at the tennis court. That was a bit disappointing for Anu, but on the bright side, Pete had said she was now looking like a below-average player after two days of practice. That was a great improvement from pathetic.

On Friday morning, Anu decided to beg Pete to go with her for admissions. His grandkids were in the same school. Also, white people received a good reception in India.

'Why do you want me to go with you? You are the native here! I am the foreigner.' Pete protested when Anu called him and asked him to go along with her to the school.

'Pete, trust me. In this part of Bangalore, you are the native and I am the foreigner. I will buy you coffee at Shree Darshini. Please go with me.' Pete had told her how he loved the coffee in Darshini that was close to Verdant Green, but given how crowded the place was, he could never get in.

'Fine,' Pete agreed. 'Add two Vadas to the coffee. Both for me. Pick me up at nine then.'

'Yes, My Lord.' Anu hung up the phone. She was not like Shwetha who could go anywhere or do anything by herself. Anu needed someone by her side. But she was blessed that she always found someone right to be by her side. She had 'good people karma'.

Once the money was paid, the admission process was smooth. Everyone was friendly to her and super friendly to Pete. The principal even ordered some fresh juice for them in her chamber. She asked Pete repeatedly how they were in comparison with the schools in the US. Pete, being the diplomatic talker that he was, simply said the kids loved it there and loved it here.

'Time for me to pay your debt, Mr Pete.' Anu grinned as she drove.

Settling Pete on the stone culvert under an old banyan tree in front of the Darshini, Anu handed him a plate of piping hot Vada dipped in Sambar. 'You are my hero.' Pete smiled at her gratefully. 'But you didn't need me today.'

'Well, you were my trophy friend. I liked showing you off.' Anu bit into her Vada.

Pete shrugged. 'Fair enough, then.'

That was when Anu spotted Pooja walking on the road with her earphones plugged in. Torn jeans and a T-shirt—she looked too plain. Not at all like the designer kid she had met the other day.

'Pooja,' Anu shouted instinctively but then, realizing she had the earphone on, rushed to her and tapped her on the shoulder.

'Oh, aunty,' Pooja took off her earphone, but she did not look too pleased to see Anu grinning ear to ear in glee.

'Want to join us for a coffee?' Anu felt a little deflated looking at Pooja's lack of enthusiasm.

'No aunty, another time.' Pooja smiled curtly. She seemed to be in a hurry to go somewhere.

'Okay, call me sometime.' Anu wrote her phone number on the back of some receipt. 'Any time.' Pooja smiled, stuck the paper in her jeans and walked on.

'So, did you sufficiently embarrass the girl?' Pete asked as Anu sat down next to him.

'I think so. But where was she going on foot? This is a good two kilometres from Verdant Green. If she was going for a walk, she could have done so within the property.'

'Let her be. Don't go all sleuthing on her now.' Pete already knew Anu too well.

'I will try not to. But no promises. She seemed nothing like the girl I met the other day.'

20

That afternoon Pooja showed up at the tennis court. But she was not dressed to play, nor had a racquet with her. Anu waved to her from the court. Pooja settled on a chair and looked at her phone (with the earphones, of course) the entire fifteen minutes Anu lobbed the ball back and forth with Pete.

Panting and wiping off the sweat, Anu sat down next to Pooja. 'Glad you came.'

Pooja looked at her and smiled. An actual smile, not the fake one she had flashed earlier. 'Well, you looked very worried about me. So I came by to tell you that I am all right.'

Pete didn't approach them. Instead, he went to coach the kids. 'I was worried because you looked a little hassled,' said Anu still panting. 'And you were walking on a busy street. People in Verdant Green will ostracize you for such acts.'

Pooja laughed. 'I was hassled about something but nothing to worry about. You go on and play. I will see you around.'

When she got up to leave, Anu stopped her. 'Why don't you play? You are anyway wearing tennis shoes.'

MEET ME IN THE MIDDLE

'… and jeans shorts! I can't possibly play in these!'

Anu thrust the racquet into Pooja's hands. 'Go on. Show me what you got. Don't try to be better than me.'

Pooja had no comeback. The girl didn't talk much at all. Anu walked Pooja into the court and called Pete. 'Pete, the kid wants to play.'

Pete smiled at Pooja. 'Come on over.'

Pooja was good. So good Pete played a game with her. Anu watched them and sipped her Pepsi contentedly. She was glad Pete had another disciple. He had killed her with training on the previous day.

Friday evening came rather quickly but did not exactly turn out how Anu intended it to be. Her mother-in-law called her to say Padma aunty was back from her travel and she was going to join them for dinner. To give a bit of a story, Padma aunty was Sanju's father's widowed sister and she lived with Sanju's parents. She was like a second mother to Sanju and a mother-in-law in the true sense to Anu; she thoroughly disliked Anu and expressed it freely.

Back when Anu and Sanju were newly engaged, Padma aunty had had a private chat with Anu. 'Look, Sanju is a very innocent boy. I can't believe that he is … well he is …' She had stopped, swallowed, and completed the sentence with great difficulty. 'Going for love marriage. With you. Who is so different from him.'

Anu's mouth had opened in dismay. *Who spoke like that other than Cinderella's stepmother?* But Padma aunty neither saw her open mouth nor her shocked silence. 'You know that all my property is going to Sanju. Hope you are not marrying him for that. Sorry to be blunt.'

Anu's mouth had opened wider in shock. No wonder Sanju's mother had warned her to stay silent no matter what Padma aunty said. She mumbled something incoherently but Padma aunty had continued. 'Look, I know you asked Sanju to marry you. That is okay. You are our caste. But I prefer girls who are not so forward-thinking. Also, I would have preferred someone more academically oriented to compliment Sanju's brilliance.'

Now, where did all that come from? Anu was about to tell Padma aunty two things—she was abnormal and rude. And, that it was Sanju who had asked out. But then she had stopped and stayed quiet. *How did it matter anyway?* If she wants to think her Sanju to be an innocent boy, let her. But that was only the beginning. Padma aunty, since then, had never let go of a single chance to be a nuisance in Anu's life.

Breaking away from her thoughts, Anu followed Geetha to the kitchen when she arrived. 'Geetha, make four or five types of vegetables. Anything you like but without garlic.'

Geetha pursed her lips thinking. 'I will. But—'

Anu sighed. 'Yeah, I know. I will pay you extra for the cooking. Three guests and us.'

Geetha perked up. 'Don't tell my mother that you paid me extra.'

Sanju's parents were simple folks who were easily pleased. As soon they arrived, they gushed about how beautiful the house was. *Looks like the White House,* said Sanju's father, though the house was painted pale blue. But Padma aunty, who as always returned Anu's hello with nothing, walked around hawk-eyed. 'This furniture needs to go, Sanju. This worked for your small flat but not here.' Stressing on *your* because that flat was technically Anu's.

Sanju jumped in. 'Yes, aunty. We will replace all this soon.' Anu almost asked Padma aunty if she was going to sponsor the furniture, but didn't.

'Beautiful house, Sanju. Someone with a sense for interiors would have done wonders to the place,' concluded Padma aunty.

'You should stay with us and deck the place up, aunty.' Sanju purred, making Anu seethe silently. *Is he really that thick? Can't he see she was taking a dig at me?*

Anu quickly got the dinner going. The sooner it was over the better. Padma aunty unleashed a barrage of verbal firing all through dinner.

'So much food. We have to have a sense of proportion when we cook.'

'Why keep a cook? I cooked even when I worked.'

'Is Sanju even getting any proper south Indian food? This looks too fancy.'

The final firing was just before she left. 'Vicky is such a bright boy but because of the school, he can't even spell simple words.'

Anu was exhausted by the end of the night. Such hatred from Padma aunty because she believed Anu was not good enough for Sanju. Nobody on earth was good enough for Sanju in her view. But there was another reason too for aunty's hatred. Anu had broken off the engagement when Sanju had insisted that they live with his parents. Then, after about six months, they had got back together when Sanju had agreed to move into a separate flat.

Padma aunty, who was much relieved when they had separated, was devastated when they got back together. Her Sanju was not only marrying beneath him, but he was also moving away from the house.

It was altogether another story that Sameer had proposed to her in the meanwhile and Anu had almost agreed to marry him. She often wondered if Sanju's change of heart was because of that proposal, though he denied it vehemently. But that had marked the beginning of Sanju's disapproval of Anu's friendship with Sameer.

21

By the time everyone left for the night, Anu was a wreck. Setting up the table, getting extra salt for someone, pickle for someone else, cold water for some and hot water for Padma aunty—well, none of this would have left her this dead if the house wasn't as big as the Mysore Palace. In the middle of this, Vicky had gone into superhero mode flying from the sofa to window to what-not.

Padma aunty did not leave before firing a final salvo at Anu. 'Sanju has done so well all by himself.' Then, for good measure, she added. 'With a single income.'

Sanju's mother was the only one who caught it. The father-son duo was busy arguing about the best route to get home. Sanju's mother then mildly corrected Padma aunty. 'Padma, Anu stopped working only now. Also, because of her flat, they have saved a lot on rent.'

Padma aunty's nostrils flared. 'Because of that tiny flat, Sanju moved out of our nice house. And, Anu, you should do a B.Ed and qualify as a teacher.'

'Yes, ma'am,' Anu muttered to herself, closing the door behind them. Vicky came bounding to her full of stories.

Some of them got so intermixed, Anu didn't understand them at all but that didn't matter. She hugged him close and that was all he needed.

It was truly a manic Monday having to get Vicky ready for school after more than a fifteen-day break. By the time Anu managed to get him onto the car, she was ready for a nap. There was school transport, but Anu or Sanju would have to sell organs to include that in their expenses.

They had visited the school over the weekend and Sanju was over the moon. He took pictures of the building from all angles and shared them to the family WhatsApp group. Unfortunately, Anu was a part of that group. Padma aunty immediately sent friendly smilies and thumbs-ups. 'Send a picture of you and Vicky at the school,' she wrote.

There was a reason behind Padma aunty ignoring Anu even on WhatsApp. When on her travel, she uploaded a thousand pictures a day. Anu got so tired of seeing photos of Padma aunty in different salwar kameezes and the same sneakers, she had stopped downloading them. That Padma aunty had figured out and was now on a mission to ignore Anu digitally. Breaking away from her thoughts of Padma aunty, Anu parked on the roadside and walked inside the school building. It looked so much like a five-star hotel, Anu instinctively started to look for a pool. Vicky looked bewildered. When she asked the receptionist for his class, she gave a curt smile and called a coordinator. Vicky looked at the beautiful, smiling woman who offered him her hand. 'Come on. Let me show you to your class.'

Vicky eyed her suspiciously and then declared. 'I will go with my Mumma.'

Anu felt unnecessary tears sting her eyes. She always left him in his class and then went to hers. 'Mumma isn't working here, Vicky. You go with ma'am.'

'But you should work here. I can't go to school if you don't.' Vicky wasn't making it easy. The coordinator distracted him with the 3D picture of a lion and signalled Anu to leave.

Anu decided to hang around in the area for the next four hours. What if Vicky got upset and they called her? Walking into a Coffee Day, Anu dug out her book. A Poirot mystery. Agatha Christie was her comfort read when she was upset.

So, what was she going to do now? How was she going to spend her time in that beautiful alien land called Verdant Green where the house still did not feel like home?

Anu shut the book after a few futile attempts to read it. She was done feeling unhappy. She could reserve that for when they went bankrupt, which could be a few months away. Until then, she was going to have a good time. Just then her phone rang. It was Sumitra aunty.

'Anu! I have some good news.'

'Tell me soon, aunty! I could really use some!'

'The seller called. He said whatever games we played, it has worked in his favour. Says many schools have come to him for materials citing that Dew Drops recommended him. So, he says as a thank you to us, he is taking back the materials!'

Anu laughed. 'I never intended it that way but who is complaining! I am so happy he came to his senses!'

'Anu, thank you for the help and care. Take care, child.'

Feeling light and happy, Anu downed her Cappuccino and walked into the Internet Café next door. First things first, she needed a job and a resume to get a job.

She downloaded a sample resume for teachers off the net and filled in her details. She had worked in only two places, which meant her resume was about two-and-a-half sentences. Then she added an internship at her father's office. She did give him coffee whenever he worked in his home office. So that should count. Anu decided to fill the rest of the page with a Statement of Purpose. She had helped her friends with those when they applied for schools abroad. It didn't make any sense on a resume, but it had to be at least a page. It took her two hours and three visits to Coffee Day before she had her resume ready.

But Anu was very happy with her writing. She had explained how teaching young minds warmed her heart, how the kids loved her unorthodox methods of teaching, and listed how Indigo could and should make school more fun for kids. Anu dreamed the next sequence of events. She was going to walk into the principal's chamber, hand over the resume and bowl her over. The Principal would smile at her witty statement of purpose and offer her a job on the spot. And she would also tell Anu how the teachers' kids studied for free at Indigo.

Anu asked the Cyber Center owner to print her resume. He looked at it intently. 'I have seen only black borders on resumes. Nothing pink and blue like this.'

Anu beamed. 'Let it be. Nice on the eyes.'

Feeling all confident, Anu walked into Indigo International 'I need to see the Principal, please.'

The receptionist raised her brows ever so slightly. 'You need to make an appointment.'

Anu felt deflated but did not let that affect her. She had expected the same treatment the other day had Pete not joined her. 'Can you please call and ask the Principal? It is important.'

The receptionist made a few phone calls in a very hushed voice. 'No, ma'am. The Principal is busy. You can meet her on Thursday at eleven.'

Taking an off chance, Anu asked the receptionist. 'Forgot to mention. Pete Dunsworth will be joining me too.'

There was a change in the pretty girl's demeanour. 'Let me ask again, ma'am.'

A few more hushed calls later, she smiled, 'Please go straight down the corridor and take a left, ma'am.'

The Principal looked at Anu and nodded but craned her neck to look at the door. 'Miss Anu, please have a seat. Will Pete be joining us soon?'

'Oh, I am afraid not. I was the one who wanted to meet with you.'

The Principal looked visibly irritated. 'How may I help you?' She had turned ice cold. 'If this is this about your son, please talk to the coordinators.'

Anu wanted to ask her if she was born cold and sinister or just groomed herself to be one. But she instead showed her the resume. 'I would like to work here as a teacher.'

The Principal, without even glancing at it, pushed it back towards Anu. 'We are not looking for one. I am very busy right now. Please leave the resume with the receptionist.'

Anu knew she had to shut up and leave. But words tumbled out of her mouth, 'If Pete had asked for a job, would you reject him?'

The Principal turned red in anger. 'Miss Anu! What are you hinting at? Your son studies here and that is where it all ends.'

Anu hadn't felt more foolish in her life.

Pete laughed and laughed some more when Anu told him what she had done. 'Why were you so desperate to work there?'

'I wanted to be with Vicky. That is how we have been for two years.' Anu sat down with the racquet by her side. Vicky was playing tag with Pete's grandsons.

'Nothing wrong with that intent.' Pete sat down next to her. 'You did what you thought was right. It is not entirely untrue that the Principal likes me a little better than others.'

Anu smiled for the first time that day. 'You should become a motivational speaker, Pete. I feel better already. The Principal adores you. Why? Why not me?'

'I don't know. Maybe because I volunteer there?'

Anu felt even more foolish. She had convinced herself that the principal liked Pete because he was white. 'Could be.' She smiled and got up. 'This place is turning me into a lunatic.'

Pete patted her back. 'Hang in there. These are the stories you will tell your grandchildren.'

'Or great-grandchildren. If the shame has subsided by then.' Anu waved Pete goodbye.

22

What started the next morning, Vicky's second day of school, was soon a pattern. He would start crying that he didn't want to go from the time she parked her car. Then Anu would coax him for ten minutes, then bribe him with something new and different every day. A meal at McDonald's, a pizza treat, a bike ride on the road, the best one that worked every single time was that he could pet the gnarly puppy that curled up next to the car at the school. Most parents flashed Anu a look that spelt part pity and mostly disgust at the sight of Vicky all over the puppy. *Oh, come on! This is an adorable puppy, you snooty people!* Anu wanted to shout at them but thankfully, hadn't reached that state of insanity yet.

After somehow shoving a half-sobbing Vicky into school, Anu sat at her usual chair at Coffee Day and sipped Cappuccino with a book. The staff knew her well by then, the woman who entered the shop in a state of semi-daze but left looking normal after an hour.

That day, ten minutes into her coffee, Anu's phone rang. Sameer! 'Hey, sorry didn't return your call yesterday.' Anu

174

felt happy to hear from him at a time when she didn't have
to rush anywhere or do anything.

'What is new with that! Listen, can you meet me for
dinner tomorrow?'

'That is perfect! I am coming to Vijaynagar today evening.
Meeting Shwetha today. Sanju is travelling, so I am spending
the weekend there.'

'See you tomorrow.'

The phone rang again. That was Kavitha who was put
on bed rest. 'Anu, I am dying of boredom, ya. Bed rest will
kill me.'

Anu smiled. 'You will have a healthy baby if you stick
to the bed now. I will see you this weekend. Hang in there,
soldier.'

The moment Anu entered Vijaynagar that evening, she
started to feel better. The familiar shops, street vendors who
sold anything from food to clothes to sunglasses that said
Rayybon, a fender-bender accident that had a gathered a
crowd. Home! Mom's coffee, grandmom's snacks, dinner
with Shwetha and the grand finale—the new chick-lit she
had just started to read. Life was going to be bright and
beautiful. And that was only the beginning of the weekend.
She was going to be there for two nights. Sanju was going
to join them on Sunday afternoon, and they were all going
to drive back together.

When she took her usual parking spot near her parent's
house, Anu knitted her brows. Parked a little ahead was her

father-in-law's car. What are they doing here? *God, please, at least spare me Padma aunty.* Then, some memory, buried deep inside the subconscious, surfaced for Anu. Oh no! Panic rose in her heart and reached the pit of the stomach. It was as though she was in a wild ride in Wonder La, where she was held upside-down and shaken.

It was her father-in-law's birthday and she had offered to host a party for him at his favourite place, Jake's Club. But she had made that offer fifteen days ago! In her overzealousness, she had even called her parents and invited them to the party too. And, her father-in-law's two best friends. She had sent them Whatsapps asking to save the date.

But nobody had reminded her of that in the past fifteen days. Not even her mother! And they all miraculously remembered her offer? Why hadn't her father-in-law said anything when she wished him in the morning? Maybe she was panicking for no reason. Probably, nobody remembered and they were there to see Vicky. That was it. They probably brought along some sweets too. Anu began to relax and let Vicky out of the car.

Vicky rushed inside when her phone rang. It was Sanju. 'Hey Anu, heads up. My parents are at your parents' house. Apparently, you are hosting a birthday bash at Jake's Club for my dad.'

'Yeah. Right. That is why I am here early. Wish you were here too, Sanju.' Anu lied with sweat pouring down her back. She didn't want Sanju to think she didn't care or was forgetful.

'Hmm … are you sure, Anu? You never mentioned it to me. Have you called the club? They won't have seating for all of you on a Friday evening.'

'Called the place and they have agreed even to do a bit of decoration. Don't worry. I will send you the pictures.'

Anu wanted to turn around and run. Run fast and far. What on earth had she gotten herself into?

She called Shwetha and explained the situation quickly. 'Anu! What will you do?' Shwetha half screamed.

'Hey, help me here, will you? Don't wash your hands off me.'

'Hmm, let me think. You know, you are the one who can wing such situations. I am no good at that. I am a planner, not a winger.'

'Think, okay? I will too.'

Anu contemplated calling Sameer. But it was better to call the restaurant first. It was a club with a fair amount of seating inside and out. They could always put a table for eight or so people, right? It was not like they were a party of eighty. A smooth sounding man picked up the phone and Anu asked for a table for eight at eight.

'Sorry, ma'am. We are full for the night. IPL night. RCB is playing.'

'This is for my father-in-law, please. Can you please accommodate? It will mean a world to him. He is a really big cricket buff.' Anu tried to sound sweet though she was both panicking and getting frustrated.

'No, ma'am. Sorry.' The man was now waiting for a chance to hang up on her. He was of no use.

Anu called Sameer who did not pick up. So much for close friends. She called Shwetha back. 'Listen, get some balloons, streamers, and a cake with the picture of a cricket bat. Come to Jake's at eight, okay?'

Anu then walked inside the house with a bright smile. All faces turned to her expectantly. Padma aunty too did not sport her usual I-hate-your-guts look.

'Anu, you are late.' That had to be her mother. *Late for what? The birthday party I haven't planned but invited people to?*

'Not late at all. Jake's is only a half-hour drive.' Anu rebutted.

Anu's mother-in-law, looking visibly happy, spoke. 'Instead of everyone going separately, we thought we can all go together. Your father-in-law's friends will come there directly. They all want to watch IPL on the big TV at Jake's.'

Anu smiled as brightly as she could. 'That is the plan, aunty.'

The caravan of cars started. Anu drove alone and sent Vicky with her parents. She had to reach there before all of them. Cutting, swerving and swearing, Anu reached Jake's in a record twenty minutes. She was sure her father and father-in-law would take at least forty. Calming her breath, Anu stopped at the reception. Thankfully, Shwetha was already there. 'Table for eight, please.' Anu panted.

The woman smiled. 'Under what name, ma'am?'

'Anu.'

The woman looked and looked again and then spoke, looking very perplexed. 'No, ma'am. I don't see it here.'

'That is very careless.' Anu put on as stern a face as she could. 'I called and made a reservation.'

Shwetha was playing along well by dawning an angry face. The woman made a call and a man walked to the reception. Can't these women handle anything by themselves? Something as simple as setting up a table?

'Are you the one who had just called, ma'am? I told you there are no tables.' It was the same voice that had spoken to her over the phone.

'I made a reservation is what I know. This is my father-in-law's ninetieth birthday and he is an ex-army man. Is this the respect you pay a veteran?' Anu couldn't believe herself for the lies that tumbled out.

The man looked highly unconvinced but luckily, he didn't argue. He instead turned to a waiter and mumbled something. 'Follow him, please. We will arrange something.'

There was no sign of her troupe yet. So Anu, finally smiling at Shwetha, followed the waiter. The man walked past the lawn, then past the large dining area with a wall-to-wall TV blaring IPL, past a tastefully decorated smaller dining area and stopped at a closed door.

'Is he taking us to the toilet?' Shwetha whispered. 'To murder us there?'

'Shh…' Anu waited for the waiter to open the door. The man stood at the door and said politely, 'Please wait here, ma'am. I will be back.'

Anu and Shwetha rushed inside the room and stopped short. It was a storeroom! With cans of oil, flour and potatoes stacked all along the wall. In the middle was a table with three proper legs and one broken short. The dim light in the room was what her father used to call a zero-candle lamp.

'Well done, Anu. Hope your invitees are blind and have lost their senses of smell.' Shwetha began to laugh.

Anu turned to the waiter who was now bringing in the chairs. 'Look. Please don't send in the old people who are waiting at the reception. Not yet.'

'Shwetha, go get the balloons and the cake. Go from the garden entrance.'

In the next fifteen minutes, Anu begged the waiter to cover the storage area with table clothes. It looked as though people were hiding behind curtains, but still, it was better than seeing sacks of potatoes. She then asked him to turn on the wall-mounted TV . It was a tiny one, but as long as her father-in-law could watch IPL it was all right.

Shwetha placed the balloons here and there and put the cake on the table. Then she looked around. 'Anu, this place still looks like a dreadful dump.'

Before Anu replied, everyone walked in. Anu scanned the faces for disapproval. But the great thing about old folks is that they are not hostile. 'Oh ho! A cake for me!' Her father-in-law laughed in glee, his friends joining in.

Thankfully, none of them noticed that the picture of the cricket bat on the cake was drawn with icing or that the table had only three good legs or that that was a room where the staff slept!

'Winger,' smiled Shwetha. Anu smiled contentedly. She had saved the night after all. When they were all about to disperse, Anu's father-in-law stopped to talk to her. 'Thank you, Anu. For all the effort.'

Then, Padma aunty whispered in Anu's ears. 'Next time, try not to forget.'

23

'Everyone knew I had forgotten about the party and they were nice enough not to mention it. Except, of course, Padzilla,' Anu gulped her beer down.

Sameer chuckled. 'Why do you have to lie? Just say things as they are!'

Anu shook her head. 'I lie only to those who make me feel miserable.'

'Why do you hide from Sanju that we meet?'

'Only to avoid a zombie war. If I tell him I am having a drink with you, his face will grow so tight, it will split at the seams. Then he will grow deathly silent. Then he will either boil the air around him or freeze it for the next couple of hours.'

'The air thing did not make a lot of sense.'

'Well, just emphasizing.' Anu chewed on the masala peanuts.

'Do you lie to me?' Sameer asked.

'No. You are cool because you make a million mistakes yourself.' Anu munched on more peanuts. If she ate more, she drank less. 'Do you lie to me?'

Sameer shrugged. 'I don't lie to anyone. But you are a forgiving one. I have cancelled on you so many times but you still meet me.'

'That is not a compliment. That sounds like I am desperate to meet you! Anyway, tell me what's going on with you.'

Sameer grew serious. 'I am moving to Dubai.'

Anu choked on her peanuts. 'What! Why? You had this blockbuster news and waited till now to deliver it?'

'I am investing in some real estate there with a friend. Maybe, I will even hone my photography skills.'

Anu stared at him. 'No offence. But where do you have the money to invest in Dubai? And, what will you photograph there? You can capture the deserts and Burj Khalifa only so many times.'

Sameer laughed. 'And, both are already done to death by all my Dubai-returned relatives!' Growing serious, he added. 'I will be a working partner. My friend Jaggi's uncle will put in the capital.'

Anu suddenly felt empty. 'Once I get over my sadness, I will be happy for you. Can't digest you being so far away.'

Sameer smiled. 'I may not even last there! So feel sad if I stick around for at least six months. Now tell me your stories. Pete, that girl, Vicky's school, the mean mommies.'

Anu was always the talker and Sameer the listener and she liked that equation. A conversation was more fun when she was the one talking, 'Well, Pete and Pooja are good and nothing much to report. Except I have a very sore arm from playing. The bad thing is, Vicky is so unhappy with the school he cries every day.'

'Then pull him out of that school. Bring him back here along with yourself.' Sameer ordered his third beer while Anu was still working on her first. He had the metabolism of a bull.

'Sameer! Your last name should be extreme solutions! Just listen to my distress, okay. Don't give me suggestions.'

'I am extreme? How about when you changed from Science to Humanities and didn't tell your parents for six months? How about when you broke up with Sanju but let your mother keep planning your wedding? How about—'

Anu cut him off. 'All right, all right. That was then. Now, with a kid, I can't make random decisions.'

'Do what makes you happy. You will anyway, eventually!'

Anu pursed her lips. 'I won't miss you one bit when you are gone. Precisely for such insensitive remarks.'

Sameer smiled at her. 'You will miss me precisely for such remarks!'

He was right. She missed him already. He told her what he felt without ever sugar-coating his words but he meant well. And, he also said a lot of good things about her. That helped blunt his blows.

'Call me when you want to haul yourself and Vicky back to real Bangalore,' Sameer concluded paying the bill.

The next morning Anu had a spring in her step when she went to her old apartment. She was going to visit Supriyaji and Kavitha. Yashoda aunty was visiting her children in the US. The familiar trees, pathways with the most colourful oleanders, people she knew smiling at her and enquiring about her. Anu exhaled in delight and sat on the stone platform built around an old peepal tree.

'Anu! How are you? You forgot about us.' That was Mrs Rao offering flowers to the tree. Usually, such remarks irked Anu but not that day. People were nice to her here!

'Anu! Is everything all right?' That was Murthy uncle. A nice man who had been greeting her the same way for as long as she knew him.

Anu finally got up after a good fifteen minutes to first visit Supriyaji. She was dressed in a crisp white and blue salwar kameez and had the warmest smile.

'You have become thin, Anu,' she said with concern.

'That is the only positive of moving to Verdant Green, ma'am!' Anu smiled.

'That can't be true,' Supriyaji flashed and ethereal smile. 'You have to find things that give you a positive vibe.' Anu wanted to drop everything and move back here to take her classes and listen to her wise words.

Anu sipped the lime juice handed to her, which was just so perfect. How does Supriyaji do everything so perfectly? Her clothes, house, food, even the simple lime water spelt divine.

'I am trying, ma'am.' Anu spoke at last. She became very unhurried and calm after being with Supriyaji.

Carrying that sentiment, Anu went to Kavitha's. Okay, it was the exact opposite of Supriyaji's house. Kavitha loved gold and glitter and did not at all believe in being subtle. She had done up the house with green walls, orange vases, and golden chandeliers. Kavitha's mother ushered Anu inside flashing a big affectionate smile.

'Come in, come in, Anu. It has been so long since I saw you.' Then she whispered to Anu. 'You are the only one who can put sense into Kavitha. Every day she orders things. Look at this!' She pointed at a large, ghastly vase that was of a shark spewing water.

'Please tell her to stop this madness.'

Anu could see what Kavitha's mother meant. The house was filled to the brim with tacky decorative items that weren't there before. To name a few, there were two gigantic elephants on either side of the front door as if it was a King's court, an immense statue of Buddha with an attached water-fountain, tables of all sizes and plastic flowers of all kinds. As Anu gaped baffled, Radha came running from the kitchen and almost toppled hitting against a stone pedestal.

'Akka! Where is Vicky?' Radha smiled and then sobbed. 'I miss you both so much.'

'I miss you too, Radha. Here is something I got for you. And Vicky made this card for you.' She had bought a big box of dry-fruits for Radha. Vicky had drawn a stick man and named it Vicky.

Radha smiled in happiness. She loved fruits of all kinds. She compensated for Anu's bad eating. 'Show me Vicky's photos, Akka. I will bring you coffee.'

Wading through the home decors, Anu entered Kavitha's room.

Kavitha had sprawled on the bed with a dozen home decor magazines all around her. 'Anu! So good to see you!

Sit here.' She pointed at an ornate bench seat that had taken up half the room.

'Did you see my decorations? I have so much time on hand, I am doing up the house big time, ya,' Kavitha said with a dimpled smile.

'Kavitha, how much money have you spent on all this?' Anu pointed at a vase, a night-stand, a dresser, and a carpet—all brand new, large and gaudy.

Kavitha was taken aback. 'Err … I don't know. I am using Aravind's credit card.'

'Isn't he objecting?'

Kavitha grinned. 'He is afraid to, I guess. I am on bed rest and I have made sure he feels both sad for me and scared of me.'

Anu chuckled but only briefly. She had to be firm with Kavitha. 'Listen, all this must go. You have a tiny two-bedroom flat, not an Ambani mansion!'

In the next two hours, Anu and Kavitha's mother packed all the new arrivals and Anu, snatching the phone from Kavitha's iron grip, put in return requests on all the items.

'Kavitha! You have spent sixty-thousand on all this garbage!'

'Must be six. See properly,' Kavitha knitted her brows at the phone and Anu smacked her on the head lightly.

'No more online purchases. Not even clothes till you deliver. Here, I thought we can twin in these!' She draped Kavitha in a faux-Kashmiri shawl and wrapped a similar one around herself.

Kavitha burst into tears. 'This is so pretty, Anu! Once I deliver, I will reduce my weight and we can twin properly.'

Kavitha's mother handed Anu a plate with a dozen pooris and chole. 'I know Yashoda is not here. She would have made this for you otherwise.' Anu felt suddenly sentimental. Everyone here cared to know so much about her! Then she wondered if she had some sort of a split personality. A loving one for here and another that elicited hatred from everyone at Verdant Green.

Pete had come to Bangalore as an IT consultant but had stayed on since his daughter wanted to spend a year in India after her divorce. He had now sent his daughter and his wife on a tour of North India and Bhutan for a month. He had invited Anu and Pooja over for lunch at his place that afternoon.

'How do you work, cook, clean and care for the kids, Pete?' Anu gasped walking into that ultra-tidy house. Pete seemed like a superhero to Anu.

'Because I come from a land where there is no help. No cooks, no maids, no housekeepers unless you write out your paychecks to them.'

Anu shuddered. 'God! That is precisely why I didn't want to live in any western country.' Then she grew thoughtful. 'Then again, Verdant Green is no better for us. We are writing out our paychecks and more for the help we are getting!' A sudden worry gnawed at her. She had to pay

Rathnamma's extra salary and the gardener's wages from her savings. Did she have any savings by the way?

Sitting at the dining table, waiting for Pooja to join them, Anu looked around the immaculate minimalist house. 'Pete, such neat spaces depress me.'

'Then feel free to scatter things around,' Pete shouted from the kitchen.

Anu laughed. 'Very funny. How do you keep things this tidy?'

Pete brought out a steaming hot pot of soup to the table. 'Hmm, let me think.' Setting it on the table, he knitted his brows and narrowed his eyes as if thinking deeply. 'Maybe by actually tidying up? Pick things up, put things away, throw things out. That sort of highly glamorous tasks.'

'I wish the houses were self-maintaining.' Anu bit into a nacho. The Table (without even the food on it yet!) looked inviting with matching cups, plates and serving bowls.

'Soup and nachos with salsa for starters. And, make-your-own tacos for the main course, ma'am.' Pete sat down facing Anu. 'So how was the weekend?' He asked.

Anu sighed. 'Long story for another time. I always bother you with my woes.'

'Please do bother me with your woes! They are highly entertaining, to say the least.' Pete opened a beer for himself and Anu refused. Alcohol made her put on weight almost instantly.

Before Anu spoke, Pooja walked in, taking out the ear phones. Setting the phone on the table next to her, she let out a mild exclamation. 'Oh! Mexican. Where did you order from?'

Anu laughed. 'From his kitchen! He cooked all this if you can believe it.'

While Anu and Pete talked, Pooja mostly ate and kept checking the phone each time it beeped. Finally, Anu couldn't resist asking. 'Expecting a message from someone?'

Pooja shrugged. 'No, just that some of my old friends are planning to meet in the city.'

'I have never seen you hang out with the kids here. Are they aliens or vampires in the disguise of humans?'

Pooja laughed. 'Most of them are! But I don't hang out with them because they don't want to.'

Pete cleared his throat; that was an indication for Anu to back off. But she pretended not to hear him. 'Why wouldn't they? Because you are not a vampire or a werewolf?'

Pooja grew serious. 'Long story.'

Anu pulled the chair closer to Pooja. 'Oh, do tell. Pete is in no hurry to get rid of us.'

Pete cleared his throat again and Anu pushed a glass of water to him, flashing an innocent smile. 'Drink water, Pete. Your throat will feel better.'

'A guy who is in my lane asked me to join him and his friends for a night party last week. Never thought their night would go on till beyond midnight. My mom, in a state of panic, rushed into the pub where we were, yelled at me in Tamil, and I left with her like a lamb.'

Anu knitted her brows. 'That should make them not want to be around your mother. But why not you?'

Pooja flashed Anu a look of incredulity. 'Are you serious? Who wants to be with someone whose mom yells at the top of her lungs? I never got near that group again. I hide when I see the guy who invited me.'

Pete sat right there but pretended to be not too keen on the conversation. But Anu was sure he was very clued in. She turned her attention back to Pooja. 'You should talk to that guy and laugh about it. All mothers are lunatic to some degree. His mother will be too. It comes with motherhood.'

Pooja sighed. 'You think so?'

'Hey, I know so! I was a teenager only a decade ago. My mother still embarrasses me.'

'Let me think. Maybe when I see him again, I might talk to him.' Pooja smiled. 'If he runs away, Pete has to make you play half-an-hour extra for a full week.'

'Deal,' said Pete raising his cup.

24

The next morning was not any different with Vicky. On the other hand, it got a lot worse because the puppy had developed the courage to leave its habitat and had wandered away. Anu finally had to promise Vicky that they would look for puppies in other streets and he could play with them for ten minutes.

'I want my old school, Mumma. I don't want to go here,' he sobbed.

Anu's heart sank. 'Vicky, what do you not like here?'

He mumbled many things but what she could gather was he had to do too much writing, could not talk in the class or walk towards friends. He did not like his separate desk and chair. He wanted to sit on a bench with a long table like in his old school. Anu sighed. Does he need to be educated this vigorously? The school coordinator had explained how they had a new method of fast-track teaching. But Vicky was happy in his slow-track school. Sumitra aunty's school was anything but old fashioned. She had created a very open and friendly environment for learning.

As Anu sipped her coffee sitting in her usual spot at Coffee Day, she looked around. All those waiting for someone had their heads buried in their phones, those with a special someone took selfies, and the ones with ordinary everyday friends intermittently checked their phones. The waitress made coffee while checking her phone, the window-cleaner hanging from a rope listened to music on his phone, the maid mopping the floor was busy chatting with someone. Anu had a wild thought of taking away all their phones and dunking them in the bucket of water the maid had. What would happen? Someone would murder her for sure.

She began thinking about her life. She had to do something. Maybe give her resume to schools in and around that area so that she could work till Vicky's school ended. Or, work in a library or part-time somewhere. None of the thoughts was appealing. Maybe she should just enjoy her time for a while as Sumitra aunty had suggested. Just when her thoughts began to exhaust her, the phone rang. Pooja. Well, that was a surprise. The girl only messaged at best!

'Aunty, are you busy? Can I talk to you?'

'All yours. I am at Coffee Day.' Anu sipped her coffee.

'Can you go shopping with me? Like now?'

Anu spilt a little of her coffee. *Why would Pooja want to go shopping with her?*

'Hmm … we could. But no shop opens before eleven, Pooja. It is only eight-thirty now!'

'Oh … didn't think of that. I want to talk to you too. Can I come to Coffee Day?'

'I will come back home instead. Let us meet at the coffee shop there.'

'I thought you don't want to pay for the coffee there.'

'I don't. But that is a good meeting point!'

Anu walked to the cake shop next door and got six blueberry muffins packed. Both Pooja and Pete loved those.

Settling down on the bench (Shwetha had told her it was made of expensive Italian marble) that rimmed a large circular gazebo, Anu handed Pooja a muffin and helped herself to one. That gazebo was so beautiful; the dark black granite flooring, the sloped roof of Mangalore tiles and wooden pillars with carvings holding the roof up. That entire structure sat bang in the middle of a lush green lawn.

'Aunty, I spoke to Akash, that guy who invited me to the party. And I am joining them today afternoon for a movie.' Anu saw Pooja that excited for the first time.

'That is so fantastic, Pooja! Is that why you wanted to go shopping?' Anu exclaimed.

Pooja bit into her muffin and nodded. 'Yeah! But they are starting at twelve. So I don't I have the time to shop. The problem is, all of the girls there dress very differently from me.' She looked at herself. 'They wear tiny shorts and tank tops. Not full jeans and round-neck T-shirts like me.'

Anu hummed and hawed and let Pooja continue. The girl had more to pour out. 'My mother is quite conservative. Also, I grew up in Muscat. So I don't dress like the others here.'

'Different is fine,' Anu packed up the rest of the muffins for Pete. 'You look great any way.'

'No way. I am so dorky.' Pooja sounded convinced about what she said.

'Let me see.' Anu gave Pooja a deliberate and slow once over. 'You stand at five feet seven inches. Slim. Your designer jeans and D&G top fit you like a second skin. You can model for hair and skin at any time of the day. So yeah, you are very dorky.'

Pooja laughed. 'You are so funny, and you are quite cool for your age.'

Anu smiled at her. 'Thank you. Next time compliment me without the age bit. Also, Pooja, all our lives, women are told to fit in—fit into a pretty dress, fit into a good-girl group, fit into a family. Instead of sawing your edges off to fit in, search for what fits you

Pooja sighed. 'That is so true. Thank God for you and Pete!'

They saw Pete jogging towards them. Anu had asked him to join them after half-an-hour. Given how little Pooja talked, that was more than enough time for their girl talk.

'There goes my jogging,' Pete sat down and picked up two cupcakes. 'Go on with your discussions. Don't mind me.'

Anu turned to Pooja. 'Here is what you can do. Get your hair and face done by eleven. Then start trying outfits from your super-filled closet. By eleven-forty-five, panic starts hitting you because you are running out of time. That will force you to settle for something comfortable and head out. Your mom will yell at you for messing up the room, but you can handle that after you are back.'

Pooja started to laugh again. That girl looked so good when happy. 'That is your advice?'

Pete chimed in. 'Why agonize for forty-five minutes? Start trying only ten minutes earlier.'

Anu shook her head. 'Works in a man's world. For us, an hour of agony is ideal.' Then she got up and stretched. 'Shilpa Shetty would have shot her yoga videos here. It will be so nice to do yoga here than in that hot hell.'

'Why don't you?' Pete asked, wiping his hands on his face towel.

'Yeah! Why don't I?' The idea started to appeal more and more to Anu. 'Will you both join me?'

'I have never done yoga before,' said Pete. 'But I can try.'

'I don't know. If someone spots me stretching here in public, it will be quite humiliating,' said Pooja. 'Can we do it after dark?'

'Sorry, Pooja. It has to be at this hour. When Vicky is at school, or else he will be climbing all over me like a monkey each time I hold a pose.' Anu turned to Pete. 'Pete, you wait here. I will change and bring two mats. Pooja, you are right. You will look dorky stretching with us in a gazebo. You run home and agonize over outfits.'

Pooja stood there looking doubtful. 'How long will you do it?'

Anu shrugged. 'Half hour max.'

The day had started to look good already! Yoga in a gazebo. How nice is that!

25

Pooja, despite her concern about peers, joined them with a mat. While Pete was pathetic, Pooja was very graceful and lithe, and Anu was somewhere in between. That was the first day. It was quite a herculean task to teach Pete Surya Namaskaras, but Anu was not one to give up.

Then it was Day two. Though she was dying to know the details of Pooja's outing the previous day, that had to wait till after . They were going to meet at nine-thirty every morning for their 'Gazebo Yoga'.

'Let us start with Surya Namaskara again.' Anu began.

'I can't remember the sequence of stretches,' Pete sounded a little dejected.

'Didn't you Youtube it?' Pooja sounded surprised.

'Nope.' Pete shrugged. 'Why would I spend time on twice in a day? This will do.'

'Let us do only four sets of Surya Namaskara.' Anu suggested. 'What do you say, Pooja?'

'Perfect. I hate it when I have to go on and on and on a thousand times.' Pooja rolled her eyes.

Anu taught Pete four postures and asked him to do only those. A proper guru would be horrified at that sort of teaching and maybe even curse Anu, but it worked for Pete. He touched his knees instead of toes, he mostly bent his neck backwards than his torso, but Anu smiled approvingly. Any kind of bending was better than no bending, right?

They did a quick and easy ten minutes of Asanas and then five minutes of Pranayama. In twenty minutes, they were done and had rolled up the mats.

'Is what we did of any use?' Pooja was doubtful. 'The sessions elsewhere usually last for an hour-and-a-half.'

Anu grinned. 'Look, it will give us enough flexibility to scrub our own backs. That is enough, right?'

'Yeah, whatever. My mom is off my case for now since I am doing yoga and tennis! So works for me.'

'I have never done yoga. This more than works for me.' Pete waved goodbye before taking off.

When Anu and Pooja got down the steps of the gazebo, Anu saw a familiar face staring at her. The Meanie Meena! Anu groaned inwardly. She had begun to forget about her existence.

'Done with yoga?' Meena asked.

'Yeah. Done.' Anu smiled as well as she could.

'There is a proper studio, you know. But it is a little expensive.' Meena attacked. Anu expected it though.

'It is expensive! Why pay and suffer in that sweltering heat?'

'So, would you be in the sweltering heat if it was free?' Meena laughed at her own words.

'I wouldn't know because it is not free!' Anu walked on.

Pooja started to laugh. 'No, you wouldn't get into that hell even if they paid you! But who was that woman?'

Anu sighed. 'I call her Meena the Meanie in my head. You can call her that too.'

'Totally a meanie! But you are not bothered by her.'

'The one perk of getting older is you worry less about what others say. Now spill the beans about your outing yesterday.'

Pooja shrugged. 'It was okay. They are a clique and it is too much effort to break into their group. I may not go again. When my results are out, who knows where I will be going to be.'

Anu nodded. 'That makes sense. If you are not even going to be here, why invest energy in belonging to the clique.'

'Aunty, was yours a love marriage?' Pooja asked out of the blue.

'It was.' Anu smiled. 'We were neighbours.'

'That is nice,' Pooja added after a pause. 'I knew this guy in high school. We sort of went out for a couple of years. But it was too hot and cold.'

Anu nodded. Pooja talked only if the other person was quiet. 'He called me yesterday. Asked me if we can meet sometime.'

'Oh, okay.' Anu gave a very noncommittal reply, though a hundred questions bubbled inside her.

'We brought out the worst in each other and the best in each other too. Don't know if I want to meet him now.' Pooja chewed on her lower lip. 'Should I meet him?'

'Do you want to meet him?'

'I don't know. Would you meet him? I mean, if you were me?'

'Hmm, may be as a friend.' Anu patted Pooja on the back. 'Sleep on it. See how you feel tomorrow. And, don't text him tonight!'

Pooja smiled and nodded. 'That is sane advice.'

Anu felt relaxed as she started walking home. She had begun to feel comfortable in the new place, but Vicky's agony about school bothered her.

Sanju called as she was walking. 'Anu, we are going out tonight with Dave and a few colleagues. At 7 p.m.' He sounded too excited to Anu's ears. 'Be ready.'

'Who are the colleagues?' Anu asked suspiciously. After the dinner debacle from the previous time, she dreaded these groupie dinners.

'None from the last time. Relax,'

God, let there not be another fiasco this time! Anu prayed silently. She had to get Geetha to babysit Vicky, which meant she had to cough up more money.

The dinner was sombre. It was a new and swanky lounge bar. The gathering was mostly single people on a short visit to India from the US, which meant the conversation was all office gossip. Anu managed her time wisely between listening and tuning out. The music was retro, and the furniture was elegant, wooden and uncomfortable, and very un-lounge-worthy. But Anu quite enjoyed the music—The Beatles, The Eagles and Pink Floyd—being played. Occasionally the guy next to her asked her something out of politeness or because he was drunk. He was Scottish and Anu couldn't understand a word of what he said. She simply smiled at everything. She was sure she smiled away at his questions too.

She felt all warm and fuzzy until the bill came. Anu peeked at Sanju's share on the credit card machine. Eight thousand for what they ate and drank! It was not more than three even if you added a twenty five per cent tip! Why couldn't everyone pay up for what they consumed?

While she and Sanju walked out, someone at the far end of the table caught up with her. 'So I heard you have started a class? Is that allowed?'

Anu almost tripped and fell. What kind of wild rumour was this? 'We just stretch together. That is not a class.'

'Oh, is that so? But my neighbour Meena told me you have started a class. She was worried you may not have taken the property manager's permission.'

'It is a public space! If we don't need permission to sit, we don't need permission to stretch!' Anu sounded a bit too defensive to her own ears but who was this woman? Everyone was walking around them, pretending not to hear them but the woman had made sure everyone had heard her.

Sanju was angry. She knew it by the way he sat and drove. Well, his pursed lips and knitted brows were quite a giveaway too. If she had any doubts left in her, his next words confirmed his anger. 'What is all this nonsense, Anu? People will think we are classless.'

'I told you I am doing yoga with Pete and Pooja. Why is that classless? That Meena who is spreading these rumours is classless. Not me.' Anu's eyes started to well up against her will.

Sanju drove quietly the rest of the way. She was well-liked in her circles—be it when she was studying or at work. Nobody hated her. Nobody thought she was classless before. Especially, Sanju.

26

Anu tried her best not to let out a sob. That would be so uncool. She stared out of the window and tried to register the shops and the streets that buzzed past her. Though her mind kept slipping and going back to the *classless* remark by Sanju, she fought tenaciously not to dwell on it. She was tempted to text Shwetha but refrained. Sometimes talking about your hurt would only further the pain. It is better to swallow the hurt like a bitter pill and hope for it vanish forever. There she was advising Pooja that she didn't bother with what people said. Such hypocrisy! Then again, Sanju was not people. He was her soulmate – what he said had to matter.

Her vision blurred as they passed by half-shut hotels, bars and humongous malls with glass facades. She saw riders on small scooters zip right next to monstrous trucks and double-decker sleeper buses. Everyone coexisted, mostly peacefully too. Why was it so hard for her at Verdant Green? Why did Meena dislike her so much? Should she talk to her? The very thought was as appealing as jumping off a multi-storeyed building.

As she watched absently, Sanju not uttering a word, they were almost home. It was eleven-thirty and she had to call Rathnamma to pick up Geetha. When she picked up the phone to make the call, Sanju spoke. 'Anu,' he sighed. 'Don't be bothered by all this. You will be fine. You are fine.'

Sanju never apologized but he always made up quickly. Anu nodded. 'I know.'

'Shall we watch a movie?' Sanju offered.

'Yeah, if Vicky is asleep.' Anu smiled.

The following Monday, Vicky's blues hit a crescendo. He didn't want to get up. Anu coaxed him saying the little puppy at the school would be waiting for him. That got him till school. She made sure they were a good twenty minutes early. To her distress, there was no puppy. Anu looked under the drain and over a compound wall, with Vicky trailing and mimicking her actions. No sign of the puppy. Vicky crawled back into the car. Anu heard the first bell ring and her heart started pounding. The coordinator had reprimanded her in a gentle voice that Vicky cannot miss the assembly every day.

'I think the puppy went to its mom. It will back in the afternoon.'

'Okay. We will wait here then.' Vicky was clear about his decision.

'Vicky, it will be too hot to wait here. You get inside the school till the puppy is back.'

'No. I will not go until the puppy is back.'

'If you don't go to school, how will you get a job? How will you get a house?' Anu tried reasoning now.

'I don't want a job. I already have a house.' Then he added. 'Rakesh also does not like this school.'

'Is Rakesh your friend? He will be waiting for you, Vicky. Go now.' Anu tried every arsenal in her kitty.

'No. Rakesh has many other friends.'

Anu's patience started to wear thin. But losing it with Vicky had no happy ending. He would wail and then she would have to coax him for another hour. Maybe she should put him on the school bus but she laughed at the thought. Unless the bus driver got a crane to separate Vicky from her, the boy wouldn't get inside that bus!

Leaning against the car, Anu looked at the imposing and cold school building. Its high compound walls, the security guards pacing as they did in front of the Buckingham Palace—the school felt intimidating to her. What about her poor Vicky? She looked at him slumped in the backseat. Her heart melted. Vicky was hyperactive and never gave them a moment of peace, but he was never morose. He hardly cried but in the last month, he had cried enough for a year.

Anu made up her mind. Right then and there. She picked up the phone and called Sumitra aunty. After a ten-minute chat, though Sumitra aunty wasn't at all convinced by Anu's plan, she agreed to help her.

Anu turned to Vicky. 'Fine then. No school today. We will go someplace else.'

She drove for thirty minutes and landed at the school she had visited with Shwetha. The simple homely building with a sleepy guard on a chair. Vicky walked beside her happily. He was wide-eyed at the play area that looked like his old school. He looked curiously at the kids in the common area sprawled on the floor drawing. Anu walked into the principal's chamber.

'Come in, Miss Anu. Sumitra had just called me.' The principal, Janaki, looked as kind as Sumitra aunty.

'Hi, Vivik.' She flashed a wide smile at Vicky.

Vicky smiled and shook his head. Anu felt deliriously happy. Sumitra aunty had told the principal that Vicky gets amused when someone mispronounced his name.

'Hi, Vivith.'

Vicky shook his head with a wider grin.

'Hi, Vivek?'

He started laughing but shook his head vigorously.

'Hi, Vivikth, then.'

He nodded and sprawled on the chair.

'Anu, don't apply for TC yet from Indigo. Let us see how he takes to our school. If he is okay, then you can put him in here.'

'I am sure he will be fine here,' said Anu and she knew he would be.

'I hope so too. This school is run almost like Sumitra's. But what concerns me is the fees. You will be losing it at Indigo and will be paying here again.'

Oh, she hadn't thought of that! The fee here was eighty thousand, Anu remembered. She mustered her courage and asked. 'Can you give us a concession? Whatever you can.' She wanted to dig a hole and crawl inside it. She hated asking for discounts at reasonable places.

'I will be able to waive the twenty-thousand registration fees. But can't help with the fee component. I am answerable to the board.' Janaki truly sounded helpless.

'It's more than enough discount, then. Can he attend from today?' Anu smiled at the friendly woman.

'Certainly. You be with him until he settles down. Let me walk you to the classroom.'

It was a small classroom with kids working with various contraptions for a maths class. Vicky's eyes brightened at the sight of those.

'Pink Tower!' He rushed inside and settled down next to a child. Soon, Anu was all but forgotten.

Anu smiled at Janaki. 'I think I will leave. He seems fine.'

'Tell him and go. He should not panic not seeing you.'

Anu agreed. 'Vicky, bye, sweetie. I will pick you up later.'

Vicky waved a happy hand without even looking at her. He was busy assembling a tower and chatting with his neighbour.

Anu drove back feeling relaxed. Vicky was happy! But soon that happiness began to morph into a small worry. By the time she was home, that worry had turned into a full-blown panic. How was she going to tell Sanju about this? Already things were so tense between them. If she could somehow manage the fees, she need not tell him about this at all for the time being. Vicky mostly talked in the middle of running or biking and panting, so even if he managed to tell

Sanju about the change of school, he would not understand him anyway.

Now, she only had to pay Rathnamma's ten thousand and this sixty thousand. And Anu's account, as of that day, had fifty rupees.

27

That night Anu observed the father-son duo. While Vicky went hiding, Sanju kept finding him. There was no talk about school that evening, not yet. But it was bound to come. Sanju always asked a few customary questions about school and Vicky gave highly irrelevant answers to all of them.

'Enough hide-and-seek. Sit with me. We will watch cricket.' Sanju forced Vicky to sit next to him on the Sofa.

'Let us play cricket!' Vicky got a new idea for running around. 'Watching is boring.'

'We will watch for half-an-hour and then play. Sit now.' Sanju wouldn't give up on making Vicky sit.

'I will play with Mommy then.' Vicky came running to Anu.

After chucking the ball at him a hundred thousand times, Anu sprawled on the floor exhausted. She had to keep her energy for a food battle with Vicky still. Though she made him sit on a high chair and strapped him to it while feeding him dinner, he still managed to make it a prolonged and messy affair.

Just as she got up, mustering the courage to bring out Vicky's dinner, Sanju's phone chimed. Reading his message, Sanju broke into a happy smile. 'Anu, Padma aunty says she has a surprise for us!'

Anu had a minor heart attack. Padma aunty's surprises were never good news; they were mostly some large and fanciful gift that she hoisted on them. In her favour, she bought expensive things but they were quite ... hideous. It started when she had bought a matching saree-and-kurta combo for Anu and Sanju for the wedding reception. It was bright pink! Anu had her reception outfit carefully selected for both of them but Sanju had fallen in love with Padzilla's gift.

Luckily, Sameer had averted that catastrophe. 'Wear a suit. If you wear this pink number, people will think you are a music teacher from the seventies.' Anu was never more grateful to Sameer. For Sanju, though he never admitted, Sameer's words were his commands. Anu's mother-in-law had shoved the receipt to the saree into Anu's palms when Padzilla wasn't looking and had whispered. 'Exchange the saree for something humans wear.'

Padma aunty's next was a western-style large crib for Vicky. It was bigger than their bedroom and Vicky screamed the moment they put him in it. Anu had sold it to a US couple on OLX. Padma aunty's list of gifts was endless. A very large oven that could bake five kilograms of cake. 'Why should I bake a cake when they had bakeries on every street corner?' was Anu's reasoning. Then there was the plush floor carpet. It was so big and red, Anu had felt claustrophobic at the very sight of it. Finally, she had donated it to her maid, who had cut it to pieces that she used as foot rugs.

So, now what? What was the surprise?

The next morning, after dropping Vicky, Anu started stretching with Pete and Pooja. A few minutes into the session, two elderly ladies stood around tentatively, holding their yoga mats. Must be the middle-class mothers of some nouveau riche.

'Can we join your class?' One of them asked in Hindi. 'We have not done any yoga before.'

God, this *class* tag was starting to get to Anu. 'This is not a class but you can do yoga with us.' She replied in her broken Hindi.

The women didn't understand her. 'How much fees?'

Pooja took over. 'No fees. Just do it.'

The women looked delighted. 'Free class!'

They both spread their mats and looked at Anu expectantly. Sighing, Anu taught them Surya Namaskara. They were more awkward than Pete, to say the least. Once they wound up the session, one of them opened a box full of homemade biscuits. 'Please eat. These are Nankathais.' She offered it to the group.

Pete looked a little doubtful at first but once he bit into them, pure delight spread on his face. 'Well done, Anu. Keep recruiting. Make sure your prodigies pay you with food.'

Pooja smiled. 'This class is turning out to be very interesting.'

Anu rolled her eyes. 'This is not a class!'

The women, before they left, spoke to Anu in the earnest. 'Take some fees, beta. You are very good. Why are you doing the class for free?'

Pooja began to laugh and mimicked Anu. 'This is not a class!'

In the following days, Anu's non-class had four more elderly men and women for students.

'Shall I make a sign that says the "Enter the waitlist for Anu's Yoga and leave a box of homemade sweets?"' Pete asked Anu as they sipped coffee after tennis. Pete insisted on paying every time and Anu had stopped even the tentative objecting.

'Pete!' Anu rolled her eyes. 'Why did we become so popular?'

'Among Octogenarians!' Pooja groaned. 'Why do I even come there?'

'Anu's Low-intensity Yoga for those who can't bend! It might catch on,' Pete nodded his head thoughtfully.

'Given the number of sweets we are gorging on, it is more like Anu's Weight-gaining Yoga!' said Anu remembering that one of the women had brought Rasmalai that morning.

Pete raised his coffee cup. 'To unpronounceable yet delicious Indian sweets.'

Anu walked home feeling happy and contented only to spot a large truck parked in the driveway. Sanju came scurrying out. *Oh god! Did Padzilla buy them a truck as a surprise?* Anu stepped inside the house fearing what awaited her. A large seven-seater sectional sofa stared at her in the living room. It had a matching centre table and two side tables. And, the whole ensemble was bright orange!

Anu's jaws dropped. Sanju chirped in excitement. 'Look at this Anu! So perfect for our living room. Padma aunty has spent close to a lakh on this.'

Anu found her voice with great difficulty. 'But we can't accept such an expensive gift from her. She is retired and she needs to keep her money.' Anu prayed fervently for that logic to work.

Sanju looked thoughtful for a moment. 'You are right. I should pay for it.'

Anu was horrified. 'Sanju, we don't need a new sofa now. Where is the money? It is almost the first of the month and have you thought of the bills we need to pay?'

Four delivery men stood around looking uncomfortable. If those men left, Anu knew she would be stuck with the orange monstrosity forever.

Before she knew it, her pleasant reasoning tone got replaced by a brutally honest one. 'I don't really like that sofa. Our living room looks like an orange setting sky!'

Sanju looked shocked at first and then hurt. 'Hey, what do you have against Padma aunty? She tries to win your affection but you keep rejecting her.' He added after a pause. 'I lived in the house your father gave you! So you can accept the sofa my aunt is giving me.'

Anu felt incredulous. 'My father did not have an orange house delivered to you, Sanju. You need not have lived there.'

'Well, your father had a little chat with me and explained how it made economic sense not to rent a place but live in the one he already had! So, yeah, no pressure there!'

Anu started to feel drained. 'Fine. You want this sofa so badly? Then we will keep it. But it is going to the basement.'

Though Sanju tried to look hurt and stern, Anu swore what she saw in his eyes was a relief. As the sofa got moved section by section, Anu wished she could return it for money.

28

Shwetha came by the next day. They were going to have a beer at this small garden pub outside Verdant Green, a place mostly the drivers from the community frequented. But who cared. Neither she nor Shwetha was in the mood to shell out big bucks for beer and boiled vegetables—that is all they ate when they drank midweek.

'Anu, where is your TV? Neither in the living room nor the family room. Whatever is the difference between the two anyway?' Shwetha sounded annoyed after walking from one room to the other.

'Hmm …' Anu shrugged taking away the magazines from the sofa. 'I don't know about the other houses but our living room had a TV and the family room Vicky's bicycle.'

'And now? There is only air and sunlight in your living room. I want to catch at least a bit of the Grammy rerun.' Shwetha sat on the sofa with a thud.

Anu placed a plate of homemade biscuits one of the women who joined her for yoga had given her. 'Sanju moved it to the basement.'

Shwetha got that can-you-get-more-weird look. So Anu further explained. 'I asked him to move the sofa his aunty gifted us. He said if that is the case, the TV moves too. To make the basement a complete entertainment room.' Anu grinned biting into a biscuit. 'But the joke is on him. Since he moved it to the basement, he has almost stopped watching TV. I bet the big orange sofa scares him!'

Shwetha sighed. 'Your lives are too complex for me to understand. Let us head out for that drink then. They might have a TV in the sitting room.'

It was only eleven but the garden bar was open. One of the neighbour's driver nodded at Anu, looking highly embarrassed. There was also the gardener, spending the money Anu gave him the previous day. He should be treating her for the money he charged her.

'Madam, you are in our place.' The gardener belly laughed.

'All because you were at mine.' Anu mumbled and Shwetha duly broke into a giggle.

The gardener said something sheepishly and turned back to his drink.

'So why this surprise visit in the middle of the day, Shwetha?' Anu took large gulps of her cold beer.

Shwetha leaned closer to Anu smiling. 'Guess what? I am getting married in a month! Then, I am moving to London with Dini.'

'What! You can't do that! Sameer is moving to Dubai and you to London?' Anu almost broke into tears. Spirits made her feel too much.

'Hey hey, at least congratulate me first! I will be there for only six months. Then Dini has agreed to move to Bangalore for good.' Shwetha squeezed Anu's hand. 'What is going on with you?'

Anu thought of pouring out her woes but decided against it. Shwetha would never back her decision to change Vicky's school without telling Sanju. She couldn't talk about the money problems because then Shwetha would jump in to help. Anu never took money from friends. She couldn't tell Sameer any of her problems for the same reason.

Anu smiled bravely. 'Things are not too bad. The yoga, tennis, walks with nannies—getting used to it all.' Mothers in Verdant Green sipped their tea by the poolside while their nannies played with the kids. Anu knew more nannies than moms. One of those nannies had even asked Anu how much she got paid because she dressed so well.

'Good, Anu. I am hoping for some luxurious time in London myself. But Dini says he leads a very below-average life there. How can he when he lives in such a rich country?'

Oh, Anu knew it! She could in fact write a book titled 'How to successfully lead a poor life in a rich neighbourhood.'

After Shwetha left, Anu felt severely empty. She will have neither Sameer nor Swetha close to her anymore. Maybe that is why fate pushed her to Verdant Green so that she had more to worry about than her friends moving away.

It was a week into the new month when Rathnamma talked to Anu. She had avoided talking to Rathnamma all week. 'Madam, when will you give me the rest of the salary?'

'My husband says by the fifteenth. Half on the first and the other half on the fifteenth.' Anu pushed her hair back and tried to sound confident.

'Then, please ask your husband to clean the house for fifteen days. I am not a bank to take money in instalments.' Oh boy, Rathnamma looked scary the way she stood with her hand on her hips with her nostrils flaring.

'Okay. Fine. I will talk to him.' Anu mumbled. Rathnamma looked angry enough—not to mention strong—to kill her with bare hands.

Anu had roughly spent an extra five thousand on the gardener and Geetha for babysitting. The last time she had tried to withdraw a thousand, the machine had rebuked her with a message that said she had no money left.

Vicky's Principal Janaki had asked her gently to complete the formalities at the school and pay the fees. So, now the money problem was real.

That evening, as she sat watching Vicky ride his bike, Anu's phone chimed with a message. Since she had the phone in hand, she opened it right away. What was that she was seeing? A lakh and a half deposited into her account! Such things happened only in fairy tales, didn't' they?

Once her initial euphoria died down, Anu's memory returned. The money was from her father. Well, he had started some yearly investment for Vicky and every year he deposited money into her account. That amount got auto-deducted a few days later and vanished.

Except for this year, Anu thought, if she could stop that auto-deduction, the money could be hers! For the time being, of course. She knew nothing about either the investment or where that money went. She thought of calling her father casually. But the two of them hardly spoke on the phone. It would be too suspicious if she did so now.

Where was her bank statement? She remembered all those emails she got from the bank telling her how to open the attached statement. Well, she deleted them all. She liked a clean inbox.

How about going to the bank? But her account was in Vijaynagar and the manager knew her father too well. Could she go to their branch here? She felt the itch to call Sameer but he would not help her with the bank. He would simply give her the money, somehow. She could not let that happen.

She had worked in the bank after all. Well, for a year where she mostly sent people to wait in a queue. But she should still be able to handle a simple affair like this.

'Hey Anu, what is the deep thought?' Sanju shook her gently. He had parked his car five feet from her and Anu hadn't even noticed.

'Oh, nothing. Go on inside. I will make coffee.'

'Anu,' Sanju hovered around her in the kitchen. 'Do you have any money in your account?'

'What!' Anu jumped back in horror. *Did he read her mind?* 'I don't. I have nothing.'

'Calm down! That is why I asked. You will need some for your expenses, right? You don't have your job now. How much do you need?'

How about seventy thousand? Anu was tempted to ask. But then, she was also really touched by Sanju's gesture. 'I don't know …' She trailed off. She had never asked him for her expenses so far. Whatever she earned, she spent.

'I will transfer five thousand. I know it is less than what you made. But you know how it is now.'

Anu handed Sanju his coffee and asked gently, 'How are you doing money-wise? This is a crazy month.'

Sanju said weakly. 'I am fine. When is the next instalment of Vicky's fees?'

Anu had another wicked thought. Could she take that fees money from him and pay at the other school? God, this was how criminals and frauds were born!

29

Anu found a branch of her bank near Vicky's school the next day. She could not find her account number but she knew they could pull up her records based on the name. Luckily, she could find photocopies of her PAN card and Aadhar by rummaging through a stash of papers Sanju had kept.

'Can you please tell me where my auto-deduction is going?' Anu asked the dapper-looking young man assigned to her.

He flashed her a strange look before asking. 'This is your account, right?'

'Of course. But only one of my accounts.' Anu smiled indulgently. 'So I can't remember the details.' Lying was an art and she had mastered it by practising it on her mom all her life.

'It is not an auto-deduction, ma'am. It is by cheque and it is going to …' He kept typing away. 'Let me see. To your post office account.'

What was that? Dad was investing in stamps?

Probably her cluelessness showed on her face making the man continue, 'To a yearly RD probably.'

Okay ... at least not stamps. Still, it sounded too complex to her.

'Can you stop that deduction? Just this once?'

'It is not an auto-deduction, ma'am. If you don't present the cheque, it won't get debited.' Now impatience had begun to show on the man's face.

Cheque, he said? Suddenly Anu remembered signing one for her father the last time she was in Vijaynagar. *Oh boy, he will present the cheque soon. I am doomed.* She had assumed it was all going to be between her and the bank.

Despite the man ushering in the next person in line, Anu asked. 'Look, I have already presented the cheque. Can you stop it?'

'Give me the cheque number, please.' The man was now visibly irritated. Did she see him roll his eyes at the pretty teller next to him?

'Hmm ... I don't know. I don't have it.' Even as she said it, Anu suddenly had a brilliant thought. 'I will withdraw all the money in my account. Now.'

The man knitted his brows. 'Your cheque will bounce. You can be in trouble.'

Anu narrowed her eyes at him. 'What kind of trouble? Like pushed-into-jail kind?'

'Maybe not. Do as you wish.' He was in a hurry to get rid of her now.

As Anu walked back home with a lakh-and-a-half in hand, she had never felt so fraudulent in her life.

That Friday was another dinner with Sanju and friends. Anu's mother was quite miffed that she was giving them a miss even that weekend. Anu had to lie to her that it was a business meeting for Sanju and she had to be there.

After getting off the phone with her mother, Anu decided that no matter what it took, she was not going to be in any trouble at that dinner. She was going be like those rare people who only nodded and stared and and never filled silences with talk. Because no social calamity can befall someone quiet. Or, so she thought.

Anu chose a corner chair where she had Sanju to her left and a palm tree to her right. She was all set to be trouble-free but she also decided not to be conservative with her drinks and food. They were paying big money anyway. So they might as well have a good time over-consuming. That was the idea behind dinner outings, right?

Anu began with two White Wine Sangrias back to back with a plate of loaded nachos, Potato Jackets, and a few other artery-clogging starters. Sanju had leaned away from her to be a part of a discussion on ERP, SAP and other similarly abbreviated technologies. Nobody cared much about her, which suited her fine. She took out her phone and started watching *Gilmore Girls* on mute with just the subtitles. Someone ordered a pitcher of Sangria and kept it before her. Nice of him or her or whoever.

'Anu ... Anu,' she heard someone call her name and shake her shoulder. *Oh boy, where was she? Why was she so sleepy?*

Lifting her head which weighed a hundred kilograms, Anu stared into Sanju's horrified face. 'Wake up, Anu. Clean your face.'

It took her a moment to realize she was still at dinner. Utterly groggy, Anu held a selfie camera to inspect her face. Oh boy! She looked like she was straight out a ghost movie—her face had a mixture of green and white paste with embedded crumbs of nachos. She had fallen asleep on the plate of nachos! She stole a glance at the concerned faces around her as she tried to wipe the guacamole and sour cream off her cheeks.

Sanju didn't speak to her either in the car or at home. Was it her mistake that she had had a bit too much Sangria and fallen asleep? Didn't it speak volumes about the conversation around her?

As she twisted and turned in the bed, sleep eluding her, Anu began to think. What kind of life was it? A change had to be for the better, wasn't it? They had a good life and now they were bent on ruining it.

Pete and Pooja began to laugh (Pete modestly, but Pooja uncontrollably) when Anu narrated to them what had transpired the previous night. Eyes watering with mirth, Pooja asked if Anu had a photo of her guacamole face. To her chagrin, Anu had in fact clicked one when she had used the selfie camera to fix her face. As Pooja continued to laugh, Pete patted Anu's hand. 'You fell asleep, big deal! Cheer up now.'

'Wish Sanju felt so. He hasn't said a word to me till now.' Anu felt terrible. Sanju had never gone silent before. Even when she had broken up with him, he would send a message now and then.

'He will come around.' Pete finished his coffee. 'By the way, my wife and daughter will be in Mysore day after tomorrow. I am joining them with the boys. So, I want to take the two of you out for lunch tomorrow.'

Anu rolled her eyes. 'You are a brave man taking me out to eat after my recent history with dinners.'

Pooja sipped her coke and winked. 'Let us order a large plate of loaded nachos.'

Pete smiled. 'Give Anu a break, Pooja.' He got up to leave. 'We will take a cab. So Anu can have some Sangria.'

Anu banged her head on the table. 'What have I gotten myself into!'

That evening when Sanju continued to be silent and cold, Anu stood before him blocking his TV. 'Sanju, don't act like I masterminded my insult.'

'Your insult?' Sanju moved to the side and continued to watch TV. Anu moved with him, blocking the TV again.

'Of course, my insult. I was the nacho-head if you remember.' Anu glared at Sanju.

Sanju tossed the remote on the sofa and got up. 'Anu, why are you so bent on making this miserable for me? I know it is always your way or no way but I thought just this once you might give in.'

'If you don't see how much I am trying, then you must be newly blind.' Anu looked away before he saw her eyes welling up.

'Then, maybe, you should stop trying.'

They rarely fought before and now all they did was bicker.

Anu paid off Rathnamma the next morning but waited before paying the school fees. She was yet to get the TC from Indigo. In the meanwhile, her heart thudded each time the phone beeped, fearing it could be the message from the bank that her cheque had bounced. Each time the phone rang she jumped in horror thinking it was her father who had called to ask about the money.

But all those disasters spared her that day, leaving her free to enjoy Pete's lunch. He had chosen a good restaurant in the upscale UB City mall. When they burped happily after a spicy, cheesy Mexican meal downed with a few shots of Tequila, Pete handed Anu a package. 'Here is a small present for you.'

'Oh, but why?' Anu was genuinely surprised. When she opened it, it turned out to be a Kindle. 'Oh, Pete. No … I can't take this. This is too expensive.'

'I insist. You can now read all the romances without first wrapping them in a newspaper.' Pete gave her a thumbs up and handed Pooja a package. It was a sweatshirt.

Anu looked at him quizzically. 'Pete, are you going to Mysore or running away someplace? Why are you making this a goodbye lunch?'

Pete shook his head. 'Not running yet. I will be back in a week but I am going to get busy with work and travel after that. Also, I am here only for another month-and-a-half before heading back to Florida. Pooja might be leaving too by then. So I thought this was a good time for presents.'

Anu's heart sank. What kind of cruel game was the universe playing with her? Shipping away everyone dear to her to different countries? But she smiled at Pete. They only had fun times and she was not going to ruin it by getting all emotional.

She fiddled with the Kindle. 'Pete! You have loaded it with books!'

Pete smiled. 'Mostly what you like and some, what I want you to like.'

30

From the next morning onwards there was no Pete at the class. His work had become painfully intense, in his words.

'I had forgotten that he is here on work,' said Pooja spreading her mat.

'Same here! Thought he too was on a holiday like me!' said Anu and looked around.

'But you are not on holiday here. You live here.' Pooja corrected Anu.

'Pooja, darling, no need for truths, got it?' Anu's reprimand elicited a giggle from the teen. Anu was going to miss that too.

Sitting down on the mat, Anu glanced at her new family. A few had already gathered and more would join in within minutes. The elderly were very punctual. Well, most of them. Those who brought food were sometimes late, but nobody minded that.

'This yoga you make us do is is so weird it is kind of cool,' Pooja said looking at the people around her. 'What an odd bunch!' Most men were in sweaters and dress pants, and women in track pants and kurtas.

Anu couldn't help gushing. 'I can't believe we are twelve of us here now!'

One of the gentlemen, Mr Ranganath, a retired bank manager, replied. 'That is because all other classes kill you. I went to one but had to crawl back home on all fours. This is nice and low-intensity.'

'Almost like the laughing club exercises.' Another Gujarathi woman, who routinely got high-calorie sweets or dhokla smothered with ghee, chimed in. 'Good exercises. I have got Rasmalais for all of you today.'

'Did you hear it? We are like a laughing club!' Anu whispered to Pooja.

'We should start laughing at the end. That would be cool!' Pooja suggested.

'You are a very brave teenager now.'

'Yup. Once I decided not to try fitting in with the crowd here, I feel liberated. Maybe this is how Buddha felt.' Pooja declared solemnly.

'Start a sermon after the class, then.' Anu laughed at Pooja. 'This can be your Sarnath.'

Anu started the class. Despite her many protests, it had become her class and she a teacher. As they started slowly rotating arms by way of warm-up, Anu noticed an elegant woman walk up to the gazebo.

'Can I please speak with Miss Anu here?'

Anu recognized her by the saree. She was an employee of the Karma Yoga studio. *What did she want? Collaborate with me? Ask me to give a talk?*

Anu walked down the gazebo smiling proudly. But the moment she saw a murderous expression on that pretty woman, her smile vanished. That woman was pretty in an evil way, like Cruella de Vil in *101 Dalmations*.

The woman's nostrils (she had a very pointed nose like Cleopatra) flared. 'Miss Anu, I am Rajani. I own the Karma franchise here.'

'Okay …' Anu trailed and noticed the woman. She felt very underdressed before that woman who had a diamond shining off her nose and two more from her ears. Her saree, though the same uniform as the others, was of superior silk. She oozed money and attitude.

'Do you know how much I have to pay this complex to run Karma here?' Wow! Anu smelled blood and heard battle cries. The woman was there for war.

'I don't know. Should I?' Anu asked suspiciously.

'You should. I have paid twenty lakhs as a franchise fee. And every month—' The woman stopped. 'You need not know. But what you are doing here is illegal.'

'What?' Anu was now honestly horrified. 'What is illegal? Yoga? Then Ramdev is illegal too.'

'Look, abandon this class. Or, I will escalate the issue and have you evicted from your house. You cannot run a cheap class and take my clients.'

Anu felt a rage rise through her. 'It is not a class. I am not a teacher. We are a group of people—'

'Oh, cut the crap.' The woman now looked ready to punch Anu with her toned arms.

Anu backed up a little. She was not the brave sort. Even in school, Sameer fought all her battles. The woman wagged her manicured finger at Anu. 'Stop this right now. Ask these people to go home or join Karma.'

Anu, to her shame, actually got scared. Angry people scared the daylight out of her. When she was still handling the blood rush to her head, she heard a voice.

'Madam, you are very rude. You cannot speak to Madam Anu in this manner. She hasn't done anything wrong.' Mr Ranganath! He looked sterner than Miss Karma.

Now, the warrior queen looked taken aback. Way to go, Mr Ranganath! He continued. 'As Madam Anu pointed out, we are all gathered here for a friendly chitchat and some exercises. By the way, none of us is your clientele. Our households run with the fees you charge.'

Now Menaka aunty, a retired teacher, spoke. 'If you object to us being here, we will report you to the management. I am a long-time resident.'

The woman nodded her head evilly at Anu and walked away, while Anu's mates stood around her protectively. Anu had never felt so hated and loved at the same time.

Pete did come for the tennis session that afternoon. Once Anu and Pooja briefed him about the eventful morning, Pete shook his head. 'I don't come one day and I miss all the drama?'

'That is what happens if you put work before exercise.' Anu reprimanded him. 'Don't you have twenty minutes to invest in your wellbeing?' She tut-tutted. She was joking but she missed Pete.

'I missed all the sweets too. What was today's special?' Pete asked.

'What happens in the class remains in the class, mister,' said Anu packing her shoes. Then her eyes fell on a little boy standing around Pete's twins and Vicky. There was a woman, probably the boy's mother, holding on to what looked like invites. The next minute the little boy was walking away with his mother, the twins had invitations in their hands, and Vicky ran to her crying.

'Mumma, that boy did not give me the card. He gave it only to Jason and Justin. I want one too.' He wailed.

Justin handed Pete the invite and said, 'They have a bouncy castle and a cotton candy machine. It is that boy's birthday party tomorrow.'

'Mumma, I want to go to that party too. But the boy did not give me a card.'

Anu consoled him. 'I am sure he missed giving you the card, Vicky. He will give you later.'

Vicky shook his head. 'No. His Mumma asked him not to give it to me.' Anu could not believe her ears. Could someone be nasty to a child? Then she felt incredibly sad, angry and shocked. Now the meanness is directed at Vicky?

Pete picked up Vicky. 'That is not a nice party because they made you sad. Tomorrow, nobody will go to that party. I will take the three of you to a place with bigger bouncy castles, larger cotton candy machines and also racing cars.'

Pooja whispered to Anu. 'I have seen that woman hang around with your nemesis Meena.'

Anu felt a wave of dejection wash over her. What had she done to Meena that she harboured such hatred for her?

31

That Friday, Sanju made no dinner plans. *Wonder why*, thought Anu wryly. She and Sanju had begun to talk but there was still tension in the air. Simply put, they talked very abnormally in monosyllables. Anu decided to pack herself and Vicky off to her mother's place for the weekend. She texted Sanju the same and got back a thumbs up for a reply. She hated emoji replies. How hard is it for people to type a few words?

The moment Anu entered her parents' house, her mood started to liven up magically. Her mother and grandmother were in the kitchen. Father was as usual on his chair going over some papers but the moment he saw Vicky, the papers went flying. Anu said a quick hello to her father and moved towards the kitchen. She was very afraid of the money thing coming up. But she had convinced herself that the bankers did not write nasty letters on weekends.

Anu stood at the kitchen door still unseen by her mother and grandmother.

'You are charring the parathas, can you lower the flame?' That was Anu's mother.

But her grandmother was not a fan of being instructed. 'I am not charring them. You are rolling them too thinly.'

'You get off and make the chutney. I will finish these. Anu hates charred parathas.' That was her mother being thoroughly impatient and making no efforts to hide it.

'Who likes charred parathas? You make no sense when you are angry.' Her grandmother huffed and Anu decided it was the right time to enter the battlefield to propose a truce.

'Anu!' Her mother exclaimed. 'You are early. The sun will set in the east today!'

'Anu, you look so pretty. Is that a new haircut?' That was her grandmother.

'Mummy, why do you never greet me nicely like Ajji does?' Anu sighed. Usually, she would be cross with her mother for such remarks (though they were truthful), but not that evening. She was just happy to be home.

'I don't garnish my words like your grandma but see, I made your favourite Aalu Parathas.' Anu's mother was like a child. She never filtered her thoughts.

Anu watched her grandmother plop large dollops of butter on the Parathas before serving them. Dollops big enough to make stomachs swell and arms jiggle and Anu ate every bit of it; then licked her fingers for good measure. As she washed it all down with a large cup of strong filter coffee, she wondered why she gave up on this life of luxury by getting married. Well, six years too late for that pondering!

She waddled slowly to the garden where her father was playing cricket with Vicky. Her mother was scurrying around stuffing Vicky with bites of Parathas whenever he took his microsecond-long breaks from running. Anu looked at the time. It was only six in the evening! What was she going to do for the rest of the night?

She missed Sameer, who had left for Dubai two days earlier. Shwetha was busy shopping for her wedding. And none of Anu's other friends lived in that neighbourhood anymore. Only their parents did. Anu picked up the Kindle and went upstairs to her room. She pondered whether she should just roam the streets, buy something cheap and kill two hours. Or, change into nightwear, drink more coffee, and go over what Pete had on Kindle. She settled for the latter.

Around ten, Anu's phone pinged. 'Got any good dinner stories?' Pete!

'Dancing on the tables. Can't type right now.'

'You had promised to buy me an out-of-the-world Masala Dosa.'

'Anu always pays her debts. Tomorrow morning at nine in Gandhi Bazar. By the way, it is Masale Dose. Valar Morghulis.'

'I stand corrected. Valar Dohaeris.'

Too bad Pooja wasn't there. Their *Game of Thrones* references left her fuming. 'You both are like Mean Girls. Talking in code to exclude me.' Anu smiled at the memory. Thank God, they still had a month of all that fun before Pete left. She was going to lap up every moment of it.

'Pete, listen to me carefully. For that to-die-for Masale Dose, you have to be aware of a few ground rules.' Anu met Pete at the Gandhi Bazar circle.

'I am listening.' Pete walked next to Anu carefully. 'But not if my feet get squished under one of these.' He pointed at the vehicles zooming by next to them.

'Oh, don't worry. Nobody steps on anybody's toes here.'Anu hauled herself up onto the footpath. Pete followed her sporting a look that was part afraid and part amused. Anu continued. 'Now, first of all, expect a half-hour wait to be seated. Then, expect a twenty-minute wait inside to get the food. Be forewarned, in a table for four, we will have two strangers eating with us.'

'I could live with that.' Pete sighed.

Anu grinned at him stopping at a small nondescript eatery with a large crowd gathered ahead of them. 'We have arrived.'

After the highly anticipatory wait (all the while getting roasted in the sun), Anu heard the old usher call her name. 'Oh boy, my name sounds so sweet coming from him,' Anu murmured and grabbed a table that had two empty seats.

'How are we to squeeze into these two tiny chairs?' Pete looked bewildered.

'Oh, please sit down before we lose the table.' Anu glared at Pete, making him scoot to the wall. She took the other seat.

Anu ordered three Doses for the two of them. Otherwise, they would have to wait another twenty minutes. When the Doses arrived, Pete finally smiled. Biting into the Dose (holding it in his hand like it was a wrap) he said dreamily, 'How can something so crispy on the outside be so soft on the inside? This is heavenly.'

'This is an art perfected here for over seven decades, Mister. Told you it was worth the wait.'

When they sipped their coffee, their tablemates changed. A youngish guy and a middle-aged man, obviously unrelated to each other. Anu thanked all her stars that the older guy hadn't come in when they were still eating. He coughed nonstop like a sputtering engine.

The younger guy politely asked the cougher to move to another table.

'If you have a problem, you move.' The man coughed his words.

'If I move, I have to wait again for the food. I don't have the time. You are spreading your germs all over here, so you move.' The younger man was now furious. Anu leaned back into her chair and covered her coffee cup subtly.

The older man settled snugly into the chair and coughed more vigorously. The young man muttered to himself but knew it was hopeless to argue more. When the cougher got busy with his phone, Anu tilted her cup to spill the coffee closer to him. As the brown liquid neared him, threatening to drip all over his white pants, Anu shrieked. 'Sir, watch out.'

The man jumped out of his seat in horror. 'You mad woman! Do you have Parkinson's to spill the coffee?'

As he coughed his way to the sink to wash the stains off, Anu got up to leave. But not before emptying more coffee onto his seat. She smiled at the young man and whispered, 'Enjoy your Dose.'

Following her out of the hotel, Pete looked heavenward. 'You are one of a kind!'

After a bit of strolling and shopping, Anu took pity on Pete. He looked just about ready to have a nervous breakdown amidst the vehicles, potholes, street vendors and dogs. Leading him inside a Coffee Day, she laughed. 'Relax your frazzled brain now.'

Pete sighed. 'This was nice and adventurous. But I can only experience this chaos very briefly.'

Anu ordered two lattes and plonked on a sofa. 'Takes a different mindset to live in real Bangalore. Nothing seems to work but everything works. There is a hidden method in all the madness which only a local can decode!'

Pete sipped his coffee and smiled at Anu. 'I wouldn't say this to your face but you are a remarkable woman! And, a great mom.'

Anu smiled back. 'I wouldn't say this to your face either but you are one of the nicest people I have met.'

'I have got some news, though.' Pete swirled the coffee. 'I heard from my brother that my mom isn't keeping well. So, I am leaving tomorrow night.'

Anu gasped. 'So sorry about your mother, Pete. You are going to be back again, right?'

Pete shook his head. 'No. We are moving back for good. There was not much to pack since it was a furnished house. We lived minimally, as you saw.'

Anu felt a knife pierce through her. 'I knew you would leave soon but this is sudden. I am going to miss you.' She fought back her tears.

'Thank you for your friendship and for showing me a Bangalore I never would have seen on my own.' Pete patted Anu's hand. 'Stay happy and don't resist change too much.'

Anu smiled at him. 'I will try. By the way, I read ten pages from each of the eight books you want me to like.'

'And? The verdict is?' Pete looked at her curiously.

'I will read a few of those. Definitely Lee Child.'

Pete picked up his bag to leave. 'I promise to read Leanne Moriarty for you. Let us see who finishes first. Stay in touch, kid.'

32

Anu did not want to go home yet. She strolled the busy streets, drank more coffee, then went to the Big Bull temple. The large stone bull staring down benevolently at her made it easy to submit her wishes. Once her panting from climbing the small hillock came to a halt, she prayed. At first, for money to materialize from somewhere, then for her to get out of Verdant Green, then for Vicky to be happy, then for her to drop a size and fit into her size 30 pants again. Her endless list began to exhaust her. 'Well God, give me peace of mind. Erase the previous list and keep just this one.' She offered a final prayer and walked to the eatery right opposite the temple that sold some great snacks. God had to work very hard to slim her down. Or, close down the eateries.

When she got back home, her mom greeted her as usual. 'Anu, I called you ten times. Where were you?'

That was when Anu realized she hadn't checked her phone at all for hours. 'What was the emergency that you called ten times?' Anu asked taking her shoes off and heading to the bathroom to wash her feet.

'You said you would be gone for two hours. Wash your hands and feet. The streets are so dirty.'

'Mummy! I am thirty and it is broad daylight! Also, if not to wash my hands and feet, why am I heading to the bathroom?'

'Would it kill you to just say okay?' Anu's mom started serving her lunch. 'Made your favourite Rotti and Kalu Palya. The TV remote is on the sofa.' Anu hated sitting at the dining table to eat. She was either with a book or with the TV, but on the sofa. That, by the way, had appalled Padzilla. Sanju's was a very let-us-sit-together-and-eat type of family.

'For all the noise you make, you are a good mummy.' Anu hugged her mother from behind knowing well that it irritated her. She was not the huggy-kissy type. That was her grandmother's department.

Just when Anu finished her lunch, her father walked in with Vicky. Both of them had turned red like tomatoes after whatever activity they had done. 'Mumma, we went to see some puppies in grandpa's friend's house. He said we can take one. Can we take one?' Vicky was breathless. 'Grandpa said we can take one if you agree. Can we go now and take one?' He tugged at her shirt.

'Daddy! Who is this friend bent on ruining my nap?' Anu rolled her eyes at her father and began to construct a lie on the fly for Vicky. 'Vicky, they are too little to be away from their mummas. They will cry all night if we take them away now.'

'You become its mumma.'

'I can. But I have to turn into a dog then. Then you won't have a mumma. Is that okay?'

Vicky giggled. 'You can't turn into a dog!'

'Oh, I can. If I have to become the puppy's mumma, I must.' Now there was doubt in Vicky's eyes. He left it at that and ran inside.

As Anu began to go up the stairs, her father's voice stopped her. 'Anu, take this and file it.'

Anu took the envelope her father handed her. *What could that be?* The moment she read the address on it, her heart sank. It was from the post office. She opened it slowly as her father got immersed in his paper. It was a receipt for payment of one-and-a-half lakhs. *What did that mean? Had daddy paid up?*

'Daddy,' Anu began to speak before her father cut her off.

'Keep the receipts because they have the account number.' He spoke without looking up from the paper. 'I have transferred another fifty thousand to your account.'

Anu's eyes started welling up again. *She did not deserve such good parents.* 'Daddy, sorry I used up—'

She was stopped mid-sentence again. 'Turn on the AC when you sleep. You need to run it at least a few hours every week.' He knew she loved to keep the AC on and cuddle with a blanket. Her parents cared to know everything about her and went out of the way to make her happy.

'Okay, thanks,' Anu murmured and started up the stairs.

'Anu,' her father again. 'Ask me if you have expenses. You are between jobs so it is okay to ask.'

Anu flopped on her bed and did not try to stop the tears. She did not know why she was crying but she had to get the silly tears out of the system. They threatened to come out too often lately.

Sunday morning Anu visited Sanju's parents. While her parents' house spelt food, entertainment and mirth (not to mention healthy bickering), Sanju's did calm, orderly and neat. Nobody raised voices, laughed too loudly or played TV on high volume. A combination of those two households would be utopia, mused Anu.

'Good morning, Anu.' That was her father-in-law wishing her politely. He took Vicky by hand to show the squirrels in the garden.

Anu's mother-in-law greeted her with a friendly smile, as she always did. 'Sit down, Anu. Watch some TV while I make tea.'

Anu followed her into the kitchen. Until she saw that kitchen, she had not believed that working kitchens could be so neat and organized. She thought only the model kitchens looked good.

'Are you leaving today evening?' asked her mother-in-law. Suma was her name. Very befitting because it meant a flower and she always had a flowery fragrance about her. Well, she was also soft natured.

'Yes, aunty. After lunch. Sanju said he can't come today. Some emergency call.' Anu wanted to roll her eyes even as she spoke because she did not believe in techies having emergencies. Not like they were life-saving surgeons.

'He told me so. I hope his crisis resolves soon. He must be so stressed.' Anu wondered how she could be so empathetic. Her mother would have yelled and asked her to haul herself to visit them. Anu smiled at the thought. Sanju was so shocked the first time they had stayed over at her mother's house. The noise, the non-stop food and coffee, the blaring TV, a parade of visitors—he was not exposed to any such hazards in his house.

'Shall we sit on the terrace? The garden is thriving now.' Her mother-in-law offered.

Anu nodded and followed her with the tea tray. *How does she remain so slim*, Anu wondered watching her mother-in-law's slender frame.

It was a slice of heaven up in the terrace. Blooming flowers, vegetables and herbs, hanging pots—that place was verdant green! Anu breathed deeply. No wonder her tardiness got to Sanju.

'You look a little pale, Anu. Is the house too big to manage?'

'I guess so, aunty. Also, too many changes too quickly,' Anu took a sip of her tea.

They generally chatted for a while and then stayed silent for some. Anu had never really gotten close to her mother-in-law. They were friendly and civil like good neighbours. But that evening Anu decided to ask her a few hard questions.

'Aunty, why does Padz ...'—she corrected herself quickly—'Padma aunty dislike me so much?'

Anu's mother-in-law almost spilt a few drops of tea on her immaculate white and pink cotton saree. 'She does not dislike you. It is just that she likes Sanju a lot.' Anu smiled, nodded and waited for more explanation.

'Padma is overprotective of Sanju and his father. So she does not trust anyone, including you and me, to do right by them! But she is not a bad person.'

Anu nodded more while her mother-in-law continued softly. 'For a long time, she was not happy with the way I took care of your father-in-law. She even cooked a special breakfast for him! But that is her love for her brother.' The mother-in-law trailed off a little but regained her composure quickly. 'But now we are friendly...'

Anu narrowed her eyes. 'How recent is *now*? Because you and uncle have been married for over thirty-five years.'

Sanju's mother laughed heartily. 'She lost her husband very early. She has been living with us for almost thirty years and helped me raise Sanju. When she was working, she was not this controlling but once she retired ten years back was when she began to fuss a lot.'

'Weren't you uncomfortable that she was so possessive of Sanju and uncle?'

The older woman shrugged. 'Not really. Love is abundant. You should give and receive it freely.' Okay, Anu's mother-in-law read a lot of spiritual books and she spoke like that sometimes. But it sounded quite nice and not tacky coming from her. 'But Anu, don't worry about all this. Padma aunty, as you said, is over possessive of Sanju and he adores her. She has nothing against you.'

Except that she makes sure to tell me how I am just not enough for Sanju—thought Anu but did not voice it.

Just as she was leaving, Padma aunty arrived. Anu smiled as brightly as she could and got a small nod in reply. But Vicky got ample bosomy hugs and wet kisses.

'Look Suma, I got Sanju's baby videos converted to DVDs. We should play now so that Vicky can see his father.' She was so excited she squeaked her words.

Anu knew there was no escaping the video. For the first fifteen minutes, it was very endearing. Little Sanju looking dapper in suits, Krishna costumes and girl outfits. Then it began to feel highly boring. Anu looked at her mother-in-law helplessly who came to the rescue. 'Anu, you can watch it another time, or I will give it to you after we watch it. Now you carry on since you said you have plans.'

Anu wanted to kiss her mother-in-law. Padzilla looked visibly upset. 'It is fun to watch it with Vicky. I also got my Europe trip video. We will watch when Sanju comes home.'

When Anu walked out of the house, Anu suddenly felt guilty. *Sanju is so loved here and he gets nothing but angst from me lately.* She remembered Sanju standing by that very gate most mornings and evenings when she went to college and came back. Later, he had confessed that he stood there only to see her. The first time he invited her home she had spilt a large cup of Bournvita on the sofa and he had only smiled and asked her not to worry and the cleaned up the mess. And the time he had invited her home when he was alone ... As the memories came crowding, she wanted to run home to Sanju and make everything perfect between them.

33

When her Uber stopped in front of the gate, Anu felt mildly deflated. Sanju's car was not in the driveway. Yanking the phone out, she checked her messages. There it was—a message from him a good three hours ago. He had gone out with friends. Now she felt majorly deflated. They hadn't seen each other for two days and she had come prepared to have a good time, like the good old days—pizza, beer and a movie. She could ask him to come back early. Anu called but Sanju disconnected the call.

That is mature, Anu muttered to herself, making her way into the house with Vicky. Her immediate instinct was to run away. Coming from the warm world of cosy houses full of people and noise, the large space around her seemed cold and scary; like in a Stephen King novel. Maybe King could write a book where a house ate its inhabitants and grew bigger. As if sensing her discomfort, Vicky had gone unusually quiet too. Turning on the TV to *Oggy and the Cockroaches* (Vicky had some eclectic taste), Anu settled down next to him.

'Mumma, shall we play tennis with Jason?' Vicky's question brought her to the harsh reality that there was no Pete anymore. Now she felt not only deflated but also depressed.

'Too late now. We will play tomorrow.' There was no need to break Vicky's heart just yet.

As she went upstairs to their bedroom to get a book she was reading, there was a printed note on her bedside table. As Anu read it, she couldn't believe her eyes. It was a note from the Verdant Green property manager.

'Dear sir/madam, it is brought to our notice that the residents of this house are misusing public spaces for commercial activities. Also, we have been informed that the residents are using the tennis court without an ID card. These cards are issued to the owners of the property and the tenants will have to pay for the same. If these shortcomings are not rectified immediately, you may face eviction.'

The room spun around Anu. This was so vicious. That was why Sanju hadn't even called all day yesterday and now he had left before they came. He must be hopping mad. Who is this faceless property manager sending the letter? She wanted to punch him in the gut. Instead, she took a picture of the notice and contemplated whether she should send it to Sameer, Shwetha or Pete. She settled for Pete. He would have a funny comeback while the other two would also want to punch the manager for her. Pete's flight was not until midnight so he might check his message.

He didn't disappoint her. 'Ask them to take the public space and the tennis court and stick them where the sun doesn't shine.'

250 Vani Mahesh

Anu began to laugh. 'Will do. Then again, eviction isn't too bad either.'

There was a message from Pooja asking her if they were going to do yoga the next day. Anu sent her the picture of the notice. 'Do you think we should?'

'We definitely should. See you at nine tomorrow, aunty.'

Sanju did not show up until after she was fast asleep. The next morning when she was making her coffee, he walked in. He looked stressed and she hoped it was because of work. He quietly made his coffee without a word. When he was about to head out of the kitchen, Anu spoke. 'You know that they are false allegations, right?'

'Are they?' Sanju spun around. 'Why did you have to do yoga in that godforsaken gazebo? Why did you have to play tennis now when all you wanted in high school was to run away from it?'

Anu stared at him. 'What happened to you after moving here? Can't you see right from wrong? Shouldn't you be supporting me instead of that property manager?'

'That is Sameer for you, Anu. Whether you are right or wrong, he will jump in to support you. I have brains.' Sanju shook his head in what looked like part disgust and part distress.

'That is so mature and kind and—' The right word came to her after Sanju was gone —*modest*. Which Sanju was anything but at the moment. Fuming, Anu gulped her coffee and made another tall cup. She needed all the caffeine to get her through the day.

When she showed up at the gazebo, the old folk had already gathered and were warming up. Pooja was there as well with someone who looked eerily like an older and a stern version of her. The woman had her hair in a braid, wore a bindi, track pants and sneakers. 'Hi aunty, this is my mom. Mom, Anu aunty.'

Oh god. What now? Is she going to accuse me of derailing Pooja? To Anu's relief, the woman smiled. A nice and friendly smile. 'Thank you, Anu. You have been a great influence on Pooja. So I thought I would say hello to you before going on my walk.'

Anu blushed. 'Oh, no. I ... well, Pooja is a great kid. You have raised her well.'

'I saw the note you got from the management. Don't worry. They are all empty threats.'

Anu nodded. 'But threats, empty or otherwise, scare me!'

'Don't worry. I will meet you after my walk. We will have coffee together.'

'I thought your mother was here to yell at me,' said Anu rolling her mat.

'Well, my mom is happy that I am off the bed before noon and moving my muscles.' Pooja grinned. 'She might give you a reward!'

When they sat down for coffee, Anu looked at the tennis court. It held no charm without Pete. She sipped her coffee silently, letting Pooja's mother talk.

'You know that Meena is behind that notice, right? The property manager is a good friend of hers.'

Anu took another sip of the hot coffee. 'I guessed so. But why is she so angry with me? All I did was meet her for one disastrous dinner.'

Pooja's mother shook her head. 'If Meena does not like you, that always means you are good. She gets vindictive if she feels threatened. That someone might take away her unofficial crown of being the Queen of Verdant Green.'

Anu laughed. 'We are the poor tenants of Verdant Green. Where do I have the army to take away her throne? Can I go tell her that?'

'See, Pete was very aloof and kept to himself here but he took to you. You both became great friends. That was unbearable to Meena. How could someone pass her up for you? Then, your yoga crowd adores you. That was another blow to her pride. So she is just resorting to all means to be nasty to you.'

Anu didn't know whether to laugh or to cry at this saga that was getting fiercer than the war of the Mahabharatha. 'Hope Meena realizes soon that I am not here to take away anybody's non-existent throne and crown! I am barely surviving.'

As she walked back home, all the fight had left her. Sleeping in her old bedroom at her parents' house began to feel so appealing, it was scary.

When she reached home, Sanju's car was in the driveway. Why is he back? Did he forget something? Or, was he going to apologize to her and take her out? That might happen if the pigs flew! But nothing had prepared her for what she saw. A Sanju wild with anger. A Sanju she had never seen before.

'Why are you being so vengeful, Anu?' Sanju's face and eyes had turned red. 'I have never been anything but nice and accommodative in this relationship. What did I ask of you after all? To live in a mansion and spend my money?'

Anu was speechless for a moment and then enraged. 'That is such a below-the-belt comment, Sanju. I am trying to be happy. Keep you happy. Keep Vicky happy.'

'I can see that. I got a call from Indigo International when I was at work. To collect Vicky's things from his cubby as he is no longer a student there. Where is Vicky?'

Anu cursed herself for not taking the mobile along. They would have called her first. Sanju's was a backup number. She tried her best to explain why she did what she did but Sanju looked stony.

'You know what, if you don't want to live here, you don't have to. Feel free to leave anytime.'

'Sanju! What does that mean?'

'You know what that means.'

34

'Are you breaking up with me, Sanju? Do you know we are now married and you can't just break up and walk away? Like you did seven years ago? Why is there no middle ground with you then or now?'

'I broke up and walked away? Life is always about you, isn't it, Anu?' Sanju stormed out of the house. Anu heard him start the car.

She sat feeling nothing for a long time. Her mind had gone blank. She didn't want to think about the present. So she thought about what Sanju had just implied—that he was not the one who had walked away before.

They had been dating for three years. Anu had somehow made up her mind that she wanted to be married at twenty-five. But her family never thought what she said had to be taken seriously. They kept bringing the so-called alliances and Anu kept turning everyone down.

'Sanju, not to brag or anything but you got a catch in me, man.' Anu would laugh showing him the pictures of eligible grooms and their parents asking her parents for her hand.

'Really?' Sanju was always a good sport. He would laugh. 'I will build a temple for you like they have done for Khushboo and worship you for bestowing yourself on me.'

But at one point, Anu started to get tired of battling her parents. Her I-wont-marry-till-twenty-five was not getting any attention.

'Anu, we must tell the parents. So that they stop looking for grooms for you!' Sanju had convinced her when his mother had begun to suggest prospective grooms for Anu.

When they told the respective parents, there was nothing filmy about their reactions. Anu's parents were disappointed that she had found someone herself. But other than that there was no objection. Except, big trouble came in the most unexpected form.

'If you both are keen on each other, you must marry immediately.' Anu's father was firm. 'We can't have you see each other out of wedlock.'

'Daddy! Please don't use cringe-worthy phrases like "out of wedlock".' Anu had scrunched her face. 'We have been seeing each other for three years. Just because you know about it now, you can't force me to marry immediately.'

But her father, usually a very forgetful man, hadn't forgotten his stance on the matter even after weeks. For heaven's sake, he forbade her from meeting Sanju! Well, that was a bit filmy and unnecessary because she was working by then and was meeting Sanju after work. He had finished his M.Tech from IIT Chennai and was working for an IT company in Bangalore. He had turned down offers to go abroad because Anu was averse to the very idea.

Sanju had convinced her father that he was applying for Ph.D in the US and getting married too quickly would hamper his plans. He had asked for a year more to settle down.

Sameer had surprisingly kept himself out of this. He met her but Anu sensed that he did not want her to talk about her wedding. Shwetha was working with her at the bank and they had bonded big time over shopping and eating. She kept asking Anu to get married soon. 'For me, Dini is in London. So getting married changes my life. What is your problem? You will only be moving out of your parent's house and gain the freedom to live on your own.'

That actually kind of sounded good. Though Anu was working, her father had set a strict 8 p.m. curfew. Not to mention her over paranoid and overprotective mother and grandmother cramping her style. That was when she spoke to Sanju and all hell broke loose after the talk.

'Sanju, if we have to get married in a year, we must look for a place to live.' She had said enthusiastically slurping ice cream. She was already dreaming of house shopping.

Sanju had looked confused. 'Why? We will live at my place, right?'

'Oh no! I am not escaping my parents to live with yours!' That had sounded a bit harsh but she was horrified by what he had suggested.

Sanju had not been happy. 'I have passed up opportunities to go abroad because you don't want to. I at least want to live with my parents. They would be too hurt if I move out.'

'If you lived abroad, how would you live with your parents?' Anu was not one to give up.

'I would sponsor them to come live with me.'

They had gone back and forth for weeks on the issue. Finally, Sanju had declared.

'This is an impasse, Anu.' He had choked his words and looked pained but had said they had to part ways.

Anu was at first shocked, angry, devastated and eventually wanted to kill Sanju. How could he call off their relationship of three years just like that? But he had. Anu did not have the heart to tell her parents that the wedding was off. So she hadn't, for almost six months.

Sameer and Shwetha were her crutches. They had made sure she hadn't fallen apart. They fed her food and beer and made her laugh. On one such dinner with Sameer, he had asked her what her plans were. 'How long are you going to wait for Sanju to crawl back, Anu?'

'I feel we are not over. Not yet.' Anu was convinced.

Sameer had stayed suspiciously silent for a while then he had asked. 'In case, just hypothetically, if Sanju doesn't come back, do I stand a chance with you?'

Truth be told, Anu was flabbergasted. But her quick reply to his question took her by surprise. 'Without batting an eyelid,' she had said and she had meant it. She used to get annoyed when Sameer went dating everyone on earth but had friendzoned her. But after she and Sanju became a couple, she was the one who had friendzoned Sameer. But, maybe, deep down somewhere, she still had a crush on him. Why would she agree so quickly otherwise? But Shwetha had begged to differ. According to her, Anu had agreed only because she liked staying well inside her comfort zone and Sameer spelt comfort with a capital 'C' for her. What is wrong with comfort zones anyway? Anu never understood.

However, a month later Sanju had met her. 'Anu, I spoke to my mother. She is fine with us moving out.' He was never one to confess love but Anu knew he had missed her. As much as she had missed him, at the very least. Or so she wanted to believe.

'What brought about this change of heart?' Anu had secretly fished for some confessions and he hadn't disappointed her.

'There is only one Anu in this world. I don't want to lose her.'

That was when he had casually mentioned that he had dated Kshama for a couple of months. 'There is no other woman like you, Anu. Crazy, mad, but also sane!'

'I moped for you like Meerabai while you went around dating women!' Anu was genuinely angry, more with herself than with Sanju.

'We were on a break!' Sanju had mouthed Ross's famous line from *Friends* and then had said seriously, 'Kshama and I were friends all through undergrad. Dating was nothing more than a continuation of the same friendship, okay? I am not a serial dater like Sameer.'

Anu had then made the mistake of telling him what Sameer had said. That had changed everything. Sanju, that instant, had turned hostile towards Anu and Sameer's friendship. But what neither Sanju nor Sameer had told her

(her mother-in-law had later) was that it was Sameer who had brokered peace between Sanju and her. He had spoken to her mother-in-law about this breakup who had then spoken to Sanju.

Anu had asked Sameer why he had done so, while he wanted a chance with her!

He had cracked some bad joke at first (something like when she had agreed, he had developed cold feet) but then had come clean with the truth. 'I needed a chance with you only if all the doors between you and Sanju were closed. Evidently, no door was closed between you two! You are the creepy Romeo and Juliet of this century.' He had ended with a bad joke.

Anu's alarm jolted her out of her blast from the past. It was the 'Pickup–Vicky' alarm. What would she do after picking up Vicky? Stay back and make peace with Sanju? The thought of staying back revolted her. She did not belong there. She did not want to belong there. Then again, moving away from Sanju was equally depressing. Would he come back to her if she moved out? Or was that it for them? She still wondered if it was not for Sameer's interference, would Sanju have come back to her at all. Should she take that chance now?

35

Anu's phone rang when she had just picked up Vicky. It turned out to be Pooja's mother, Dharini.

'Hi Anu, I am meeting some of my friends for lunch at the restaurant. Please join us.'

Anu hesitated. Even a shared lunch meant damage of at least two thousand. As if reading her mind, Pooja's mother spoke quickly. 'It will be a simple veg-and-no alcohol kind of lunch. None of us wants to spend too much.' She gave a small awkward laugh.

Anu couldn't do anything but agree. But she felt depleted. She knew money was not an issue for Dharini. Pooja's track pants cost more than Anu's best evening dress! Anu sighed as she drove. Now even nice people like Dharini had to downgrade their lifestyle to accommodate her!

Leaving Vicky with Rathnamma, Anu changed into a decent pair of jeans and a T-shirt that made her look nice to herself. Anu made up her face quickly and admired herself for a quick moment. God, was she a narcissist!

When she reached the restaurant, Dharini waved to her. Anu stood dumbfounded for a moment. The entire table, with around six women, looked the most resplendent in crisp cotton sarees and gorgeous jewellery. Anu groaned inwardly. Would she ever fit in anywhere in this darn place?

'We are all cotton saree buffs, Anu. So when we meet, we wear only those. But don't bother with us oldies! You look beautiful.' Dharini was a genuinely nice person. Her friends weren't bad either. Everyone was friendly and even asked Anu about her life—past and present. Anu began to relax. Not everyone in Verdant Green was an ogre after all.

Soon the conversation turned to the vacations they were all planning that year. One was going on the golden chariot train journey with family that costed around four-lakh rupees per person. Another was going to London to watch the India–England cricket match. The third was going to Mauritius to stay in a luxury resort and spa. Nobody was trying to be mean. They were simply sharing but Anu had nothing to add. They had no vacation planned. And the vacations they had taken were better not mentioned here—Simla, Agra, Ramoji Film City! How commonplace and mundane!

Anu swallowed the low-fat vegetarian food—tofu, millets, and lots of salads, the women were all very health conscious—with great difficulty. Why eat at all if one had to eat this! The conversation then moved to where their kids were going to do their undergrads; one to the USA to pursue pre-med courses, another to Germany to pursue a major in economics, yet another to Hong Kong to join the UC Berkeley Dual Degree Program. They were all talking about at least a two-crore rupee expense to get a three-year degree. Anu wondered if those kids were better off taking that money from their parents and attending KLE as she did. In between, the women did politely try to include Anu in their conversation but she felt as out of place as a vegan at a steakhouse.

As Anu walked back home, she glanced around at the driveways. Mercedes, Audi, BMW—any luxury car you could think of, you could spot it there. Where the drapes were open, she could peek inside to spot furniture worthy of admiration more than comfort. And, of course, the perfect gardens. Anu's gardener waved to her zipping by on his brand new motorbike that cost more than her old Santro. When Anu reached home, Vicky was asleep. Anu thanked Rathnamma with a five-hundred rupee note. The woman grumbled, 'You were gone for two hours and you are giving me only five hundred.'

Anu plonked herself on the ground and looked around her mansion. She wanted to cry! Their unremarkable furniture made that grand house look miserable! Nothing about her was enough to live there. She checked her phone to see if Sanju had texted. He usually did at that hour. Anu thought of texting him but that seemed more energy-sapping than the lunch she had just had.

Her mind reeled back to that morning. Sanju had asked her to leave! What could she text him now? Beg him to let her stay? Yell at him for what he had said? Send something meaningless and neutral? She would have opted for the last if not for the hurt that was still too raw—Sanju had asked her to leave him and the house.

By the time Vicky woke up, after a good two hours, Anu had made up her mind. She pulled out her large suitcase and started packing her clothes. Then she took another smaller one and packed Vicky's clothes and toys. She sauntered into the kitchen and picked up two vessels and a cooker. Two plates and two cups. Her coffee and Maggi were taken care of with those. Then she called Radha. She was not sure if what she was doing was right or wrong but it seemed natural.

Vicky was jumping all around assuming they were leaving on holiday. 'Where are we going, Mumma? I want to go to Wonder Land. And then Zoo. And then—'

The innocence of a child! Anu did not bother to correct him. His ideal holiday spots What he wanted were all in and around Bangalore and she could very well give him the holiday he desired!

Dragging the suitcase, managing Vicky riding on the big one, Anu lugged it to her Santro and shoved it in the backseat. She gave one last look at the house and bid a silent goodbye. *Should she leave a note for Sanju?* She went inside and got a piece of paper. Stopping for a moment to think, she scribbled. 'Meet me in the middle.'

As she walked to her car, she felt quite impressed with her clever note. Well, it was not her original thought but a song by Jessie Ware, but she used it so aptly. Then, as an afterthought, she took a picture of the two suitcases in her car and sent it to Pete, captioning it 'The End.' A bit dramatic, but then again, as far as Anu was concerned, Verdant Green ceased to exist the moment she locked the front door.

She looked for Vicky who still ran in circles in the driveway. The house that was hers (well, again a bit dramatic because technically it was still hers) looked marvellous. For the first time, Anu admired the stony front façade, the lawn, the driveway so big they could fit four cars in it. The French door, the long and clear glass windows—she wished she was only visiting that house. Then she could have, would have, admired it wholeheartedly. Like she did all the resorts they frequented, from Chikmanglur to Coorg to Goa.

'Hey, Anu,' she heard someone pant next to her.

'Hi Dave, should you be jogging now? Shouldn't you be at work?'

Dave grinned. 'Don't tell the boss. By the way, you will sell this tin box when you get your BMW, right?' He patted her Santro. 'Oh, you have some big cases in there! If you had waited a week, you could have travelled in style in your BMW SUV!'

Anu's head reeled. Now, she could respond in two ways— act as if she knew or act ignorant (which she was, so that was not an act).

She chose to act. 'Oh yeah. Why is my BMW taking this long?'

Dave wiped the sweat off his sleeve. 'Because Sanjay insisted on black. Did you test drive it? He said he was going to take you.'

'Yeah … Yeah, sure,' Anu mumbled and bid goodbye to Dave. So, where did Sanju have the money for a BMW? Wouldn't it cost like something obscene like 100 lakhs? Or at least forty-fifty lakhs? Once the wonderment came down, the worry started. *Is he adding more to the already full EMI?* Once that worry came down, anger built up. *Didn't he think he had to ask me before taking such a big step?* Once that anger subsided, a form of cloudy depression began. *Have we ended as a couple?* She remembered the countless test drives they took before Sanju bought his XUV two years back.

She had no clue how she reached her apartment despite having a nonstop conversation with herself. But she did. She was home. Radha met her at the parking lot with a wide smile.

'Vicky! You have become so tall in three months!' She picked up Vicky and kissed him despite his many protests.

'Akka, so good to see you. I missed you.' Her eyes were moist. Anu smiled. She really was home.

'I have kept the house clean. But there is nothing much there. How will you stay here until your furniture comes? Shall we ask Kavitha akka for some stuff?' Radha spoke the words that were straight out of Anu's worst nightmare. How was she going to live there? Forget the furniture, what about the money?

'No. Don't even tell Kavitha I am here. She will worry too much.'

36

'What on earth!' Shwetha shrieked the moment she walked into the house. 'Is this your chosen life?' She pointed at the flat cotton mattress on the floor in an otherwise empty living room.

Anu pouted. 'Don't mock the poor friend. Have you brought the drinks?'

'Where is Vicky?' asked Shwetha taking out the Sprite and Smirnoff and mixing them into their glasses.

'Have left him at my mother's place. Tomorrow I am talking to Sumitra aunty to get my old job back.' Anu took a deep sip of the drink. The best part about drinking at home was that she didn't have to worry about driving.

'Have you told your parents yet?' asked Shwetha. She had agreed to spend the night with Anu.

Anu rolled her eyes. 'God, no. I need a break from the world. If I tell them, they will badger me into moving in with them. Then they will badger me into moving back to Verdant Green.'

'A single Meena cannot scare you away, Anu. I will help you all the way but I don't support what you have done.'

Shwetha was now serious. 'You are not a saint to give up a good life to embrace poverty.'

Anu flashed her phone before Shwetha to show her the messages from the bank where she and Sanju held a joint account. 'Look at this, Shwetha. I hadn't read any of these in the past two months thinking they are routine messages from the bank.'

Shwetha read through the thread and knitted her brows. 'Three fixed deposits have been broken. The third one for twenty lakhs. Who keeps money in the FD anymore? Maybe Sanju is breaking the deposits to invest in mutual funds or stocks.'

Anu shook her head. 'Sanju is the last person to invest in the market. He is breaking the deposits to sustain a lifestyle we can't afford. The twenty-lakh-rupee one must be for the BMW. I can't be a part of that artificial living.'

Shwetha leaned against the wall and stretched her legs and waved her hand around. 'Is this a natural living for you?'

Anu grew sombre. 'No. But this is temporary. I feel Sanju will move back soon.' But she sounded very unconvincing to her own ears. *Why would he? He was leading the life of his choice after all.*

'Shwetha, enough about me. Why did you postpone the wedding again? You even shopped for the bridal gear.'

Shwetha twirled her drink and looked away. 'This time it was Dini. He wasn't sure if he wanted to marry now. Says his job is dicey.' She gave a wry smile. 'Maybe, he has moved on. I kept postponing the wedding for nearly three years now. I won't blame him.'

Anu was horrified. 'Absolutely not. Dini will not move on. You both are meant to move together. You sound upset, Shwetha. Why didn't you tell me anything?' Anu shook her head. 'I am so selfish. I only keep throwing my woes at you and never asked about yours.'

Shwetha shook her head. 'Don't be silly. You are the best listener in the world. I just didn't want to talk about it. I don't even know if I should be upset yet. Tonight, let us both pretend to be single and happy.' She got up, turned on the music in her phone, and started doing her animated gyrating. Anu began to giggle but joined her soon.

The next afternoon, when Anu entered her apartment, she didn't know if she was relieved, sad or anxious. Probably a mixture of all feelings (mostly the bad ones) that humans go through. She had just come back from meeting Sumitra aunty. Anu sighed looking around her living space. A tattered bed in the living room, no TV, two utensils and two cups in the kitchen. Another tattered bed in the bedroom. How long was this living going to last? Those were precisely Sumitra aunty's words.

Anu had felt exhilarated as she walked down the simple school corridor that morning. Every teacher she met, gave her a genuine so-happy-to-see-you smile. Some hugged, some shrieked. The nursery kids she had taught had refused to let go of her hand. They had all talked simultaneously for ten minutes before their class teacher broke the party.

Sumitra aunty had been her usual warm self. She was never Anu's boss. She was always Sumitra aunty whom she knew since she was an infant.

'Anu, how good to see you! Thought you forgot all about me in your new life.'

'Well, aunty, about that—' Anu had faltered at first but then had managed to tell her about what happened to that new life. To her credit, her eyes only moistened and she did not bawl.

'Aunty, please take Vicky and me back.' She had asked in earnest. Well, it was more begging than asking.

'Anu, you can have your old job back any day. Vicky is of course more than welcome to study here. But—' she had looked at Anu doubtfully. 'Are you sure you want to uproot yourself from your current life and Sanjay?'

'Not from Sanju. Only from Verdant Green, aunty.' Anu had tried to sound confident but ended up sounding like a shivering wet dog. The fear that Sanju and Verdant Green might be a package deal was her worst nightmare.

When Anu had asked her not to tell her parents yet, Sumitra aunty had smiled. 'Your mother will be angry with me. But I am giving the job back to one of my best teachers. Not to my friend's daughter.'

That was when Anu had to fight back her tears. That was the nicest thing someone had said to her in a long time!

Now back in her empty house, Anu tried to break away from thoughts and fought hard not to feel depressed and lonely. She was too restless to focus on a book or a show or even to take a nap. That was when she decided to text Sanju.

She would do anything to hear from him at that moment. 'Have you told your parents anything about us? Can I visit them and not be bombarded by questions?'

Even after three hours, with Anu checking the phone a thousand times, there was no reply from Sanju. *Was he going to come back ever? Or in a very filmy manner, was she going to receive a courier with divorce papers? Oh god! Divorce!* Anu started to panic. *Did she make a mistake?* She tried to imagine moving back to Verdant Green. That thought was as depressing as getting the divorce papers in the courier.

Deciding to visit her parents, Anu picked up her handbag. That was when the phone rang, giving her a near heart attack. Could it be Sanju? She began to rummage through her bag furiously to dish out the phone. She peered at it all hopeful but immediately felt like someone had punched her in the gut. It was not Sanju. It was some nameless person.

'Madam, we have a delivery for you. Can we send it to your flat?' That was the security at the gate.

'Sure. Please do.'

Anu waited at the door to pick up the package but a large truck got parked before the building. While a man looked at her and waved, another two started to unload the truck. It was all their stuff! What was happening? Sanju had sent the furniture back! Was he going to jump out of the truck too?

As things arrived one by one, Anu watched in silence. *Was he moving back or was he getting rid of her?*

37

As soon as the truck was unloaded, Anu knew it was not good news at all. There was nothing of Sanju's in the haul that had arrived. Not his desk, not his recliner, not his clothes, and not even that hideous orange couch that Padzilla had gifted. Anu directed the men numbly to place things into their places. Sanju, being his meticulous self, had packed every single item that belonged to the house, Anu and Vicky. By the time the men left, Anu had no air in her lungs. She collapsed on the sofa staring at the blank TV.

What started as despair soon began to turn into anger within her. *How could he not reply to my message? What is he so mad about? That I did not live in a place that made me miserable? That I asked for a life that suits our income? He travelled six months a year, and did she ever complain? Did she ever nag him to take her places or get her gifts?*

She soon made herself a martyr in her head and Sanju a complete villain. Just when she thought her head was going to explode with anger, her phone chimed. She picked it up with hope surging but it was a friend. Anu quickly turned

271

off the notifications. That pinging never suited her, especially not then.

She got up to head out. She was going to bring Vicky back from her parents' house and start her life. If it had to be without Sanju, so be it. She checked her phone one last time before starting the car. There was a message from Pete. 'Still trouble in paradise?'

'Trouble has replaced paradise.' Anu wrote a reply explaining briefly how she thought her life was over.

'You are both hurting. Give yourself time to heal. In the meanwhile, watch some Netflix and eat junk food. Distraction is the best medicine for a muddled mind.'

Another fifteen days of desperate waiting went by, but nothing happened. Vicky was happy to be back home but asked for daddy more frequently than ever. Anu placated him saying daddy was in the US to get them both gifts.

'Will he bring me a robot this time?' Vicky asked with eyes opened wide. 'I want to tell him to bring me a robot.'

'What kind of robot, Vicky?' Anu smiled and ruffled his hair.

'The walking one. The one that can play cricket and make a sandwich,' Vicky kept adding to the list, making Anu laugh till her eyes water. 'That is what Mumma does for you, Vicky. Why do you need a robot for that?'

'Hmm … robot doing all that is nice. You can also play with the robot, Mumma. We will call him Lucky.'

Days moved quickly with Vicky keeping Anu on her toes. She had now force stopped herself from overthinking about Sanju. She had also realized that Sanju hadn't told his parents anything about them. So she decided to spin her own story. She told both sets of parents that they had decided to move back to the old apartment and Anu was shuttling between here and Verdant Green. Anu's mother prodded once in a while about why Sanju wasn't visiting them at all but she bought it when Anu said he was travelling. Her father only asked her if she needed anything (meaning money), but she had enough left from what he had already given her.

That Sunday evening, Anu walked inside the gate to her in-law's house. They had Vicky for a day and she was there to pick him up. Before knocking on the door, Anu stood still to admire the tidy garden her mother-in-law maintained. Everything about that woman was calm and organized. She suddenly felt sadness envelop her. *What was this place without Sanju? Only he made that house hers.*

'Hello, Anu,' Padma aunty's voice jolted her out of the reverie.

'Hello, aunty. How are you?' Anu avoided looking into the eyes of that sharp woman.

'Come with me. I am going to the temple. Vicky is playing with his grandmother so he won't miss you for now.' She dictated her terms like a true Padzilla and closed the door shut behind her.

A walk with Padzilla? Wasn't her life already bad enough for God to make it worse? Anu gave a mental eye roll but followed the woman who was already at the gate. Instead of the temple, they entered a park and found a bench. Anu knew they were going to have a 'talk'. How did she hate these talks!

'What is going on with you and Sanju?' Padzilla never minced words.

'Hmm ... Well, nothing—' Anu looked at her own hands and studied them intently.

'You are living here and Sanju in that Verdant place. Why?' Padzilla looked at Anu through her glasses. Her hawkish face looked sterner than ever.

'Didn't you ask Sanju?' Anu braved asking.

'I did, of course.' Padma aunty was now visibly irritated. 'He said nothing much. But his story didn't exactly match yours. So tell me.'

Anu thought of just getting up and going off but decided against it. 'Are you asking because you are curious or because you are concerned?' She didn't know where that question had come from! Padzilla might kill her now for that insolence.

But to her surprise, the older woman placed her bony hand on Anu's shoulder. 'Because I want to help.'

Anu looked at her in surprise. She saw a softness in her eyes that she had never seen before. Anu's eyes welled up at that concern. It was so difficult to bottle it all up and pretend like nothing was wrong. Once she began to talk, there was no stopping her. Anu told her everything—things that had happened, what she had said, done and felt. By the end, she was crying so profusely, the park walkers kept glancing at her, concerned. Padma aunty offered her a clean white hanky to wipe her face.

'Anu, from where I stand, you both are being very immature.'

Padma aunty was now back to her stern self. 'You could have tried harder to stay there and make a home. Sanju, after all, did come back to you every time you both had a difference. He even moved out of our house to live with you.'

Anu got up. 'I should have known that you wouldn't take my side, aunty. You never did like me.'

'Sit down, Anu.' Padma yanked at Anu's hand and made her sit down. 'Sanju is being very foolish by choosing to live in that place that looks nothing like a house but like a star hotel. But how could you leave him and come back here? You should have stayed, fought, reasoned and moved back here together. Running away is not an option in life.'

Padma aunty was mouthing all the clichés in the world but she made sense. Why hadn't Anu tried harder to make Sanju move back with her? Or better, why had she given up so quickly on Verdant Green?

'Think about what I said, Anu. Do the right thing.'

With that, Padma aunty was gone. Anu sat there with her head absolutely devoid of any thoughts. The mosquitoes buzzing, the walkers dwindling, the lights coming on—she noticed nothing. Then she picked up the phone and dialled Sanju. Five rings, six rings, Anu knew it was hopeless. Just when she had given up, she heard Sanju's voice. He said a simple 'Hi!'.

Anu's eyes welled up all over again. She so missed his voice; she so missed him.

'Sanju,' she managed not to break down. 'I am coming back. Please, this is horrible. I will not embarrass you. I will not pull any more Anuisms. I will not—'

'Hey, Anu! Are you crying?' Sanju sounded wounded. He hated it when she cried. 'Stop crying, Anu. Are you still at my parent's house? Mom said you were going there to pick up Vicky.'

'I am coming now, Sanju. I will drive to Verdant Green right away.'

'Go home, Anu. We will talk tomorrow, okay? I am still at work.' He sounded too eager to hang up on her.

He spoke politely but seemed to have no intentions to get back with me. He does not want me back at Verdant Green! Is his life so good without me? Am I the only fool missing him? Anu felt dejected as she walked to her in-law's house. Thinking back on their conversation, Sanju had said nothing to indicate that he wanted them to be together. Anu messaged Pete. 'Why can't life work the way we want?'

Pete: Because you have to lose some to win some.

Anu: But I want to win all!

Pete: Then someone else has to lose all!

Anu sighed. Now she was willing to lose some to Sanju but he seemed determined to win all.

38

By the time she reached home, Anu had decided to just let things be. As Pete had said, she had to heal first. She had to become whole again. An intense sadness kept creeping up on her but she fought back hard. She had told Sanju how she felt, and he had said he would call tomorrow. She didn't want to think about what happens if he didn't call. That was a worry for later. With Vicky next to her and a large bag of chips between them, Anu settled down to watch *Finding Nemo* for the hundredth time.

When the doorbell rang around nine at night, Anu's ears perked up. Vicky dashed to the door crying a long 'Daddyyyy'. Tacky, but both Anu and Sanju had their own ways to ring the bell. Anu felt numb. Just when she thought they were over, just when she thought Sanju would never come back, there he was. Then it occurred to her—probably he was there to end it all. Vicky was jumping up and down at the door to get to the latch. Anu picked up the courage to open the door.

'Hi,' she said leaning against the door. The good news was that he carried no papers with him. That meant no divorce that night at least.

'Hi,' he stopped at the door. To Anu's eyes, he looked exhausted. *He has missed me*, said her confident mind. *He looks like death only because he has come from the office*, yelled her logical brain. Then it yelled more. *Get a grip, woman.*

'Want to come in?' Anu looked at Sanju quizzically. Okay, that was a stupid question when he was at the door.

Sanju looked slightly irritated. 'What do you think?' He came inside, closed the door, and hoisted Vicky into the air.

Vicky giggled and Sanju played some more with him. Anu stood uncertainly. What was she to do? If it was like before, she would make them both coffee. She decided to do the same.

'Anu, wait.' Sanju stopped her with a hand on the shoulder, turned her around and stared into her eyes. He cocked an eyebrow and gave a half-smile. A smile that said he was amused. 'What is the middle?' He took out the note she had left for him. *Meet me in the middle.*

Anu smiled despite her eyes beginning to well up. Then she pointed at the living room. 'This right here is the middle.'

Sanju laughed. His hearty, happy laugh that made his nose crinkle. 'Really? Looks to me that this is your end.'

Anu shook her head. 'Nope. This is the middle.'

Sanju sat on the sofa and stretched his legs on to the centre table. He pulled her next to him and rested his head on her shoulder. 'You are the most stubborn human I have ever met, Miss Anu.'

Anu felt all jelly inside. So Sanju had come back to her! She felt relief like never before. Vicky was back to playing with his Hot Wheels. Anu snuggled closer to Sanju. Sitting up straight, Sanju put an arm around her. Anu breathed his scent deeply. She had given up on ever being this close to him. 'Fine. If you don't think this is the middle, let us find a place within five kilometres from here.'

'Ten,' said Sanju.

'Six.' She countered.

'Seven,' said Sanju.

'Sold,' Anu smiled. 'I don't see what is wrong with this place. But a deal is a deal. We will move.' She had so much to ask him but at that moment, nothing seemed important. Sanju was back. They were a unit again.

She turned on the TV and switched to Romedy Now. *You Got Mail* was playing. Perfect romantic movie for a make-up night.

Sanju snatched the remote and changed it to a News channel where people were screaming.

Anu snatched it back and changed it to Star World where *The Big Bang Theory* was playing.

Sanju nodded and smiled. 'Now, that is more like it, babe.'

After a pause, Anu asked. 'Sanju, why did you ask me to leave you?'

Sanju groaned. 'I hoped you wouldn't start this line of inquiry now. It is not important. I was angry, you were angry. Leave it at that, Anu.'

Another ten minutes passed. 'Sanju,' Anu had to know. 'Would you have come back if I hadn't called you today?'

Sanju yawned. 'Maybe not tonight. But sometime this week.'

Another ten minutes passed. 'Sanju, how much money are we going to lose on the house?'

Sanju turned off the TV and faced her. 'Three questions, Anu. I will answer only three tonight.'

Anu nodded solemnly. 'For tonight, I will take that. Now tell me.'

Sanju smiled. 'Not much, actually. A new guy came from the US office, and he returned the deposit I had paid. He will take up the house next week.'

'The BMW?'

'Who told you about that?' Sanju knitted his brows. 'I never got it delivered. Cancelled the booking after you left.'

Anu smiled indulgently. 'You couldn't enjoy it without me, right?'

Sanju started laughing. 'What are you expecting, woman? A full-blown love confession like in the Karan Johar movies?'

'Yeah, do you mind? Would it kill you to say "Anu, life without you isn't life at all. Anu, life without you—"'

Sanju stopped her with a finger on her lips. He looked into her eyes and declared. 'Anu, life without fighting with you, groaning at you, rolling my eyes at you … isn't life at all.' Then he hugged her and kissed the top of her head. 'Not to mention laughing with you.' He always ended things rather nicely.

Before Anu could reply, Vicky got wind of a good moment between his parents that did not include him. He ran towards them, pulled Sanju's hands off Anu and wedged himself firmly between them. 'Don't touch Mumma, Daddy. Not nice.'

Anu picked up Vicky and chastised Sanju. 'Not at all nice, Daddy. Go to your room for a timeout. Vicky gets his TV with dinner because he has been a good boy. I will bring your dinner to the room. No TV for you.'

'Yes, ma'am.' Sanju stretched and smiled. His timeouts were how they stole time for themselves.

Anu asked him before he left the room. 'What about the orange sofa?'

Sanju groaned. 'I said I would answer three questions, Anu. Your quota is over.'

Anu pursed her lips. 'If you don't bring that couch back, I can reduce your timeout.'

Sanju shook his head. 'No. Sorry. The couch is coming.'

'More timeout for Daddy then! Mumma, more timeout for Daddy!' Vicky's excited squeal soon got drowned in Anu and Sanju's laughter.

Wiping at her eyes, now watering in mirth, Anu texted Pete quickly: 'Trouble over in paradise!'

Acknowledgements

Abhijith Ramesh for being my reading, writing, and ideation companion. This book was born only because of our coffee evenings.

Neethi Mahesh and Akshara Mahesh, for being the first readers of everything I write and for your smart feedback. And for making me look good as a mother.

Shinie Antony for being my constant friend and for finding this book a home. Thank you for making me rewrite the first chapter. Took me five attempts but when you finally approved it, it was my Eureka moment.

Preeti Shenoy for reading my draft and for giving the book such a beautiful blurb. Thank you for all the handholding through my writing. I cherish our friendship.

Pradeep Sriram, my brilliant cousin for pointing out that I had too many parenthesized sentences. I have removed most.

Ravinder Singh for accepting the book for publication.

Swati Daftuar and the rest of the editorial team at HarperCollins India for such superior editorial work.

My parents, Nagesh and Ramamani, and my husband, Mahesh, for always letting me be me.

About the Author

Vani Mahesh is an avid reader and she believes that all that reading combined with her unusually keen interest in other people's lives led her to writing. The novel *Meet Me in the Middle* happened in her mind years ago though she got around to writing it only now. Vani loves humour and she hopes she can make her readers laugh through her unlikely protagonist, Anu.

Vani is best known for writing mythology. She is the author of Creation Tales – stories from Brahma Purana, Saptarsh – The Seven Supreme Sages, and Shiva Purana. Vani feels thrilled to spot her books in bookstores and she also instantly falls in love with those who have read her books.

Vani began her career just like any Bangalorean – a software engineer in the Silicon Valley. Since she was always jealous of a librarian's proximity to books, she quit her job to start EasyLib.com, the first online library in India. She ran it for over a decade before getting bitten by the writing bug.

When not reading or writing, Vani cannot be caught gardening, baking, or running. But she can be caught watching OTT, eating, and playing badminton. She lives in Bangalore with her husband and two daughters.